MW01126352

TREACHERY

TREACHERY

R. T. LUND

Copyright © 2019 R.T. Lund

All rights reserved.

ISBN-9781793185693

DEDICATION

To ATL and NKL, neither of whom would want her name associated with this book.

"Oh, what a tangled web we weave when first we practice to deceive."

—Sir Walter Scott

1

F ALLON HEARD THE familiar, soothing call of a mourning dove as he checked his alignment one last time and unleashed a compact yet powerful swing with his ancient persimmon driver. Without expression, his eyes followed the arching white sphere as it drew slightly inward and landed in the middle of the lush, green fairway, nearly 300 yards from the tee box.

"Nice shot, Judge," fawned David Liscomb, Fallon's former law partner and an occasional member of his Saturday morning foursome at St. Paul's venerable Town & Country Club. "I can't believe a fat-fuck 60-year-old can still hit it that far." Liscomb was a 15-handicapper trending towards a 20 but was competitive as hell and loved the game with a passion.

"Lauren keeps him vigorous," chided Fallon's younger brother, Patrick, "while the rest of us deal with erectile dysfunction and depression."

Fallon smiled self-consciously and shook his head as he picked up his tee and tossed the driver to his bored but now bemused teenage caddy.

"Watch your language in front of His Holiness," scolded Fallon, referring to his former college roommate and permanent Saturday morning guest, Father Kevin Daly.

The shortest hitter in the group, Daly was also the best golfer. A former parish priest and English professor with an MFA from Notre Dame, he was the President of St. Thomas University, conveniently located about a block from the course. Daly was one of the few members of St. Paul's Catholic brotherhood who still enjoyed a high level of respect and influence outside the Church. Even so, he couldn't persuade the Fallon brothers to return to the flock.

The fourth hole at T & C was an unforgiving par 4, about 440 yards from the back tees but on a steep incline heading east away from the Mississippi River and directly into the morning sun. The narrow, elevated green was nearly impossible to reach in two by the average member. Two steeply-banked sand traps guarding the green's entrance prevented hackers like Liscomb from running a skulled worm-killer onto the putting surface.

Patrick's duck-hook off the tee darted into a shallow bunker that bordered the left side of the fairway. While he and his caddy discussed which club could accomplish a miracle, Fallon gazed at the cloudless morning sky and admired the view of the Minneapolis skyline, a view that was marred by a sputtering, gas-powered golf cart carving an unsightly track across the dewy third green and heading straight for his group.

"What the hell?!!" exclaimed Liscomb. He recognized Clayton Miller, the Ramsey County Sheriff, in the passenger seat, chauffeured by a uniformed deputy who obviously didn't know much about golf etiquette, or physics. Miller had been an All-American defensive end at The Ohio State University in the 1980s, but a shattered tibia changed his career focus from the NFL to criminal justice. He'd been a beat cop in the tough Selby-Dale neighborhood and then a homicide detective before becoming the first African-American to be elected Sheriff of Ramsey County.

The noisy cart skidded on the wet grass before squealing to a stop between Fallon and his caddy. The four golfers closed ranks, as Miller swung his thick, muscular limbs out of the cart and slowly stood to face Fallon.

"Sorry to interrupt your game, Judge. I tried calling your cellphone but it went right to voicemail."

"No phones allowed on the course, Sheriff. It's a good rule."

"That may be so," allowed Miller, "but I need to have a private word with you. Let me drive you back to the clubhouse."

"Look around, Sheriff. There's my brother, my former partner and my best friend, who's also a priest. Whatever you need to tell me, they can hear."

Miller studied the four faces staring at him and paused to consider his response. It was a few minutes before 9:00 and already in the mid-80s with nary a breeze and a predicted high in triple digits. Droplets of sweat fell from his forehead and splashed on his polished black oxfords. He was uncomfortable in a blue blazer, dress shirt and tie, and the news he was about to deliver made his gut ache.

"OK, but the caddies need to disappear."

Fallon put his arms around the two teenagers and whispered something that made them snicker. They each grabbed two golf bags and hustled toward the small, restroom hut adjacent to the fourth green.

"I'm afraid I've got the worst possible news, Judge. I got a call early this morning from Sheriff MacDonald up in Lake County. Some hikers in Gooseberry Park discovered a naked body face down in a shallow part of the Gooseberry River between the upper and lower falls. It was the body of a woman who's been identified preliminarily as your wife, Lauren."

For a few moments Fallon simply stared at Miller, not wanting to accept the reality or finality of what he'd just heard and not finding words to respond to the news that his young, brilliant, beautiful wife was gone. Patrick squeezed Fallon's shoulder. Liscomb was the first to speak.

"Do they have any idea how she got there?"

"MacDonald says it appears she fell from the highway bridge over the river. It's about a five-story drop onto mostly rocks and a shallow stream. Someone might be able to survive that fall, but according to the Sheriff, she most likely hit head first. The Lake County Sheriff's office and other local law enforcement are still processing the scene. I understand her body will be transported to the pathology unit at St. Mark's Hospital in Duluth. They'll wait for you, judge, before they proceed with an autopsy."

"She was naked? What the hell happened to her clothes, her purse, her phone?" Fallon asked, still trying to process the horrible news while holding back tears and an urge to throw up his breakfast. "She was at a conference at Scenic Shores Resort."

"I'm sure MacDonald's office will be interviewing the resort staff and some of the other conference attendees. They assumed she'd been at the conference based on something they found in her car—they found your wife's BMW; it was parked just off Highway 61 near the entrance to the park. I don't know what else they've found at this point judge. All I know is she was naked when they found her, and MacDonald strongly suspects she didn't fall off that bridge; she was pushed."

2

L AUREN BERGMANN FALLON was born in Cooperstown, New York, the only
child of Robert and Ann Bergmann. Robert was a curator of sorts at the
National Baseball Hall of Fame and Museum. Ann was a substitute teacher
at Washington Irving Elementary School. They'd met at the University of
Minnesota where "Bobby" was a history major and third-string catcher for the
Gophers baseball team. Ann studied theater and broadcast journalism, hoping
for a career as a TV news reporter. She was smart and outgoing, a tall blonde
with wide, expressive blue eyes and an engaging smile.

Though he had his dream job and a beautiful spouse and baby girl, Robert
suffered from severe depression and probably undiagnosed bipolar mood swings.
Like his father, a career Air Force officer and jet pilot, Robert developed a passion for flying at an early age, earning his pilot's license at sixteen and graduating to instrumentation status in college.

Shortly after moving to Cooperstown, a few years before Lauren was born,
Robert bought a used Cessna 172 Skyhawk from the owner of the Cooperstown-
Westville Airport. Ann supported this extravagance notwithstanding an innate
fear of flying that was magnified in a four-seat, single-engine crate with wings
that sounded more like a lawn mower than a jet. She reluctantly accompanied
her husband on short flights to places like Binghamton, Syracuse, Watertown
and Potsdam and secretly enjoyed watching him maneuver the small plane with
a confident smile on his face.

Ann stopped riding in the Cessna when Lauren was born for reasons that
were obvious to her if not to Robert. He still took the plane up occasionally to
attend conferences and maintain his license.

In late September of 1985, a week after Lauren's fourth birthday, events transpired that would forever alter the course of their lives. During dinner one night, Robert told Ann he'd rented a cottage on Lake Piseco in the Adirondacks for a weekend getaway to celebrate their eighth wedding anniversary. He'd also arranged for Maura Hallock, a kindergarten teacher who was Ann's best friend at Washington Irving, to care for Lauren. Ann was surprised—their relationship had been strained at best for a couple of years—but she was so moved by Bobby's extraordinary gesture that she agreed to the trip. She even agreed to his plan to fly the Cessna up to Piseco Airport to give them more time on the lake.

The NTSB concluded that a thin cloud cover wasn't sufficient to cause an experienced pilot like Bergmann to miss the runway at the Piseco Airport and continue flying at a speed in excess of 100 mph before literally exploding into the side of Snowy Mountain several miles to the northeast. The authorities needed dental records to identify the couple's charred remains. The Hamilton County Sheriff was unable to retrieve any of their belongings in the black, mostly ash, debris field.

A few weeks earlier, Robert had taken Ann's minivan to a local service station for an oil change. He'd opened the glove compartment searching for the owner's manual and found a crumpled piece of lined paper stuffed to one side. It was a handwritten note from "Chris" to Ann recounting details of recent lovemaking sessions and asking when they could be together again. Robert handed the note to Ann as he flew over Sacandaga Lake and pushed the throttle forward to maximize the small plane's air speed as it hurtled toward the mountain. If he heard Ann's screams, he didn't respond.

Lauren's only surviving lineal relative, her maternal grandfather, was a kindly widower who taught World History to high school students in St. Paul. He spent a month in Cooperstown taking care of paper work, meeting with lawyers and social services, and winding up the affairs of his only child and her enigmatic, troubled husband. The most difficult and important task for the indulgent gentleman was trying to comfort and care for a precocious, bewildered four-year-old. A few weeks before Thanksgiving, he packed up Lauren's belongings and moved her to Minnesota to start a new life.

3

"NO APPETITE FOR love this morning?"

Jay McBride approached his bedmate from behind while slowly massaging his thigh and unresponsive privates.

Archbishop James Lamkin sat up, turned away from McBride and dangled his bare legs over the side of the king bed. He'd spent many memorable nights at McBride's impressive retreat on the North Shore of Lake Superior, but a hangover and a new set of worries at the Twin Cities' Archdiocese blunted his libido. Lamkin stared out the arched cathedral window that framed the ocean-like body of water. A couple of gulls were fighting over a tiny carcass on the rocky shore as the bright, mid-morning sun reflected off the lake and intensified the throbbing behind his bloodshot eyes.

"That bitch wants to take my deposition," said Lamkin. "Who could be the source of her information? She's come up with names and events that only Peter and our lawyers would know."

"And me, of course," said McBride arrogantly. "Have you ever considered that that bitch might have convinced him to betray the Church? And what if Peter knows about us? That sanctimonious little bastard would turn on you in a heartbeat."

Lamkin pondered the unfathomable while he covered his scrawny, 62-year-old torso with one of McBride's expensive lambskin robes and shuffled into the bathroom to take a leak. He was still tired, having left the chancery in St. Paul after eight o'clock the night before, arriving at McBride's place north of Tofte after midnight, but not getting to sleep until he'd consumed a few vodka martinis and some McBride. He snatched a bottle of ibuprofen from the medicine cabinet and swallowed three without any water.

McBride slid out of bed, stretched his tanned, athletic frame and headed for the kitchen, his bare feet sticking to the polished mahogany floor. He'd sunk close to $3 million into his two-story, cedar log getaway. It was constructed on a magnificent, secluded lot, thickly forested with birch, spruce and tamarack and sloping gently towards the lake.

Ten years younger than Lamkin, McBride had known the archbishop for over two decades. They first met in a small, dimly-lit bar on South Hennepin Avenue in the mid '90s. Lamkin had recently moved from Baltimore to St. Paul and was about to be installed as the seventh and youngest archbishop of the Twin Cities' Archdiocese.

At the time, McBride was a senior portfolio manager for a regional invest-ment firm that specialized in convincing upper-bracket baby boomers that they could deliver superior returns year after year. That wasn't particularly difficult to accomplish during the dot.com bubble that made Bill Clinton look like a genius. But McBride wasn't content researching mid-cap stock companies and sucking up to wealthy widows for a low six-figure salary. He had a consuming desire to be stinking, filthy rich. Not simply to accumulate assets and admire his balance sheet, but to immerse himself in a lavish lifestyle that only the one percent could afford.

McBride was raised by his mother in a two-bedroom bungalow in St. Paul's Highland Park neighborhood. His parents were married a week before newly-commissioned R.O.T.C. Lieutenant Gerard McBride left for Viet Nam, where he would drown while trying to rescue a curious native child who'd fallen into the raging Mekong River during the rainy season. His mother never remarried. She was a dutiful Catholic who made a modest living as a librarian at Our Lady of the Lakes School. She scrimped, saved and sacrificed to give her only child every advantage, so it pained her somewhat to suspect he was gay (mothers always know), though she never asked him directly, and he never said.

She was proud of his many accomplishments and tried to overlook that he was terribly spoiled (her fault), insatiably selfish, incredibly manipulative, and incurably narcissistic. He graduated with high honors from Marquette University with a degree in finance and earned an MBA at the Kellogg School two years later.

A tall, well-muscled and strikingly handsome man, with thick, curly brown hair, slate blue eyes and a long, patrician nose, McBride was an accomplished tennis player and avid fine art collector, though he was more enthusiastic than accomplished at that. He might have been bisexual. He dated a handful of the many women who were attracted to him, both to maintain a certain façade and because he enjoyed their company, though he rarely dated anyone more than once.

Nevertheless, he was comfortable with his sexuality, whatever it was, but early on decided he preferred discreet relationships with older, more sophisticated men who shared his desire or, more accurately, perceived professional need, for privacy.

More than anything, McBride was an opportunist who was accustomed to getting his way.

He recognized Lamkin from a photo in the St. Paul *Pioneer Press*, even though the diminutive cleric appeared to be seeking anonymity, sitting in a booth in the back of the bar and wearing a black hooded sweatshirt, faded jeans and sneakers.

The newspaper had reported that the new archbishop had been vicar general at the Baltimore archdiocese. Apparently, the Church had been in financial difficulty, and Lamkin, who attended St. Mary's Seminary in Baltimore after graduating from Johns Hopkins, had been credited with instituting a number of new policies and procedures that dramatically increased contributions, reduced expenses and restored the diocese to fiscal health.

At the time, the Catholic Church in the Twin Cities was on the verge of a different kind of crisis. Since the mid-1980s there had been allegations of sexual abuse of children, mostly boys, dating back to the early 1960s. Like many of his contemporaries, Archbishop Thomas Bradley, Lamkin's predecessor, believed that anyone who'd been admitted into the priesthood was capable of rehabilitation, regardless of his sins or predilections. His methods of dealing with the "pedophile problem" had been misguided in both theory and practice. Even so, by the mid-90s his cadre of administrative minions and highly paid defense lawyers had, for the most part, succeeded in protecting the Church and its assets and of shielding a growing list of wicked, predatory priests from a national crusade led by a young lawyer named Joseph P. Terranova, Jr, doing business as J.P. Terranova & Associates.

Bradley was 77 when he died within days of suffering a massive stroke. The Church hierarchy believed they needed a modern, innovative leader to clean up the growing legal, financial and public relations issues associated with the "pedophile problem." Enter James Lamkin.

McBride's mother, an optimist by nature, was hopeful that new leadership could save the Church. McBride on the other hand, agnostic when it came to religion, cared nothing about the fate of the Catholic Church; he was interested in the designated archbishop for more pragmatic reasons.

Despite his habitual wariness, Lamkin was instantly drawn to the well-dressed young professional who politely but seductively offered to buy him a drink and asked whether he was new to the Twin Cities. One night of pleasure at McBride's downtown condo led to others and to something that Lamkin had never allowed himself to experience—not just a night of booze-fueled sex with a stranger, but true intimacy. Lamkin faithfully adhered to many Catholic tenets and teachings; celibacy was not one of them. He and McBride had a common interest in maintaining a secret relationship, a relationship that would continue for years and, as far as Lamkin knew, would be monogamous.

Lamkin retrieved his cell phone from the glass-covered nightstand in the bedroom. It was already 10:00 a.m., and he had missed a call from Peter. Upset with himself, he sat on the white leather sectional that was the centerpiece of McBride's two-story great room, setting his feet on the matching ottoman. Peter had left a message at 9:15:

> "Archbishop, this is Peter. . . you won't believe this. . . Lauren Fallon has been killed. She was here. . . at my legal conference in Two Harbors, but her body was found this morning in the Gooseberry River. The police are still here interviewing people. Call me as soon as you get this."

"What is it?" asked McBride, as he set a silver serving tray with assorted scones and bagels and two steaming cups of Italian roast on the ottoman near Lamkin's feet and sat next to him on the couch.

"Listen to this," said Lamkin. He activated the speaker on his I-Phone and replayed Peter's message.

"He actually sounds upset," said McBride matter-of-factly. "She was trying to destroy the Church, to undermine everything you've worked to protect. Isn't this good news?"

"Violence is never good," sighed Lamkin self-righteously, setting his coffee cup down and brushing crumbs off McBride's expensive robe. "She was certainly a pain in the ass, but Terranova or one of his other shysters will simply take her place. I don't know what in heaven's name has happened to Peter, though. I'm beginning to think he could be the leak. Could he have been sleeping with that slut? Anyway, I need to get back to the Cities. I drove right by Gooseberry late last night. No one needs to know I was up here. And besides, I'm presiding at late morning mass at the Cathedral tomorrow."

"Relax, Jim. It's not even noon. You drove all the way up here, for Christ's sake, at least stay for lunch."

Lamkin was so lost in thought he hardly noticed McBride easing his long, naked body onto the Persian rug on a mission to soothe Lamkin's frazzled nerves. Lamkin's body shuddered, mostly with pleasure, as McBride's mouth enveloped some familiar flesh.

"I just hope he didn't tell her about the fund."

4

SAM MCDONALD WAS a light sleeper. Especially when he wasn't sleeping alone. He had just opened one eye to check the time—5:45 a.m.—when his cell phone started blasting the *William Tell Overture*. It was Ryan Hokanen, one of the young deputies on the overnight shift.

"Ryan, what can I do for you this very early Saturday morning?"

"Hey, Mac, really sorry to bother you, but we've got a possible homicide in Gooseberry Park."

"In the campground?"

"No. Below the bridge on Highway 61. A couple of early morning hikers spotted a body and called 911. Deputy Klewacki and I responded along with some EMTs out of Silver Bay. We met the callers at the scene about thirty minutes ago and found a naked female face down in an eddy, wedged between some rocks in about two feet of water. The EMTs arrived a few minutes later. It's a wonder her body didn't get swept up by the current and carried to the middle falls."

McDonald quickly processed Hokanen's words, his cell phone wedged between his right shoulder and ear, while he pulled up his jeans and tucked in a black T-shirt that read SHERIFF in bold white letters across his broad chest and back.

"Did they try to revive her?" he asked.

"Sheriff, her head was smashed really, really bad. Looks like her neck is broken, too. I mean. . . she must have fallen head first from the bridge like someone held her by her feet and dropped her over the railing."

"So you're treating it as a crime scene."

"Yes, sir. The coroner is on his way and I called Stockman. He said we might need the BCA on this one."

"Are you and Klewacki okay?"

"A little shook up but okay."

"It's still pretty early. Have Klewacki search the area around the bridge for clothes, keys, anything else that might be related to the victim and check all the parking areas near the visitor center and main entrance for a vehicle. Park's not open until 6:00, so any car would be there illegally. Maybe she met someone there. On the other hand, if she came from the campground, her vehicle and belongings may be there as well, so check over there, too."

"Will do."

"I'll be there in 10 minutes."

Awakened by the call, Hallie Bell sensed that McDonald wouldn't be coming back to bed any time soon. She listened to the beginning of his exchange with Hokanen then gently touched his chest with an outstretched hand while mouthing the word "coffee" and bounded down the stairs to the kitchen.

Bell knew where McDonald kept the coffee. She'd been spending two or three nights a week at his cozy log cottage near Split Rock Lighthouse since her divorce had been finalized in March. Tall and slender, Bell had played D-1 volleyball in college. She was blessed with alluring, smile-generated dimples, shoulder length, jet-black hair and flawless brown skin that made her appear younger than her 42 years.

After graduating law school in Wisconsin, she had offers from powerhouse firms in Milwaukee and Chicago but accepted a job with Hammond & Holden, a small, general practice firm in Superior, Duluth's sister port city, a town with more bars than grocery stores and proud of it. As a professional woman and an African American, Bell was truly a minority in the Twin Ports. Maybe that's what motivated her to take the job.

Hammond's biggest client was North Star Land Company, the largest commercial real estate developer in northern Minnesota. After making a small fortune in residential construction during the boom time following World War II, Rick Holden started buying up vacant land along the shores of literally hundreds of lakes in Minnesota and northwestern Wisconsin, including along the north shore of Lake Superior. He figured that, after moving to the suburbs, prosperous Americans would want a place to recreate with their families. Besides, the land was cheap, and he had more confidence in dirt than in stocks, bonds or banks.

Holden and his eldest son, Rick, Jr., spent the better part of the '70s and '80s building, managing and selling resorts, cabins, and golf courses on the land the old man had acquired in the '50s. After Senior died in the early '90s, Junior focused his attention and considerable capital on developing luxury condominiums, medical office buildings, and assisted living communities. His brother's law firm handled all of North Star's legal work, and his only son, Rick III, headed up the property management division.

Rick Holden III, better known as Ricky, was a typical third generation rich kid, well versed in country club activities—golf, tennis, dancing, drinking and bullshitting. He was one of the most eligible bachelors in the Twin Ports when he met Hallie Bell, then a third-year associate in his uncle's law firm. Bell was filling in for Uncle Jack at the closing of a building lease between North Star Commercial Properties and a regional logistics firm. Holden was impressed with her quick wit, command of commercial real estate lingo and, maybe most of all, her magnetic smile and sleek, 6-foot frame.

Bell noticed that Holden couldn't take his eyes off her. He literally charmed the pants off her, and within six months they were married. Ricky was successful in the family business and a lot of fun at parties, but their childless marriage ended after ten years when Bell discovered that he'd impregnated a 19-year-old hostess at Ridgewood Country Club. It confirmed her suspicion that many of his late nights with "customers" had involved alcohol, recreational drugs and gullible coeds.

Still, Bell didn't hate Ricky or the Holdens; she just needed to get away. Even though she'd made junior partner at Hammond & Holden, she quit the firm and moved into the only Holden asset she received in the divorce, a two-bedroom condominium in Silver Creek Estates, a 20-unit development about ten miles north of Two Harbors. She quickly landed a job as an assistant to Greg Thomassoni, the Lake County Attorney, making half the six-figure salary she'd earned at the law firm. Bell was one of four lawyers in the small government office, the only one who was not a prosecutor.

MacDonald was a few years shy of fifty. He grew up near Beaver Bay, a tiny tourist stop between mileposts 50 and 52 on U.S. Highway 61, the main road between Duluth and the Canadian border. His dad had labored 38 years as a heavy equipment operator at the Merritt Mining taconite plant in nearby Silver Bay before dying of lung disease at 62. His mother had been a pediatric nurse at Lake County Community Hospital in Two Harbors. She'd loved caring for sick children, but arthritis forced her to retire at 65. She lived in a senior apartment complex in Duluth, where she volunteered as a hospice aide and sang in the choir at Gloria Dei Lutheran Church.

MacDonald and his younger brother, David, were legends in Lake County. With Sam at quarterback and David at tailback, Silver Bay Regional High School won its first and only state championship. Having a glowing recommendation from Congressman Oberstar and an impressive grade-point average, MacDonald accepted an appointment to the Air Force Academy in Colorado Springs, and he made the most of it, rising from 2nd Lieutenant to the rank of Lieutenant Colonel in under ten years. With degrees in criminal justice and sociology, MacDonald became a security officer in the Air Force, which meant he led a group of soldiers and civilians responsible for the safety of U.S. bases around the world. He served a significant part of his Air Force career overseas, including stints in Kuwait during Operation Desert Storm and Saudi Arabia and Turkey during Operation Iraqi Freedom.

At the urging of a former commanding officer who was an undersecretary at Treasury, MacDonald left the Air Force during the first Obama administration to accept a position as deputy director of the Secret Service in Washington, in charge of several divisions of the Agency, including the protection of human assets. At the time his wife, Julie, was the communications director for the Secretary of Health and Human Services, and their young daughter attended elementary school a few miles from their home in McLean, Virginia. MacDonald was energized by the challenges at Secret Service, especially during the 2012 presidential election, and he and his small family were the happiest they'd ever been.

On a Friday afternoon in early January of 2013, Julie left work early to pick up their daughter at school. They were to meet Sam at home and drive to Great Falls to have dinner with Julie's parents. Temperatures falling below freezing turned a cold rain into sleet and then snow. Driving north on Highway 309, Julie was on her cell phone reviewing details of upcoming inaugural events with her boss. She was going too fast for conditions, well over the speed limit. By the time she looked up and noticed brake lights flickering on the back of a silver semi-tractor trailer, the big rig was only twenty feet in front of her Subaru Outback. She instinctively slammed the brake pedal with her right foot and felt the car slide uncontrollably on the icy pavement while the semi skidded to a stop. The Subaru was still traveling over 30 miles per hour when its hood passed under the trailer of the Freightliner 18-wheeler. Tragically, the trailer sheared off the top half of the Outback and literally decapitated Julie and her daughter. Fortunately, the terror was over in seconds.

MacDonald took a two-month leave of absence from the Service. David, a teacher and football coach in California, stayed with him for a few weeks, as did his mom. After returning to the job he once loved, he realized he needed a permanent change of scenery in order to end or at least compartmentalize the recurring nightmares he couldn't shake.

About a year later, he read that Eddie Matonich, the long-time Sheriff of Lake County and a friend of his dad's, was retiring. Over the next six months, he resigned from the Service, sold the house in McLean, bought a small log home with a view of Lake Superior, and filed the necessary paperwork to run for Sheriff of Lake County, Minnesota. No one opposed him. His natural talents, background and experience made him more than a little overqualified to be sheriff in a county where deer, bears and wolves outnumbered the roughly 10,000 residents, but that never crossed his mind. He had always wanted to get back to northern Minnesota. Lake County was where he belonged.

Hallie handed MacDonald a steaming mug of coffee and leaned against the Amish pedestal table that took up most of the old cabin's tiny kitchen. The light cotton robe she'd grabbed to cover her nakedness was untied and partially open.

"Have they identified the woman?"

"Not yet. Sounds like her skull's been crushed and, without other physical evidence, it might take a while. Especially if she's not from around here. Stockman's on his way. I'll call Greg on my way to Gooseberry and let him know we might have a murder to deal with."

"This is your first one, isn't it?"

"I don't think there's been a murder in Lake County for ten years." McDonald took a sip of hot coffee and set his mug on the table. "I'd better get going."

Sam was a big man, several inches taller than Bell, and well over 200 pounds. His close-cropped black hair and neatly-trimmed beard were speckled with grey and white. He'd added twenty pounds to the trim physique he'd maintained at the Service, which only served to make his deep voice and massive hands more intimidating to those who didn't know him well.

He leaned in towards Bell and gently kissed her neck.

"Maybe a late dinner tonight?" she asked, looking into his sleepy blue eyes.

"We'll see. I'll call you when I can."

5

MacDonald parked his squad, a black Tahoe, on the shoulder of south-bound Highway 61 just north of the bridge over the Gooseberry River. The visitors' entrance to the park was a half-mile south of the bridge, but there was a walkway on the east side that overlooked the middle and lower falls and a walkway tucked under the west side that overlooked the upper falls. Exiting the SUV, he could hear voices mixed in with the chatter of birds and continu-ous muffled roar of the falls. A cool breeze out of the northwest was subsiding, and the tip of the rising sun was visible over the lake on the eastern horizon. By mid-day the temperature would top 90 degrees but at sunrise it was barely 50.

MacDonald walked past the County Coroner's white van parked in the mid-dle of the northbound lane with its emergency lights flashing and driver's door wide open. "What a dumb shit," he said out loud as he flipped the door shut and followed the voices to the east side of the bridge. He noticed that Stockman's unmarked car, a Dodge Charger, was behind Hakonen and Klewacki's squad, taking up a portion of the northbound lane of the bridge, whereas the drivers of the highway patrol squad and Gold Star ambulance had wisely parked on the shoulder a few car lengths south of the bridge.

"Mac!" It was Klewacki, crisscrossing her arms above her head to get MacDonald's attention. She was standing behind the open driver's door of a white, late model BMW sedan parked on the shoulder of northbound 61, about fifty yards behind the ambulance. She closed the door and jogged towards MacDonald, clutching a white, plastic evidence bag.

Gail Klewacki was an excellent cop, smart, agile and analytical. In her late 30s, she began her career with the Minneapolis PD and, luckily for MacDonald, moved north after she married into the family that bought the largest ski resort in the Midwest. Highly intelligent and mature beyond her years, she was MacDonald's most thorough investigator.

"I think we've got an ID on the victim," Klewacki said, removing a small leather wallet from the white bag and gesturing for MacDonald to join her near the green iron guardrail along the east side of the bridge. He recognized most of the small crowd wading in the shallow water around a lifeless body that was partially covered by a white sheet.

"Old Doc Leeks thinks she's been dead for three to six hours. We've taken pictures and scoured the scene, the bridge area and the visitor's center. No clothing or other physical evidence in the vicinity. That Beemer back there appears to be her car. No key or fob anywhere, but it was unlocked, and I found this wallet in the console along with some information about a conference she might have been attending at Scenic Shores."

Klewacki was wearing thin latex gloves to avoid tainting any evidence. The blue wallet had a clear plastic window that covered a Minnesota driver's license. She held it up so MacDonald could read the pertinent information:

Lauren Bergmann Fallon/Female
2521 Montcalm Terrace
St. Paul, Minnesota 55105
Height: 5' 9"
Weight: 120 lbs.
Eyes: Blue
Date of Birth: July 6, 1981

MacDonald snapped a photo of the license with his I-Phone and paused for a few seconds to ponder how this young woman's naked body got from the bridge to the rocky gorge below. He scanned the terrain on both sides of the river. Though the park was densely populated with birch, cedar, white and jack pine, spruce and tamarack trees, the banks on either side of the bridge were treacherously steep and rocky with sparse vegetation.

"How'd those guys get down to the body?" he asked. "They couldn't have taken a very direct route."

"They took the hiking trail on the other side, then mostly slid down to the water on their butts and waded in the river to the body," Klewacki explained. "You should have seen old Leeks on his ass. The highway patrol has already called in a request for one of St. Louis County's rescue helicopters from the Duluth airport. They'll transport her down to Duluth."

"How sure are you on the ID?"

"The top of her skull is crushed, and Leeks thinks her neck is broken. But her face was mostly unaffected and strongly matches the photo on the license. Her height and weight check out, and I'm pretty sure I found her Facebook page. Not much there, but there is a profile picture and it says she's married and lives in St. Paul." Klewacki removed a miniature pair of binoculars from a vinyl case on her belt and handed them to MacDonald.

"Here, you can get a better look. I assume you're not going to join the others in the water."

MacDonald focused on the woman's head and torso. She was beautiful, even in death. Her head was misshapen, and her blond hair matted and stained with blood. The paramedics and state cops were preparing her body for transport by the helicopter. Stockman was talking to the coroner while Hokanen took notes on a mini iPad.

"Once the body is up why don't you and Stockman check out the campground—see if anyone saw anything or might have been involved in some way. Have Hokanen drive to the morgue so we have someone with the body. Tell him I'll call him later this morning. I assume you took a statement from the hikers who found her."

"Yes, sir. They're college kids from Duluth, in their early twenties. They camped last night in Tettegouche and got up early this morning to hike some trails in Superior National. Claim they discovered the body at about 5:15 this morning when they climbed up to the lookout above the upper falls. They were pretty shaken and left to get some dry clothes and head home. I got contact information for both and suggested they might need some professional help to deal with what they saw today."

"Nice work, Gail. I'm going to drive down to Scenic Shores and check out the details of this conference and whether our victim was registered there. I'll run a criminal check and DMV report on Ms. Fallon and call the Ramsey

County Sheriff for assistance in contacting any next of kin. Why don't you and Stockman meet me down there when you're finished here?"

"Sounds good. Unless she was super-intoxicated or suicidal, I don't get how a naked woman falls head first off that bridge in the middle of the night."

"Maybe she was already dead and someone just tossed her into the river. We'll figure it out. You OK?"

"I will be."

6

AFTER MAKING A few calls from the Tahoe, MacDonald reached Clayton Miller on his cell and described the gruesome discovery on the Gooseberry River. He knew Miller by reputation only—a tough but fair career peace officer, respected by local politicians and the public and admired, even liked, by his staff. Miller was familiar with the name Lauren Fallon.

"Pretty, blonde dynamo who works for Terranova, the lawyer who represents the Catholic abuse victims," Miller reacted. "She's married to Charlie Fallon, chief judge of the federal court in St. Paul. The Judge must be about 60. His first wife died of cancer. I think Lauren was his law clerk before they got married. Do you know what she was doing up there?"

MacDonald referred to the flyer Klewacki had found in the BMW. "We haven't confirmed this, but I think she was attending a legal seminar at the Scenic Shores conference center in Two Harbors. Something about picking the right jury in civil cases. The seminar started yesterday and ends sometime today. I'm driving to the resort right now."

"Any leads on potential suspects?" asked Miller. "I know she's not very popular with the Catholic Church down here. I assume you're familiar with that whole mess."

"In general terms," replied MacDonald. "I know the Twin Cities has had a history of abuse problems. Even the Duluth diocese has had its share of bad priests. It's sort of a nationwide epidemic. But I haven't heard much about it lately. I know the name Terranova, but I'm not familiar with anyone else in his firm."

"Terranova had a couple of big cases back in the '90s. Scored a million-dollar verdict against the archdiocese related to Father Degnan, the old priest who hanged himself in the Hennepin County jail two days before the start of his criminal trial. Archbishop Bradley had transferred him from one suburban parish to another leaving a trail of victims. But until Lauren Fallon filed a new lawsuit this spring, I don't think Terranova's office has had an abuse case against the Church down here since Archbishop Lamkin took Bradley's place. I know he's had some big paydays in Milwaukee, Boston and even in Rochester but not in the Cities."

"You said until a new lawsuit was filed this spring," McDonald interrupted. "Tell me about that."

"I don't recall the details, but your victim sued the local archdiocese and named over fifty priests. It was kind of a shocker since the media have always portrayed Lamkin as an enlightened reformer type."

"You think someone connected to the archdiocese might be involved in this?" MacDonald had abandoned organized religion in college. He'd recently read a few of Christopher Hitchen's diatribes against Christianity and couldn't argue with the author's contention that organized religion does more harm than good in the world.

"That might be a stretch but it's certainly possible," said Miller, "but for now I'll track down Judge Fallon and deliver the awful news. Where will they take the body?"

"She'll be in the morgue at St. Mark's in Duluth. One of my deputies will be there. I assume the judge will want to see her body later today. You know of any other family members? Parents? Siblings?

"I heard she was raised by her grandfather, a teacher I think, but I'm sure retired by now. Don't know if he's still around but the judge will know."

"Thanks for all your help, sheriff. I may be back to you as this develops."

"No problem. Your case has piqued my interest. Judge Fallon is highly respected around here and his wife was an impressive young lawyer, not to mention a knockout in the looks department. This is really going to upset the legal community down here to put it mildly."

By the time he finished with Miller, MacDonald was in the parking lot of Scenic Shores Resort and Conference Center. Twenty-five miles northeast of Duluth, Scenic Shores had been built in the mid-1980s and was still the largest resort on the North Shore, with over 200 rooms in the lodge, several two-story cottages with views of the lake, two restaurants, a ballroom and a handful of meeting rooms. It wasn't the most luxurious place on the lake, but it might have been the most profitable.

The lodge was comprised of two connected, four-story buildings, each with ascending sections of brick, wooden shingles and cedar shakes. The lodge and cottages were predominantly gray and white, with a coastal Maine or Cape Cod look and feel. On this Saturday morning in the heart of the summer season, the parking lot was nearly full. MacDonald opted for a space near the lodge's main entrance that was reserved for guests checking in and for the local sheriff. He hopped out of the Tahoe toting a yellow legal pad.

Scenic Shores was in Lake County but outside the Two Harbors city limits and the jurisdiction of the Two Harbors police department. MacDonald's office had responded to several medical emergencies and a few minor disturbances at the lodge during Sam's two years as Sheriff. He knew Rod Grozdanich, the resort manager, and a few of their security personnel. He walked past the twenty-foot stone fireplace that served as the focal point of the spacious lobby and knocked on the manager's office door.

"He won't be in today, sheriff," squeaked a high-pitched voice behind MacDonald. "Is there something I can help you with?"

MacDonald pivoted to his right and saw the head and shoulders of a petite, pony-tailed young woman straining to be seen above the reservation counter. No older than twenty, she wore a short-sleeved cotton golf shirt with the Scenic Shores logo (a seagull perched on a rocky shoreline) and a nametag that read "Tammy."

After confirming that Lauren Fallon was indeed a registered guest of the resort, MacDonald carefully explained that she might have been involved in a tragic accident in Gooseberry Park. He needed access to her room, copies of receipts for anything she purchased during her stay, and the names and phone numbers of the individuals presenting the legal seminar she was attending. He said he was prepared to get a search warrant or subpoena but didn't believe such formalities should be necessary.

Tammy understood the gravity of the situation and clicked through several screens in the resort's computer system. She quickly retrieved all of the information related to Lauren B. Fallon and the National Trial Advocacy seminar on "Impaneling Juries in Complex Civil Cases."

"It looks like Ms. Fallon checked in at 5:15 yesterday afternoon, sheriff. She only requested one room key. The seminar started at noon, so she may have arrived earlier in the day. She also had dinner at our Jolly Fisher restaurant last night—at least I think she did because she charged $130.00 to her room from there at 8:30."

"That's a pretty hefty charge for one person's dinner," MacDonald speculated. "Could I see the invoice?"

"Sure," replied Tammy in her most compliant voice. "The name of the person in charge of the seminar is Jennifer Gilmore. I'll give you the phone number and email we have on file, but I think I see her having breakfast in the coffee shop."

MacDonald arranged to have the assistant manager secure Lauren's room until Klewacki and Stockman could conduct a thorough search later in the morning. He then thanked Tammy for all of her help and made a quick call to Deputy Klewacki.

7

Jenny Gilmore was one of four regional directors for the National Institute of Trial Advocacy, a nonprofit organization that taught the finer points of civil and criminal litigation to trial lawyers. NITA paid successful litigators and judges a generous fee plus expenses to participate in various seminars and conferences across the country. Gilmore had been an untenured professor at Valparaiso University Law School when NITA recruited her to lead its Chicago regional office. This was her first trip to northern Minnesota. After brief introductions, the small-town sheriff rocked her with the news that one of the attendees in her seminar had just been killed in an accident that might not have been an accident.

MacDonald ordered black coffee and sat across from Gilmore in a two-person booth. She was a skinny, thirty-something woman with short brown hair and a protruding jaw a la Jay Leno, but she had kind brown eyes and an easy manner that MacDonald liked immediately. She wore a heavy black wool suit, which told MacDonald that she had packed for northern Minnesota without bothering to check the weather forecast.

I've heard of Joe Terranova," she said. "He has a national reputation for being a bulldog in the courtroom, but I didn't know Ms. Fallon until I met her at the cocktail reception yesterday. I just can't believe this, sheriff. What can I do to help you?"

"I'd like to see all the data you have on everyone signed up for the seminar," said MacDonald, "including any contact information. I'd also like to know if anyone who attended yesterday is a no-show this morning."

"You mean in addition to Ms. Fallon?"

"Is that supposed to be funny?" asked MacDonald, not amused.

"I'm sorry," said Gilmore. "It's not even 7:00 and I didn't get much sleep last night. I'll make sure my assistant gets you everything you need."

"Thank you," said MacDonald, squinting to make eye contact with Gilmore as the morning sun began streaming into the coffee shop through partially opened blinds. "What time does your meeting begin this morning?"

"Continental breakfast at 7:30. The program starts at 8:15."

"Would you object if I addressed your group before the first presentation? At some point today, I'll want to interview anyone who had contact with Ms. Fallon yesterday or saw her after about 8:30 last night."

"That seems reasonable, sheriff, in light of what's happened. Just try not to be too disruptive, ok?"

"The disruption has already occurred, Ms. Gilmore," MacDonald said, curious about her droll sense of humor under the circumstances. He stood, shook her hand, and tossed a five-spot on the table.

8

C AL STOCKMAN WAS fat, lazy and incompetent, but experienced detectives were hard to find in northeastern Minnesota, and the only other detective in MacDonald's office was on disability leave after back surgery. If Stockman weren't a couple of years from retirement with a son in college and a wife with MS, MacDonald would have taken his chances on a replacement, but today Cal was it.

At first, he and Klewacki didn't find much in Lauren's room. There were certainly no signs of a struggle. A nylon duffel bag containing running shoes, gym shorts, underwear, a sports bra and a few pairs of sweat socks was on the king bed, which was neatly made. A black personalized garment bag hanging in the closet housed a couple of lightweight business suits, black loafers, a simple white blouse and dark blue shorts, and an unzipped toiletry and makeup kit on the bathroom vanity contained the usual personal items. A cylindrical trash receptacle next to the commode was empty, except for two pieces of a foil wrapper that formerly contained a condom and, as luck would have it, a used latex condom.

"Eureka," Stockman bellowed, as he took a few pictures with his phone and used special tweezers to deposit the latex sheath into a plastic evidence bag. "Looks like our victim may have been active before she went out, but with who?"

"With *whom*, you mean, right asshole?" Klewacki didn't like Stockman for a number of good reasons. "If she did have sex with someone in this room, it must have been pretty tame, or else she tidied everything up before she left."

The only other piece of evidence worth taking into custody was a silver laptop computer sitting on a small oak work desk. Its charger was connected and plugged into a wall socket. Klewacki took photographs of everything in the room while Stockman dusted the computer and a partially consumed bottle of water for fingerprints. They noted the fact that they didn't find a cell phone either in the victim's car or her room. Whoever took her phone probably took her clothes and maybe her life as well.

While Klewacki and Stockman were completing their search, their boss was addressing a couple dozen sleep-deprived, phone-addicted lawyers two floors below in the Gitchi Gammi Room. He chose his words carefully, saying there had been an "incident" in Gooseberry Park the night before resulting in the death of a woman in her mid-thirties.

"The circumstances surrounding the incident are under investigation. We have not officially confirmed the identity of the deceased but, based on what we know so far, we are reasonably confident that she attended your conference yesterday and that her name is Lauren Fallon."

Suddenly, he had their full attention.

"I need to talk to anyone, anyone who had any contact whatsoever with Ms. Fallon yesterday afternoon, either before or after she left the conference reception. Even if you didn't talk to her, if you saw her after eight o'clock last night, I need to talk to you. And, regardless of the reason, if you have any information about her plans or visitors or whereabouts last night, I need to talk to you. I'm not going to take questions from the group, but I will be sitting in the manager's office in the lobby for the next two hours or so, and I expect anyone who has relevant information to call my cell or stop by, so we can speak in private. Whether or not you come forward this morning, members of my staff or I might contact you in the future, if we think you can help us.

"Thanks for your attention and cooperation, folks. I apologize for being the bearer of such unfortunate news."

MacDonald surveyed the faces of the sixteen men and nine women seated in front of him, looking for unusual reactions and registering two for definite follow up. This was a skill he'd refined in the Secret Service, a skill few possessed.

9

FALLON HAD HIRED David Liscomb at Wyatt & McGovern in the early 1990s. At the time, he was clerking for the chief judge of the Minnesota Supreme Court, a highly prestigious position for any young lawyer. A native of Iron Mountain, Michigan, Liscomb had been president of the law review at the University of Michigan Law School. He was also a member of the Order of the Coif, the legal honor society for brown-nosing top ten percenters who get a badge and a key and the undying envy and sometimes hatred of their fellow classmates.

As chair of Wyatt's civil litigation department, Fallon was Liscomb's boss and mentor until, at age forty-one, President Clinton made him the youngest federal judge in the history of the Minnesota district.

Everyone liked Fallon, including the aloof and egotistical David Liscomb. Liscomb eventually became President of Wyatt, a boutique firm of about sixty lawyers specializing in labor and employment law with offices in Minneapolis, Denver and Kansas City. He was quick-witted, articulate and had a photographic memory, but he was also impatient and temperamental, with a reputation for embarrassing associates and irritating opposing counsel. No one was better prepared to try a case; no one manipulated clients and judges more artfully, and no one rose to the top of a firm faster than David Liscomb, a dead ringer, physically at least, for Kevin Costner.

Fallon became chief judge of the federal district court in St. Paul in 2000, a year before his first wife, Mary, died after a short, horrific battle with ovarian cancer. The Fallons had a married daughter, Shawn, a graphic designer for an ad agency in Los Angeles. Liscomb and his wife, Beth, had two sons. Before Mary died, the two couples had socialized a few times a year. After, Liscomb and

Fallon played golf three or four times a summer, saw each other at bar association and firm events, and met for lunch occasionally, if Fallon set it up.

It was no secret that Beth Liscomb didn't like Lauren and thought Fallon was a fool to marry a woman half his age. She'd even refused to attend Fallon's small wedding in 2006—David went solo. If Fallon thought she was a complete bitch, he kept it to himself.

Declining Sheriff Miller's offer to drive them back to the clubhouse in golf carts, Fallon and his group slowly trudged back with their caddies, while other golfers stared and wondered what was up. The four men quickly showered and dressed and then huddled in the lobby.

"I'm going to drive up to Duluth and find out what I can," Fallon said quietly, his eyes already bloodshot from crying.

"Charlie, you're not driving up there alone," said Patrick, who was ten years younger than his brother and fifty pounds lighter. "I need to stop home and check on a few things for Karen, and then I'll take you."

"Thanks, Pat, but I'm just too anxious about this to wait. I'll be fine."

Fallon was surprised to hear Liscomb speak up. "I'm free all day, Judge. Let me drive you up there."

"That sounds like a good idea to me, Charlie," added Father Daly. "Is there anything I can do down here to help? Make any arrangements or phone calls?"

"No. Thanks for the offer, Kevin. Lauren had no family but me. Her grandfather was it, and he died a few years ago. It's ironic if you think about it. She was such a caring, outgoing, people person. If you're really game David, I'd appreciate the company."

10

"COME IN," SAID MacDonald, responding to a timid knock on the door of the manager's office. He wasn't surprised to see a short, pudgy, middle-age man enter the room. The clean-shaven fellow had a pallid complexion, silver wire-framed glasses and a receding hairline. He was wearing a short-sleeve, powder blue polo shirt tucked into khaki shorts that were a little too snug around the waist and thighs.

The sheriff had been sitting at the manager's desk jotting down observations and action items relating to the morning's events. This fidgety man happened to be one of the two conference attendees who, in the sheriff's view, had overreacted to the news of Lauren's accident. Before he could utter a word, MacDonald rose to his feet and leaned over the desk with an extended hand, a warm smile and a penetrating stare.

"I'm Sam MacDonald," he said, gesturing for the man to sit in one of two gray leather chairs that faced the black executive desk.

"Peter," said the man as he tried to get comfortable but was obviously nervous. "Peter Jenkins."

"You've been attending the conference, Mr. Jenkins?"

"Yes. I'm an attorney, sheriff," Jenkins said proudly, as if his status as a lawyer served to level the playing field with MacDonald.

"With a firm in the Twin Cities?"

"No. I mean, I'm from St. Paul, but I'm not with a law firm. I'm the Chancellor for Civil Affairs for the Twin Cities' Archdiocese."

"Oh," said MacDonald, wondering what, if any, connection there could be between this nervous little man and the beautiful, dead lawyer. "Does that mean you're some kind of priest?"

"No, I'm not a priest. I'm the chief administrative officer for the archdiocese. Kind of like a general counsel."

"And you knew Lauren Fallon?"

"Yes," replied Jenkins, "we have a case together." Jenkins folded his hands in his lap and stared at them, as if he were praying.

"What does that mean, exactly?" probed the sheriff.

"Ms. Fallon's law firm represents several people who are suing the archdiocese. We've discussed the case from time to time, mostly before she sued us. In one of those conversations she mentioned she was registered for this course. I needed credits to maintain my law license and thought it would be a good opportunity to get to know her better, so I signed up."

MacDonald thought there was a high degree of bullshit in that explanation. "Tell me more about this lawsuit," he prodded, trying to get Jenkins to open up.

"The archdiocese settled over two hundred claims of alleged child abuse by priests between 1996 and 2005. All of these settlements were approved by a judge, who sealed the files and ordered that the settlement terms would be confidential. Now Ms. Fallon's firm is trying to vacate the settlements and reopen these cases. It's ridiculous, really."

"Seems to me, then, that you and Ms. Fallon were adversaries, isn't that right?"

"In a way you could say that," admitted Jenkins. "But ultimately I think we both wanted what's best for both the victims and the Church."

"When did you last see her?" asked MacDonald, curious about the abuse cases but not wanting to stray too far from the events of the last 24 hours.

"We had dinner last night here at the resort," said Jenkins. "We had a seven o'clock reservation and left the restaurant between 8:15 and 8:30. I told her I'd see her this morning at the conference, and that was it. . . the last time I saw her."

"You're certain about that?"

"Yes, sheriff. Positive. I watched the ten o'clock news alone in my room and then went to bed."

MacDonald scribbled a few notes on his legal pad and started tapping the desk with the top of his expensive, silver Monteverde pen, a parting gift from his friends at the Service, while he took the measure of a potential suspect who appeared on the verge of tears. Jenkins looked to be close to fifty, wasn't wearing a wedding ring and was most definitely obsessed with Lauren Fallon.

"Did she ever discuss plans to meet anyone or do anything later in the evening, after having dinner with you?"

"No, not that I remember. I think she knew a couple of the other lawyers at the conference, but I don't know their names."

"Do you know her husband, Judge Fallon, or any of her close friends?"

Jenkins paused, trying not to misspeak. "I know who Judge Fallon is, but I've never met him, and Lauren never talked about him. As for her friends, I don't consider myself one of them and have no idea who they are. I've only known her for about six months, since she started snooping around the archdiocese looking for information."

"So, if you weren't a close friend of Ms. Fallon's, can I assume you and she were never intimate; that you weren't lovers?" MacDonald had to ask.

"What kind of question is that?" Jenkins asked defensively, his plump cheeks turning pink and the thin skin beneath his scant eyebrows even redder. "I came in here voluntarily to help you out, and you insult me with tawdry insinuations."

"I'm sorry you're offended Mr. Jenkins, but as a lawyer you must know that sexual assaults are often a part of these attacks. Based on your reaction, I assume that your answer is no, that you and Ms. Fallon did not have an intimate relationship."

"Yes, you can assume that."

"OK, thank you," MacDonald replied as sincerely as he could. "I just have a few more questions. Have any other lawyers been involved in the recent lawsuit against the archdiocese, other than Ms. Fallon and yourself?"

Andy Zimmerman of Mason & Fritch is the lead defense lawyer for the archdiocese. A couple of young associates have been helping Lauren. I don't know their names, but Joe Terranova made an appearance at the motion to dismiss hearing."

"But the case wasn't dismissed, right?"

"No," said Jenkins, shaking his head. "Not only did the judge deny our motion to dismiss, but he also granted the plaintiffs' motion to unseal the old settlement files and then tried to appease our side by issuing a lame protective order. A lot of good that will do. Now the plaintiffs will surely take the arch-bishop's deposition. I was trying to persuade Lauren not to do that. I thought she'd listen to reason and work out a deal that wouldn't cripple the Church. Terranova will want hundreds of millions. He won't stop until we're bankrupt and humiliated. It's so depressing after all we've done to help victims and still protect the Church."

"So silencing Ms. Fallon doesn't get rid of this big case," said MacDonald, more as a statement of fact than a question.

"Far from it," said Jenkins. "Terranova will be even more aggressive than Lauren."

"Then why did Terranova wait so long to try to overturn the settlements?" MacDonald asked with intentional skepticism in his voice.

"I have no idea," Jenkins quickly replied. "Maybe he didn't know about them."

MacDonald didn't believe that but would wait to pursue it further. His assessment was that Jenkins had told him everything he was willing to divulge about his relationship with Lauren Fallon, meaning he was withholding a lot.

"I want to thank you for coming forward, Mr. Jenkins. One of my investiga-tors or I will probably want to follow up with you as we gather more evidence in this case. Could you give me an address, cell phone number and maybe even email address where we can reach you?"

"Sure," said Jenkins, "but I think I've told you everything I know. I just can't believe that anyone would want to hurt her."

"I'm confident we'll find out who did," said MacDonald as he stood up, walked Jenkins to the door, and shook his now cold and clammy hand. "We'll stay in touch."

Two other conference attendees visited MacDonald in the manager's office. The first, Melinda Wegner, a lawyer with the U.S. Attorney's Office in Minneapolis, had been one of Lauren's classmates at the University of Minnesota Law School but not a close friend. She told MacDonald she chatted with Lauren for about ten minutes at the reception, mostly small talk. Lauren said she and the judge were very happy and were in the middle of remodeling their home in St. Paul. She didn't mention the archdiocese case but did say she was having dinner with another lawyer that evening. Melinda ("everybody calls me Mindy") also observed that Lauren seemed preoccupied and left the reception very early, "before 6:00."

Mindy made a point of telling MacDonald she needed to get back to the Cities because she was having dinner with Dennis Logan, the U. S. Attorney for the District of Minnesota and a good friend of Judge Fallon's. Logan had been a prosecutor in the Justice Department in D.C. when MacDonald was with the Service. He didn't know him well but remembered that he used to be married and was at least twenty-five years older than Mindy. He hoped for Mindy's sake that the dinner was purely business but decided name=dropping lawyer could take care of herself.

The second visitor was more helpful. Bill Levine, a forty-something partner with the Minneapolis office of an international law firm, had met Lauren and Charlie Fallon at a fundraising dinner for the Habitat for Humanity. He stated the obvious--Lauren was beautiful, sophisticated and much younger than her husband, but also made an observation MacDonald found interesting and relevant. He said when she engaged you in conversation, she had that rare ability to make you feel special; that you were the most important person in a room full of rich, important people; that she sincerely cared about what you did and what you thought. In other words, Lauren was skilled in the art of manipulation.

Levine had a brief exchange with Lauren during a refreshment break on Friday. She asked about his wife and kids and described a recent Habitat build in which she and the judge had participated in north Minneapolis. Though he didn't attend the reception, he did have dinner at the Jolly Fisher, where coincidently he sat in a small booth directly behind Lauren. According to Levine, he ordered a beer a few minutes before Lauren and "an odd-looking little man" were seated and immediately began arguing, the man haranguing about something while Lauren admonished him to keep his voice down. Levine said he was curious but couldn't decipher the nature of their argument, though the man kept repeating the line: "I trusted you and you deceived me."

Levine remembered leaving the restaurant around eight. Lauren and her friend were still having an intense exchange when he passed by their booth intentionally not looking in their direction.

After Levine left, MacDonald sat in the office for twenty minutes, making notes, checking emails and reviewing the headlines of the Duluth and Twin Cities papers. He still didn't have a clue who killed Lauren Fallon, but he did know one thing for sure. He needed a break from all the damn lawyers.

11

ARNEST TAMMY FURNISHED Stockman and Klewacki with a printout that contained names, addresses and contact information for the Friday and Saturday resort guests as well as a list of each restaurant guest who made a reservation or paid with a credit card. They divvied up the names, or, more accurately, Stockman pulled rank and gave Klewacki two-thirds, which she really didn't mind. They would interview everyone they could track down in person or by phone and have an analyst run criminal background checks on all the names. It was a painstaking process that early on netted little useful information.

At Klewacki's polite but insistent request, the assistant manager rounded up all resort employees who worked Friday afternoon and evening. Klewacki interviewed each employee but spent most of her time with two: the server who waited on Lauren and Jenkins at the Jolly Fisher and the late-shift front-desk clerk.

The server was twenty-three and only in her second week as a Scenic Shores employee, but she remembered the couple in booth 11. She said they didn't seem like they belonged together. The man was nervous and agitated and the woman didn't eat any of her lobster salad. The woman snatched the bill away from the man and left a big tip. She couldn't recall any of their conversation; the restaurant was full and noisy, and they clammed up as soon as she approached their booth. She confirmed what the receipt indicated—they each had two glasses of Chardonnay.

Patty Barnes had owned the reservation/concierge desk for the 6:00 p.m. to 2:00 a.m. shift on Friday and Saturday nights for more than a decade. She was a divorced mother of two girls who were now married with kids of their own.

During the week she worked as a receptionist for a dental office in Two Harbors and then netted a hundred fifty bucks on the weekends at Scenic Shores. Patty was still an eye-catcher at forty-five—shoulder-length, curly brown hair, sparkling emerald eyes (aided by tinted contacts), perfect white teeth (maybe a few caps and crowns), and a well-toned physique that competed in four or five triathlons a year.

Barnes had a raspy voice that was considered sexy in northern Minnesota and a quick smile that added to her likeability. For the past several years, she'd lived rent-free in one of the cottages on the Scenic Shores property courtesy of her part-time boyfriend, a 70-year old widower who owned an excavating business in the Twin Cities and was one of the three original developers of Scenic Shores. The other two were named Holden.

Barnes was friendly and flirtatious, always making eye contact in conversation and often physical contact if you were a man. She was known to embellish the truth for the sake of a good story, and if you wanted a detailed account of her activities during the past 24 hours, you could simply log in to her *Facebook* page, friend or not. When Klewacki showed her Lauren's photo from a law firm bio, she reacted quickly and emphatically.

"Oh, yeah, I remember her," she said. "The lobby was empty around 11:30 last night. She came in from the main hallway and sat on that blue stuffed chair in front of the fireplace. She was wearing a light gray tunic over some kind of bikini or two-piece and white sandals. Her hair was pinned up, and I think she had a small purse in her lap. Anyway, she was whispering into her phone, engrossed in a conversation the whole time."

"Did she say anything to you?" asked Klewacki.

"No. The only thing I actually heard her say was 'see you in a few.' Then she got up and walked out the front door. She was lookin' good, dressed for action in my opinion."

12

UNDER NORMAL DRIVING conditions, it takes about two and a half hours to drive the 150-miles from St. Paul to Duluth on I-35. The ride in Liscomb's Audi S7 was so smooth that Fallon had no idea they were travelling in excess of 90 miles an hour and would make the trip in under two. He stared out his side window, transfixed by the blur of passing trees and slower traffic. After twenty minutes of comforting silence, Liscomb was the first to speak.

"I understand if you don't want to talk, Charlie, but I have to say again how shocked and sorry I am about this."

"Thanks, David. It might feel good to talk a little; I feel numb right now. I'm totally bewildered about why she was out on that bridge, who she was with and who would ever want to hurt her. None of it makes any sense."

"When did you last hear from her?" asked Liscomb, hoping to engage Fallon in a longer conversation.

"About 10:00 last night. She said she'd had a good day, enjoyed the speakers at the seminar and was going to bed. But I guess that wasn't the truth."

"Did anyone else from her firm attend the seminar, anyone else she knew?"

"I don't really know. I don't think anyone from Terranova was there, but to be honest, Lauren and I haven't talked much over the past few months. She's been so busy with her big case against the archdiocese. That's not to say that things weren't good between us, because I think they were. We're in the middle of redoing the master bedroom and bathroom of the house on Montcalm, and we'd planned a getaway to Madeline Island in August."

Liscomb paused before responding, easing his foot off the gas a bit so he could focus on the conversation.

"Do you think this could be connected in some way to her case? I mean, Terranova has been trying to penetrate the local archdiocese for years—how did Lauren dig up enough dirt to start world war three?"

"She hasn't shared many of the details with me, and, frankly, I haven't asked much because in my position it's really best not to know, especially if this results in a bankruptcy or other action in federal court. I do know that about a year ago she got a call from one of her old high school classmates at Washburn. He was one of the abuse victims, a terribly tragic case, David. The guy was violated in multiple ways over several years when he was an altar boy at St. John's parish in the late '80s. He went on to be a computer techie of some kind and was married briefly and divorced. He was battling severe depression when Archbishop Lamkin contacted him probably fifteen years ago. Lamkin apparently offered to pay him ten grand along with an apology from the Church and lifetime medical care."

Fallon stopped talking and stared out the passenger side window lost in thought.

"Did he take the deal?" asked Liscomb, confounded that Fallon hadn't finished the story.

"Oh, sorry," Fallon replied, turning back toward Liscomb, "He did take the deal and then regretted it. That's why he called Lauren. Anyway, shortly after she agreed to look into his case, he committed suicide. Hanged himself in his apartment. After that, Lauren became obsessed, maybe consumed is a better word. She was on a mission to track down and vindicate all of the victims who settled with Lamkin. I don't know how she found so many, but she did."

"I heard a little bit about her suit from Andy Zimmerman at Mason."

"I know Andy," said Fallon. "He's a bit rigid but a damn good lawyer."

"Agreed. Anyway, he's represented the archdiocese for over 20 years. I got to know him when Wyatt defended Penn Chemical in that discrimination class action last year, and we have lunch from time to time. He's a big fan of the archbishop—says he cares deeply about the abuse victims but doesn't believe the Church owes them anything but compassion and therapy. When Lamkin arrived on the scene after Bradley died, he devised a master plan to oust the bad priests, find the victims and work out deals with most of them. According to

Andy, none of the settling victims was interested in talking to Terranova until Lauren came along. He says she convinced a lot of them that the adverse impact on their lives in terms of anguish and loss of future earnings was worth exponentially more than ten or twenty grand.

"Andy said Judge Kennedy, who's a Catholic himself, refused to make the confidential settlement files public but, with the victim's consent, ordered release of a summary of the settlement terms. Apparently, Lauren's theory was that the archdiocese took advantage of the victims' vulnerability in persuading them to accept the low-ball deals."

Fallon already knew that but was very interested in Liscomb's take on the situation. "I heard most of the victims who settled were represented by counsel, which makes her premise more difficult to prove. On the other hand, Lauren could be an unstoppable force when she set her sights on something, especially if it involved taking advantage of the little guy. She never told me who represented poor Billy Evans when he settled, but I assume if Lamkin is as smart as you say he provided counsel for those that didn't have one."

"I'm not sure about that, judge. I don't think the settlement documents included the name of the victim's lawyer, only the fact that they consented after getting advice and guidance from counsel."

"Really?" Fallon was incredulous. "Did Zimmerman tell you that?"

"Yeah. I think Lamkin and Zimmerman really controlled the process, and Judge Kennedy let them do it."

"I haven't met Archbishop Lamkin. Even though I was raised Catholic, I'm no longer one of the faithful. Mary was kind of a pantheist, spiritual but not affiliated with any church, and Lauren was definitely an atheist." He looked at Liscomb for a reaction, got none, and continued:

"I know Wyatt did some employment work for the archdiocese several years ago. Did that end at some point?"

Thinking that was an odd question for Fallon to ask, Liscomb hesitated briefly and then answered, "We did handle some employment litigation on a conflicts basis back in the '90s but haven't represented the Church for years. Why do you ask?"

"Just curious," Fallon replied. "My memory isn't as sharp as it used to be."

Liscomb didn't buy that for a second but noticed the Hinckley exit was fast approaching.

"I'm going to get off here, judge. I have to piss."

"I'm good in that regard," said Fallon, "but could you get me a bottle of water? I need to make a few quick calls."

"Sure, Charlie."

Fallon didn't make any calls. Something had distracted him.

13

MacDonald compared notes with Klewacki and Stockman before embarking on the 40-minute drive to Duluth and St. Mark's. He wanted to have a conversation with Judge Fallon before the media started speculating about what might have occurred over the Gooseberry River.

They all agreed that Lauren left the resort to meet someone around midnight, but who was it and where did they meet? If Patty Barnes heard right, Lauren talked to a person of interest, if not the prime suspect, on her cell phone. Even though the phone was missing, her provider should have a record of the call and the caller's number. MacDonald made a mental note to ask the judge for details about her cell—description, number, provider. And what about the used condom? Was someone other than Peter Jenkins intimate with Lauren Friday evening before she went out? Could she have had sex with Jenkins? The sheriff had a hard time with that image—maybe the condom had been in the receptacle before Lauren occupied the room and the cleaning staff simply overlooked it.

Preparing to listen to the slew of voicemail messages queued up in his cell, MacDonald adjusted the air conditioning in the Tahoe and set the cruise control to 75. Hakonen let him know that Lauren's body had made it to the forensic lab that served as the morgue for several northern counties. MacDonald knew the chief pathologist for Mid-States Medical Examiners, the private company that conducted autopsies when the cause and manner of death were part of a criminal investigation. He'd been a medic in the army during Desert Storm and decided his demeanor and sense of humor weren't suitable for live bodies. Every summer he invited the local sheriffs and police chiefs for dinner, drinks and a harbor cruise on the 34-foot Chris-Craft Catalina he kept at Hidden Cove

Marina on Barker's Island. He even invited Warren Leeks, M.D., the 75-year-old, inept Lake County Coroner.

Dr. Edward Higgins had a reputation for being meticulous, a trait most competent law enforcement professionals appreciate in a medical examiner. He also had a wicked, often morbid sense of humor that appealed to MacDonald, as did Higgins' superior intellect and interest in contact sports. Though they hadn't had a case together, Higgins and MacDonald played tennis in Duluth a few times a month.

MacDonald called Thomassoni and gave him an update on the Gooseberry case, indicating he'd decided to take the lead on the investigation rather than request assistance from the Bureau of Criminal Apprehension, at least for the time being. Thomassoni was a decent prosecutor but a twice divorced, notorious skirt chaser. In his mid-fifties, the county attorney was only attracted to women young enough to be his daughter, so Hallie was safe. She was also capable of beating the shit out of him.

MacDonald pulled into the parking lot at St. Mark's a few minutes after noon. At Fallon's request, Liscomb had already dropped him off at the morgue and had driven downtown in search of a place to eat lunch.

14

"Hello, archbishop, did you get my message?"

"Where are you, Peter?"

"On my way back to St. Paul."

"We need to talk in private as soon as possible." Lamkin was also driving back to the Twin Cities, going well over the 70-mph speed limit in his silver Lincoln Town Car. "I didn't know you were attending that conference, Peter. What the hell is going on with you?"

"Didn't you get my message about Lauren Fallon?"

"Yes, I got your message," Lamkin said, the irritation evident in his voice. "What else do you know about that?"

"Nothing new. She left the resort late last night, but no one seems to know why. Some hikers found her body early this morning in Gooseberry Park. The sheriff came to the seminar first thing this morning and told us. He interviewed me before I left."

"Why would he interview you?" After asking the question, Lamkin thought it better not to pursue the subject further on his phone. "Listen, Peter, what time do you think you'll get back at your place?"

Jenkins checked his watch. "I should be home about 4:00."

"O.K. How about if I come over between 6:00 and 7:00?"

"That's fine. Will you have eaten dinner?"

"Don't concern yourself with that."

15

FALLON SPENT TWENTY agonizing minutes in the morgue with Dr. Higgins and Deputy Hakonen. Viewing Lauren's grey, lifeless body and crushed, misshapen head sent him into semi-shock. Higgins assured him that he would perform a complete examination to determine the exact cause and approximate time of death. He was more open with Fallon about his first impressions than he would have been with most family members. He said flat out she wasn't shot, stabbed or strangled and that his best judgment was the fatal blunt force injuries to her head and neck, a shattered right clavicle and broken left wrist were all caused by an unexpected, involuntary fall from several stories. Toxicology tests would reveal whether she was under the influence of alcohol or drugs or some other poisonous substance, but those results could take a few weeks.

Fallon asked whether her fall could have been an accident. Before Hakonen had a chance to say it was really too early to know with certainty, Higgins said confidently:

"This was no accident and no suicide, judge. This was murder."

Fallon asked to have a few minutes alone with Lauren just as MacDonald opened the door to the pathology lab. He introduced himself and was appropriately deferential to the judge, stating he'd like to have a short meeting with him before he returned to St. Paul. He suggested the Lakeside Coffee Cafe, a few blocks east of the hospital in the Fitger's Complex, might be a good place to have a quiet conversation.

When Fallon didn't respond right away, MacDonald backed off. "This can wait, judge, if you'd prefer not to talk today." He was hoping Fallon would be anxious to talk, to get all the information he could despite his obvious grief.

"Oh, no, sheriff. I appreciate your understanding, but I'd just as soon meet with you now. My ride is off having lunch. How long do you think it will take?"

"A half-hour, maybe forty-five minutes, judge. No more than that. I'll get us a quiet table at the Lakeside. Walk over whenever you're ready."

16

HALLIE BELL DECIDED to make the most of the early morning wakeup call. After a light breakfast, she drove to the county courthouse in Two Harbors to work on a couple of right-of-way condemnation cases and to prepare for the next county board meeting. She had a brief conversation with Thomassoni, who had already heard about the incident in Gooseberry Park.

Bell left the office around noon, stopping at SuperOne for some groceries before heading to her condo for a long run and a relaxing afternoon in the sun. As she gathered an assortment of bags from the back seat of her Honda Accord, she noticed ominous, gray nimbus clouds moving in from the west and wondered whether the unusual heat and high humidity would lead to severe storms later in the day. She needed to get some exercise before that happened, she thought.

Leaning forward on the suede loveseat in her living room while she alternately propped each foot against a glass coffee table to tighten the laces on her running shoes, Bell was startled by an insistent rapping on the metal door to her second-floor condo. Startled, because the building had an expensive security system. Most of the residents were single women careful not to let anyone bypass the call-up procedure to get in. Startled, too, because of the earlier incident in Gooseberry.

Bell jumped up and bounded to the door, bending at the waist to peer through the spyhole when she heard:

"Hal, it's me, Ricky."

Simultaneously peeved and relieved to hear her ex-husband's familiar voice, she opened the door. "You asshole, you scared the crap outta' me! Why didn't you call from the entryway like everybody else?"

"What's the big deal?" Holden protested, "You know I have keys to these buildings."

Before Bell could react, Holden brushed past her and sat down on an antique wooden rocker, the closest piece of furniture to the door. He changed his approach and softened his tone. "Hey, I'm sorry. I was in the neighborhood and I've got some information that you and your boyfriend might find interesting."

"About what?"

"About the murder in the park this morning."

"Who told you about that?" asked Bell, now intrigued enough to settle back down on the loveseat.

"Dad and I had breakfast with your boss at the Kitchi Gammi Club this morning. We were talking about the golf course in Two Harbors. The City owns the clubhouse and runs the course but Lake County owns the land. The City is losing over half a million a year and wants the County to lower the rental fee and shorten the course from 18 to 9 holes."

"I know all about that, Rick," Bell interrupted, "and I also know that your family is proposing to buy the most valuable parcels of land on the course to build some sort of multi-use development, but what the hell does any of that have to do with the murder?"

"I was getting to that. In the middle of our discussion, Thomassoni got a call from MacDonald about the girl's body they found. Greg told us she's a lawyer from the Twin Cities who's pursuing a big case against the Catholic Church."

"He actually told you all that?" Bell didn't try to hide her disgust at her boss' lack of discretion.

"Where else would I get the information?"

"Cal Stockman, perhaps? Anyway, that can't be your big scoop—Mac already knows all that."

"You're right. After breakfast, I drove up to Tofte to meet with this rich investment banker from the Twin Cities. His name is McBride, but I'm sure you don't know him."

"I don't."

"This guy bought some buildable lots from my dad east of Cascade Mountain ski resort more than 10 years ago, about five acres with over 300 feet of shoreline. He hired Schroeder Constructors to build an incredible log home on the property.

Had to cost a couple million at least. Now he wants to add some sort of outbuilding with a steam room and sauna but needs more land. He called my dad a few weeks ago and said he'd be up here this weekend. I was supposed to call him last week to schedule a meeting, but I forgot. I needed to check on some other property up in Cook County, so I figured I'd just drop in on Mr. McBride. Anyway, I should have known something was up when I saw a huge Town Car in the driveway next to McBride's Mercedes. I didn't think they made those monsters anymore."

"I hope this is going to get better," said Bell, not particularly enjoying Holden's lecherous eyes ogling her skimpy running outfit.

"Oh, it is. I walk up the front steps to these ten-foot, solid oak double doors and through the sidelight windows I can see a half-naked man, I think it was McBride, in the great room kneeling and performing some kind of act on a grey-haired guy sitting on the couch. I make an executive decision not to ring the doorbell but take a few pictures of the Town Car with my phone and then call the PI firm we use for collections to find out who owns that monster. Turns out it's owned by the Archdiocese of St. Paul."

"And you're thinking there may some connection between the lawyer suing the Church, if she turns out to be a murder victim, and the person driving that car? Kind of a stretch but I'm sure the sheriff will follow up. . ."

"Wait, that's not all," Holden said smugly. "The land next to McBride's is undeveloped and is adjacent to Superior National Forest property. There's a service road that divides the properties and runs down to the lake. I needed to make some calls and have a smoke, so I parked my truck on the service road and walked our land, keeping an eye on McBride's front door. About a half hour later, I saw this short, grey-haired guy, dressed in black, leave the cabin and get into the Town Car. I was able to get a few pretty good pictures."

Holden got up and handed his cell phone to Bell.

"I had a hunch this guy was a big shot, so I did a little investigating with my sidekick, Google." Holden extended his hand and Bell returned the phone.

"Compare this picture of the archbishop from a story in the *Pioneer Press* with the photo I took this morning," said Holden as he held up his phone and switched between the two images. "Besides, who wears black on a day like today?"

"Wow," said Bell, somewhat mockingly, but somewhat impressed. "You're a regular Sherlock Holmes."

"Screw you, too, Hallie," said Holden, retreating to the rocker and sliding his phone into the pocket of his golf shorts.

"Seriously, Rick, send me those pictures. There might be some connection; I just don't know enough about the case. I think Mac might want to follow up with you if that's okay."

"Sure, Hal. I'll send you the pictures. I'm pretty easy to track down if the big man wants to talk."

"So, after the archbishop look-alike left, did you meet with this McBride guy?" Bell asked, rising from the couch as a signal to Holden it was time to leave.

"No," Holden replied, getting up and moving deliberately towards the door with his eyes fixed on his ex-wife's cleavage. "I didn't want him to get suspicious, so I called him on my way over here to set something up for later today or tomorrow. He wasn't very friendly. Said he didn't think he was interested in the project any longer but would call me if he changed his mind."

"What do you make of that?" asked Bell.

"I don't know. Maybe he ran out of money. Or maybe he's got bigger problems. Could this guy really be playing hide the weenie with an archbishop? This could be a major league scandal!"

"Really? Must you be so juvenile? I wouldn't start spreading a rumor like that, Rick," admonished Bell. "You're not even sure what you saw."

"I'll keep it to myself for now," said Holden, as he took a few steps toward Bell and deliberately backed her against the door. "You're really looking good, Hallie. You must be working out."

Bell playfully but with all her strength pushed Holden away with one hand while opening the door with the other. "Goodbye, Rick. Thanks for sharing the intel; it might actually be helpful. But next time call me first."

17

THE LAKESIDE COFFEE Café was located on the first floor of a cavernous, four-story brownstone originally constructed in the late 1800s as a brewery and currently listed on the national registry of historic sites. The brewery closed for good in the 1970s. The property sat vacant for over a decade when it was purchased by an investor group from Chicago and carefully refurbished as a boutique hotel with retail shops, a handful of restaurants and, more recently, a micro-brewery.

The Lakeside had been in business for a dozen years and had earned a state-wide reputation for creative, hearty breakfasts and flavorful, locally roasted coffees. MacDonald loved strong black coffee so he often patronized the place when he was in town. He was savoring a cup of French roast at a two-person wooden table with a partial view of the lake when Fallon sat down across from him with a can of diet soda.

"Not a coffee drinker?" MacDonald asked while he retrieved a legal pad from a canvas briefcase and once again shook hands with the judge.

"Not in the afternoon," replied Fallon. "Otherwise, I get even less sleep than my normal five hours."

"Fortunately, that's never been a problem for me." MacDonald leaned in, "Let me say again, judge, how sorry I am about your loss. Are you as baffled by this as I am?"

"Probably more so," said Fallon. "I can't imagine anyone wanting to harm her."

"Sadly, that's the case with a lot of victims." MacDonald tried to get the measure of the broad-shouldered, white-haired man facing him with sincere but tired eyes and a deflated demeanor. He continued with his most empathetic voice. "I might as well get this out of the way first. It won't surprise someone in your position, but at some point you're going to be asked to provide some proof of your whereabouts between sunset yesterday and sunrise today."

"That won't be too difficult," replied Fallon, knowing that he would be on the list of potential suspects until a solid alibi removed him. "I was at the federal courthouse in St. Paul until about 7:00 last night. The security staff and sign-out procedure will vouch for that. I went to my athletic club for a quick workout and dinner. I actually had a long conversation with the club manager while I was eating. I left there around 9:00 and drove home. I took our dog, a golden lab, for a short walk around midnight. Remember, I don't sleep much. Anyway, one of our neighbors, Jeff Knapp, pulled into his driveway with his teenage daughter and a car full of her friends just as I got back from the walk. Must have been about 12:30. Jeff said hello and something about a concert at the Xcel Center. I got up about six this morning and left the house at 7:00 to have breakfast and play golf at Town & Country, where my round was interrupted by Sheriff Miller. You know the rest."

MacDonald looked up from taking notes and nodded. "OK, that's very helpful." He sipped his coffee and stared out the window as he thought about how to phrase his next question. "I apologize for having to get into this, judge, but are you aware of any romantic relationships your wife might have been having outside of your marriage?"

"Maybe I'm naïve, but I think, or thought, we had a strong, loving relationship that actually got better in some ways over the ten years we were together. I know the age gap is wide but that never seemed to matter to Lauren. Even my daughter, Shawn, who was skeptical about Lauren and her motives at first, and protective of her mother's memory, came to accept her as my wife. No, sheriff, if this isn't some kind of random act, the only thing I can come up with is that it's related to her case against the archdiocese."

Something in Fallon's voice and demeanor had changed, which made MacDonald think he wasn't being completely honest about his young wife's fidelity or about what he knew.

"Did Lauren ever mention the name Peter Jenkins to you?"

"A few times. He's sort of an in-house lawyer for the archdiocese. He's definitely not a priest, more of a combination chief operating officer and general counsel. Lauren felt that he had second thoughts about the deals the Church made with many of the abuse victims; that his allegiance to the archbishop was fragile. I think he might have been the source of a lot of the evidence she accumulated about bad priests and about the identities and current whereabouts of the victims. That's just a guess, sheriff. I could be completely off base. You should know that Lauren was very secretive about her clients and cases."

"I don't think you're wrong, judge. Were you aware that Jenkins attended the conference up at Scenic Shores, and that he and Lauren had dinner together last night?"

Fallon's eyes widened but his voice remained calm. "No, Lauren didn't mention him when she called me last night."

"What time was that?"

"Between 9:30 and 10:00," he said. "She was in good spirits. Said the presenters at the conference were excellent. That she learned a lot but was exhausted and was going to bed. She didn't mention anyone specifically."

"And that was the last time you spoke to her?" MacDonald had to ask.

"Yes." Fallon replied, staring at his can of caffeine-free Diet Coke and having difficulty holding it together. A few tears escaped from his bloodshot eyes, but he quickly wiped them away with a napkin.

MacDonald decided not to mention the condom found in Lauren's room. He did tell the judge about her late-night cell phone call from the lobby and observed departure from the resort around midnight. This information might have upset the judge, but he didn't show it. He claimed more than once that he wanted to know the truth, regardless of the pain it might cause. He agreed to provide MacDonald access to Lauren's phone records, noting that as far as he knew her only cell phone was personal through their family plan and not provided by Terranova.

"So, do you have any leads, sheriff?" Fallon asked. "Is this Jenkins fellow a person of interest?"

"I'll be honest with you, judge. I believe Jenkins was infatuated with your wife and supplied her with a lot of information he wouldn't have but for these feelings. He may be a key witness, but I don't think he's the perpetrator. In fact, I don't think he left the resort last night. All that said, I haven't ruled out anyone at this point."

"This has the direct number to my chambers in St. Paul, my cell number and personal email," said Fallon, handing MacDonald a card with handwritten notations. "I'd appreciate it if you'd keep me apprised of any developments in your investigation."

"Of course, judge. And thanks again for doing this. I assume you'll be taking some time away from the bench?" For some reason, MacDonald actually assumed the answer to that question would be no.

"I'm not sure at this point," said Fallon. "It may be more therapeutic to keep working. That's what I did when I lost Mary."

"Sure," said MacDonald. "I've had my share of grief in this life, judge, and it's just impossible to know how we're going to react to the most horrible of tragedies." He stared at his coffee mug for several seconds recalling that snowy January morning when he'd lost everything that mattered.

"I promise to call you as soon as we learn anything of significance." With those words of assurance, MacDonald reached for his case and stood up, waiting for the judge to do the same.

"Thanks, sheriff. And one more thing."

"What's that?"

"Please call me Charlie."

18

MacDONALD HAD PARKED the Tahoe in a public lot near the morgue. As he walked the two blocks up 9th Avenue East, he felt a chill in the back of his neck despite the hot, muggy air. The odd feeling had nothing to do with the weather; he experienced it sometimes when his mind couldn't reconcile competing thoughts. Fallon seemed like a good guy, a smart, caring fellow whose weariness made him seem older than his sixty years. There was no question he was devastated by the loss of his beautiful young wife. But MacDonald couldn't shake the notion that he was withholding critical information, something he didn't want anyone to know. This feeling was amplified by a nagging thought left over from his morning interviews—if Lauren Fallon would sleep with someone as creepy as Jenkins, what else would she do?

MacDonald glanced up at the sky before climbing into the Tahoe. A storm was brewing to the west, and he was concerned that Hallie may have left a few windows open because he usually did. He'd call her on the way home.

He needed to check in with Klewacki first. It was 3:30. She'd been working for fifteen hours straight and sent him a text at 2:00 to call her ASAP. He also had texts from a couple of media outlets and a dozen voicemail messages. Driving east on London Road, he called Klewacki on his voice-activated, hands-free cell.

"You're not going to believe this," she said with more than a little sarcasm in her voice.

"Try me," said MacDonald, assuming she had information about the Gooseberry case.

"I'm sitting in the reception area at Lake County Hospital. Stockman's had a heart attack. Doctor says he should be okay, but their putting a couple stents in and he'll be laid up for a few weeks. I called Marlys and his son at Marquette.

"Thanks, Gail. That was thoughtful. How and where did it happen? I've talked to him about all the extra weight."

"Yeah, especially when that extra weight is banging Patty Barnes, the night clerk at Scenic Shores. Apparently, they've been seeing each other on the sly for a few months.

"After the interviews this morning, Stockman told me he had a lunch meeting and would see me at the office around 2:00. His meeting was in Barnes' little love nest by the lake. When he collapsed on top of her, she thought he was dead but fortunately called for help right away. One of the responding EMTs recognized him and called us. Of course, I didn't tell Marlys the shitty details, but in this town she'll probably find out soon enough."

"Jesus," sighed MacDonald. "I can't say I'm surprised about his extra-curricular activities, though my opinion of Ms. Barnes just dropped a few notches. Listen, you should go home and get some rest, see your family. I'll stop by the hospital and check on Stockman on my way back to the courthouse. You aren't working tomorrow, right?"

"According to the duty roster, I'm supposed to be off until Monday. By the way, we've tentatively scheduled a news conference on the Gooseberry case for 5:00 this afternoon; I figured you'd be back by then. Duluth and Twin Cities media have been swarming. Word is out that the lady lawyer who sued the Catholic Church has been murdered. Now that Stockman's laid up, you're going to need more help on this case. Just say the word, and I'll be in tomorrow."

"I appreciate that, Gail. I'll check in with you later tonight. As for the news conference, did you or Stockman learn anything of significance after our meeting at the Shores?"

"I don't know about Stockman; he talked to a few other resort staffers after our meeting, but I don't have anything new. We're sending some evidence to the BCA office in Duluth—her laptop and the used condom. Based on my review of footage from the surveillance cameras on the property, it looks like none of the overnight guests entered or left the resort property between midnight and 2:00 a.m. except for Lauren Fallon. The bar closed at 1:00 a.m., and a few local stragglers left the resort, but none of them knew our victim and, for the most part, their stories check out."

"So that would support the theory that Lauren met someone who was not a resort guest. That makes sense. I suppose you've talked to Ryan already."

"Yup. He said her husband, the judge, was pretty upset. Just sat in the morgue and cried for 15 minutes. Ryan had a hard time with it. Said you sent him home. I left a report with everything we've got so far on your desk. I'll send you a protected email copy, too."

"That's perfect. You're great. I'll be in touch."

19

PETER JENKINS LIVED in the same red brick and brownstone fourplex on the south side of historic Summit Avenue for over twenty years. It was no accident that his two-bedroom condo was within walking distance of his small universe—the corporate offices in the chancery, the St. Paul Cathedral and the archbishop's residence.

Jenkins literally grew up in the Catholic Church. His biological mother, whose identity he never learned, was a part-time waitress, part-time exotic dancer, part-time prostitute and full-time crack cocaine addict. She was stabbed to death in the back alley of a bar on Rice Street for withholding cash from her pimp when Peter was six weeks old and already in the care of social services. His mother had intended to get an abortion, but none of the half dozen or so potential fathers would pay for it. Instead, she delivered an undersized baby at Ramsey Hospital. She had hoped that the little bundle of joy would make her eligible for $600 a month in aid for dependent children and food stamps. She would have been right about that had she not left him alone in her apartment while she went out to the bars every night.

Several tenants complained to the landlord and then to the police about an infant wailing through the night. The police referred the case to child protection services. They had taken Peter into custody and were moving to terminate mom's parental rights when, by dying, she "voluntarily" gave him up for adoption.

Kathryn Jenkins never married and, given her devotion to the Catholic Church, it's a wonder she didn't become a nun. For nearly 50 years, she was the executive assistant to three successive archbishops as well as the lead organist at the Cathedral of St. Paul. She was exceptional at both jobs, though she considered playing the classic sanctuary pipe organ and the newer gallery organ to be a privilege rather than a job. She was a red-haired, freckle-faced bull of a woman who didn't have time for any lazy, messy men in her life except for Jesus Christ, the archbishop, and her adopted son, Peter.

Kathryn and Peter lived in a well-maintained two-bedroom rambler on Holly Avenue in St. Paul, about a mile from the chancery. Kathryn was forty-five when she adopted Peter in the mid-1960s, a time when few two-parent families were willing to take a chance on a "crack" baby. He attended Catholic schools in St. Paul. When he wasn't in school, he was usually with his mother either in the chancery offices or the Cathedral. To say Kathryn was protective would be a colossal understatement, but Peter never resisted her influence; in fact, he was as devoted to her and to the Church as she was to him.

When Peter was a boy, Kathryn entertained the notion of his becoming a priest, though she became disillusioned with the idea by the time he was an adolescent. Given her position inside the archdiocese, she had access to "inside" information about abusive, pedophile priests, a problem that had always existed to some extent in the Church but one that became an epidemic in the 1970s and '80s.

She believed that God was testing the Catholic hierarchy; that there was a demonic element within the Church that needed exorcism, swiftly and harshly. She didn't agree with the deny, delay and defend tactics of Archbishop Bradley, and didn't think Pope John-Paul would either, but she went along with the program, hoping that Bradley would ultimately see the light.

After graduating from the University of St. Thomas with a degree in Theology (concentrating in Catholic doctrine), Peter attended law school at the Catholic University in Washington, D.C., hoping to obtain both a juris doctor degree and a licentiate in Canon Law. Unfortunately, shortly after he graduated law school, Kathryn had a debilitating heart attack at age 70. He moved back home to care for her and abandoned the idea of getting a degree in canon law; instead, accepting Bradley's offer of employment as assistant chancellor of the archdiocese.

Kathryn never fully recovered. She died of congestive heart failure within a year of Peter's return. He sold the house on Holly and purchased the condominium on Summit Avenue, filling it with his mother's beautiful antiques, including several German clocks, an oak dining room table and a working pump organ whose origin dated back to the 1850s.

Archbishop Bradley died within a year of Kathryn and, rather than work for a new archbishop, Paul Bologna resigned as chancellor, creating the opportunity of a lifetime for young Peter. After assessing the organizational structure and condition of the Twin Cities' Archdiocese, Bradley's successor not only offered Peter the job, but sent him back to Catholic University for a year to complete work on his degree in canon law. Lamkin wanted a chancellor who would be his puppet, fiercely loyal to the Church but even more so to him. Peter was perfect for the job.

Throughout his adolescence and early adulthood, Peter was attracted to the opposite sex, but his standards were high, too high. Dynamic, professional women to whom he was drawn did not reciprocate his feelings, if they even knew he had them. He was short, plump, balding and uncoordinated, although he did enjoy bocce ball and an occasional round of miniature golf.

Shy and socially awkward around women, Peter had difficulty initiating a conversation and making small talk. Though he was conversant in three languages, could recite the *Magna Carta Liber Tatum* from memory and taught classes in comparative religion and ancient history, he knew nothing about pop culture. He didn't own a television, didn't watch movies, didn't drink anything stronger than communion wine, and didn't listen to music that was composed after 1900. Peter Jenkins was odd, or, as he preferred to say, eccentric. He did date a few single women from the Cathedral bell chorus on a platonic basis, but the only woman he truly loved for the first fifty years of his life was Kathryn. And then he met Lauren Fallon.

20

Lamkin parked the Town Car and, lost in thought, stumbled and nearly lost his balance while traversing the cobblestone walkway leading to Jenkin's building. He'd stopped at the residence to take a shower and change clothes. Listening to WCCO on the drive over, he was reminded of the main topic for discussion with Peter: A woman identified as Twin Cities' lawyer Lauren Fallon had been discovered dead in Gooseberry Park. Authorities suspected foul play. As Lamkin climbed the concrete steps, opened the glass door to the entryway, and pushed the button under Jenkins' nameplate, it was starting to rain.

Peter was putting the final touches on a tray of cheese, crackers, fruit and mini chicken salad sandwiches when he heard the entry buzzer and Lamkin's voice. He hurried into the living room, pushed the lock release to let his boss in the inner hallway and opened the front door to greet him.

"You made it just in time," Jenkins said, gently taking Lamkin's black umbrella and setting it behind the door. "It's going to pour out there."

"Let's hope that's all it does," said Lamkin, tossing a decorative nylon pillow off to the side, so he could sit on Jenkins' crushed velvet couch. "All I'm hearing on the news are severe weather warnings. That and reports of the Lauren Fallon murder. What's the real story on that, Peter?"

"Let me get a few things from the kitchen," said Jenkins as he rushed to serve the refreshments. "Would you prefer fresh lemonade to drink or sparkling water?"

"Water is fine." Lamkin considered telling Peter to forget the food, but he was famished, not having eaten since breakfast. "I can't stay very long; I'm delivering the homily tomorrow at the 10:30 mass and it needs some refining edits."

Jenkins set the tray down on a white cotton tablecloth that protected the unblemished surface of his mother's favorite oak coffee table. He handed Lamkin a plate and placed a glass of ice water on a monogrammed leather coaster on the ornate side table next to the couch.

"I'm sure it will please God and the faithful, archbishop. Your homilies are always inspirational." Jenkins took a seat across from Lamkin on a brown, leather Queen Anne chair that was his favorite. "By the way, I think it's admirable that you participate in masses during the summer to help facilitate some time off for our priests."

"I do enjoy it, Peter. But let's not get off the subject. What's your take on this murder, if it was murder, and why were you even up at there in the first place?"

"I went up there because Ms. Fallon suggested that perhaps we could discuss parameters of settling her lawsuit against us. Possibly set up a mediation session." Jenkins chose his words carefully, worried that Lamkin could explode at any moment.

"Wait a minute. Mediation? We've already addressed the grievances of these men, Peter. We established support groups for most of them. Based on the feedback I get, most seem satisfied with the resolution of their claims, and the best thing about it—we've kept most of them in the Church. All the time and effort that went into all this bullshit, not to mention the money we've spent on lawyers, and now this? I need to know how Terranova's office came up with all this shit." Lamkin was working up a good lather. He set his plate of food down and glared at Jenkins.

"From the day the complaint was served on us claiming that over a hundred victims were part of this lawsuit, I suspected you had something to do with it. I know Zimmerman's firm didn't. I know I didn't. Who else knew the identity of all these men? Only you! Were you fornicating with a judge's wife, Peter? Is that what started all of this? Did that woman manipulate you into forsaking years of the Church's work? Tell me what the fuck is going on!"

Jenkins was trembling now. Lamkin could be volatile, but he had rarely seen him this agitated. "With all due respect, archbishop, you wouldn't understand. I loved Lauren, and I thought she loved me. Over time she convinced me that we had shortchanged the victims; that they deserved more than a few thousand dollars and an apology for what they'd suffered."

"So, you betrayed me and the Church," sneered Lamkin. "What did you think—that she would leave a federal judge to be with you?"

"She never said that." Jenkins was tearing up, his voice barely audible. "She was so gentle and kind. She gave me a new perspective on a lot of things. So yes, I gave her lists of victims and abusers. She already knew about many of them. I wanted to clear my conscience, but I knew you wouldn't agree. I'm ready to accept whatever consequences . . ."

"How did it end, then?" Lamkin interrupted, knowing he needed to back off if he wanted the whole truth out of Jenkins.

"She said she would talk to her clients about participating in a mediation. She also told me that our special relationship was over. She said she was sorry, but it couldn't continue. I was terribly disappointed, but now I'm really scared."

"About what?"

"We were together Friday night in her room just before dinner. We used protection, but I don't know if the police will be able to figure it out. I'm sure my DNA is on that thing if they find it. I got the impression the sheriff thinks I might have had something to do with Lauren's death."

"Did you tell him you were with her Friday night?"

"He knows I had dinner with her but that's it."

"Why are you worried if you had nothing to do with her death?"

"Of course, I had nothing to do with her death!" Jenkins practically yelled. "I walked her to her room after dinner and that's the last time I saw her. But that doesn't mean I won't be a suspect."

"Any idea who could have killed her?"

"I've thought a lot about that today, and the only person I can think of is Billy Hutchinson."

"Billy Hutchinson? The altar boy that Father O'Malley drugged and violated back in the '70s?" Lamkin was familiar with one of the worst cases of abuse in Minnesota history.

"Yes," said Jenkins. "The boy who bludgeoned O'Malley to death with a chalice when he was fifteen and then spent ten years in a mental hospital. He's in one of our therapy groups. No one is a more fervent supporter of you and the Catholic Church than Billy. He still has serious coping issues and occasional bouts of rage, but we arranged for him to work as a custodian for Father Patterson at St. Theresa. He actually lives in a small apartment in the basement of the clergy house with Patterson and old Father Dowling. Billy has adopted the life of an ascetic in many respects, dressing in simple black clothes, drinking no alcohol, and eating only fish and bread. Unfortunately, he refuses to take any kind of medication to treat his depression and anxiety and often resorts to cutting himself.

"Anyway, as you know, I keep tabs on all of the support groups for our abuse victims. About a month ago, when Lauren's lawsuit was in the news, Billy made derogatory statements to his group about a lawyer who was trying to destroy the Church. He called her the devil's whore and worse and said somebody needed to stop her. I didn't think much of it at the time, but now I'm worried that if he got fixated on her he could have acted on it, believing he was saving the Church. Billy may be in his fifties, but he's still a big, powerful man."

Lamkin was skeptical about Billy's involvement, but wanted Jenkins to keep talking. "Do you really think he would have gone all the way up to the North Shore to kill her?"

"He has access to a car, and he's not stupid. Far from it. I know this—if he called Lauren and told her his story, she would meet with him, or would have met with him. I have no doubt about that."

"Did you tell that sheriff about him?"

"No. I was too nervous to think of it. Besides, I don't think we want that sheriff snooping around our parishes stirring up trouble."

"It's a little late for you to be concerned about that, Peter."

It was time for the archbishop to be self-righteous and vindictive. Jenkins expected it. Lamkin knew how to make him feel inept and unworthy. He folded his arms across his chest and stared at the framed photograph hanging on the wall above the pump organ. It was of Kathryn hugging him on the day he graduated from college. It was his favorite.

"You may have done irreparable damage to our Church family already by disclosing our most private and confidential information to that lawyer. I spent the first ten years of my tenure here trying to control the damage to this diocese while doing our very best for the victims. We've established protocols that are the envy of Catholic communities throughout the world. We've avoided the bankruptcies that have destroyed some of our best leaders and decimated God's work in places like Boston, Milwaukee and New Orleans. Now that Terranova smells blood he'll find a way to recruit even more victims, and then he'll start taking depositions and demanding more documents, and ultimately, ultimately, he'll destroy us, too. And to what end, Peter? So that we can transfer all the assets we've accumulated to build Catholic communities, to educate God's children, to mold followers of Christ, and to heal the sick and infirm to a relatively small group of broken men who, although they've certainly been wronged, will not benefit from it. Far from it. These men need love, understanding and spiritual healing. What will a huge financial windfall do for them? No, Peter, this is more about enriching godless, hedonistic lawyers who want to destroy the Church for their own gain."

Lamkin noticed that Jenkins was staring into space. "Peter, look at me. Please tell me you did not tell that lawyer whore about the fund."

"I would never do that, archbishop. I am so sorry about how this is turning out. At this point, I'm more confused than anything else. I believed that Lauren and I could work everything out this weekend. I know now that was naïve, but I swear she's not like the rest of them."

Lamkin ignored Jenkin's lame rationalizing. "So you're sure you haven't told a soul about the fund?"

"I swear I haven't, your eminence."

Lamkin wasn't sure he could believe or trust the man he'd trusted completely and unequivocally for twenty years. "All right, Peter. You'll remain in your position for the time being, but you won't have any further involvement with this lawsuit, understood?"

"Of course, your eminence."

Lamkin wiped his mouth and hands with a napkin and stood up to leave. "And I'll want to see you in my office on Monday morning first thing."

"I'll be there."

Forgetting his umbrella, Lamkin exited Jenkin's condo and building and walked into a downpour that included pea-sized hail. In the thirty seconds it took him to scurry into the Town Car, his short-sleeve shirt and black polyester slacks were soaked. The temperature had plummeted in the thirty minutes he was in Jenkin's condo, and he was chilled to the bone. Swiftly moving storm clouds dominated the evening sky. The metaphor of a storm brewing in his diocese was not lost on Lamkin, even though he didn't have time to ponder that kind of shit. He started the car and drove down Summit Avenue in the direction of the chancery. His homily would have to wait. He needed to call Zimmerman and check in with McBride. Time to get the defensive shields up.

21

Winton Bixby was nearing the end of his second, and by law his last, four-year term as Governor of the great state of Minnesota. He was a few months shy of seventy, so the end of this term would likely mark the end of a long and, in his mind, successful political career.

Winton's great grandfather, Bertram Bixby, opened a small butcher shop on Lake Street in Minneapolis in the 1890s. He expanded into the grocery business a few years later. Fast forward to the 1960s and Winton's father was president of Bixby Foods, a closely-held family business operating fifteen full-service supermarkets in Minnesota, Wisconsin and Iowa. By the time Winton graduated from Williams College with degrees in political science and economics, Richard Nixon was President, two Kennedy brothers had been assassinated, the Viet Nam War was raging, and Roger Bixby wanted his only son to return home to be groomed as his successor. By that time, about a dozen of Winton's relatives worked for the family business and ten owned shares in Bixby Food Enterprises, Inc. Notwithstanding that Winton and his two sisters were in line to inherit half of the company's voting shares, he had no interest in managing a chain of grocery stores. Working summers as a stock boy, cashier, and delivery driver had been enough for him. Winton wanted a life in politics.

Hoping his son would soon abandon such folly for the real world, Roger, a substantial contributor to Republican candidates and causes in Minnesota, used his influence to help Winton land a job as an aide to Third District Congressman Arlen Anderson, a six-term incumbent who chaired the powerful Public Works Committee. Anderson was a typical Minnesota Republican of the mid-Twentieth Century, a social moderate and fiscal conservative. The only problem—Winton was a typical Minnesota Democratic-Farmer-Labor liberal, a pacifist and enthu-siastic supporter of Gene McCarthy's presidential bid. Nevertheless, Winton was grateful for the opportunity and worked diligently on several constituent matters and research projects while learning the inner workings of Congress. He also took night classes at George Washington University, earning a master's degree in public policy.

It didn't take long for Congressman Anderson and his staffers to figure out that young Bixby was not a true believer, but by that time the country was distracted by Watergate and Winton had secured new employment as the chief of staff for a liberal Senator from Wisconsin. Always the opportunist, Winton started dating the Senator's well-connected, if not very attractive, daughter. He continued to suppress certain feelings he'd been having since adolescence—a natural attraction to men. Winton and Lisa were married a year later and left Washington, D.C. for Minneapolis, where they started a family and Winton took a job as assistant director of Minnesota's DFL Party.

Winton had enjoyed growing up rich, and, though he wanted to run for public office, he didn't want to give up the lifestyle that only money could buy. So after Roger died in 1982, Winton persuaded his family to buy out his inter-est in Bixby Food Enterprises in for $15 million. He and Lisa built a new house (6,000 square feet with a pool and tennis court) on Lake Minnetonka, and he personally financed an unsuccessful bid for Congress in 1984.

But his name recognition, personal wealth and persistence would ultimately pay off. He was elected to Congress in 1986 and re-elected five times, losing his seat in 1998 by fewer than five hundred votes to a female county prosecutor, the wife of a dot.com billionaire who ran on a pro-life, family values, law-and-order platform. It didn't help that Winton and Lisa had divorced a few years earlier. Lisa got the house on Lake Minnetonka, $5 million in cash, and physical custody of their 15-year-old son.

Winton grew weary of life inside the beltway, but not of politics. He bought a condominium in downtown Minneapolis and immersed himself in state and local issues, serving as a delegate to the Democratic National Convention in 2000 and distributing thousands of dollars to DFL candidates in local races. He ran for Minnesota Secretary of State two years later and was elected in a landslide for two reasons. First, he spent over a million dollars of his own money, five times more than his opponent's total war chest; and second, he had name recognition in a race about which voters don't care. Nevertheless, Bixby was back. He was determined to be the best secretary of state in Minnesota history, but more determined to move up to the governor's office in the next election. It was shortly after becoming secretary of state when Bixby met Jay McBride.

After years of kissing ass as a lowly money manager for big firms, McBride finally found the resources to start his own business in the late 1990s. An investment advisory firm, Itasca Asset Management, LLC, had two divisions, one that managed money in separate accounts for wealthy individuals and institutional investors like banks, college endowments, and pension funds, and the other that managed two retail mutual funds, a large cap value fund and a balanced fund that included both equity and debt securities. McBride's expertise was researching and predicting the future performance of health care and biotech companies based in the Midwest. Nobody was better at that. Both Itasca's managed accounts and large cap value fund contained high concentrations of these companies and, consequently, performed very well.

As Minnesota's Secretary of State, Bixby, along with the Governor, State Auditor and Attorney General, sat on the State Board of Investment, overseeing the management of several state pension, insurance, disability and cash management funds, totaling tens of billions of dollars. In 2005, McBride made a presentation to the Board, proposing that Itasca would manage a slice of the state's pension funds, about a billion dollars, in a separately managed large cap value account that, McBride touted, would consistently outperform the Russell 1000 large cap value index. At the time, Itasca had a dozen employees and $1.2 billion in managed assets, not exactly BlackRock or Goldman Sachs, but growing steadily in assets and reputation.

McBride desperately wanted the state's business to give his fledgling firm credibility with chief investment officers at the major pension and endowment funds in the region, but it was a cutthroat business, and he certainly wasn't confident the Board would add Itasca to its roster of managers. He needed to do something to improve the odds. He felt he'd made a special connection with Winton

Bixby, whose perfectly tailored, expensive suit, slender physique, neatly-coiffed white hair and beard, and manufactured tan made McBride tingle a bit in the groin when their eyes met several times during his spiel. Combining his research of Bixby's past with his intuition and perceived mutual attraction, he took a calculated risk. He called Bixby and invited him to his apartment for dinner.

Bixby accepted. Itasca got the business.

22

"THIS IS DELICIOUS," said MacDonald, as he filled both his glass and Bell's with the last third of a bottle of Ladera Cabernet Sauvignon, his favorite red. "I've never had smoked white fish tacos."

It was half-past nine, and MacDonald and Bell were finally enjoying dinner and each other on the screened-in porch on the sunset side of MacDonald's two-bedroom split-log cabin. Originally built as a hideaway for some St. Paul gangsters in the 1930s, the home was perched on a pine-filled cliff overlooking Lake Superior, a few miles east Beaver Bay. MacDonald had wiped out his 401(k) at the Secret Service to buy a little slice of heaven on earth. It wasn't lakefront property, but the views of Gitchi Gummi and nearby Palisade Head were spectacular. Even better, from his front door it took only minutes to hike into Tettegouche State Park.

MacDonald had checked on Stockman on his way to the courthouse. Marlys was there, barely able to walk and visibly upset, though she clearly didn't know about the activity that precipitated her husband's coronary. MacDonald was more concerned about her well-being than Stockman's health, though his doctor said he should make a full recovery.

The press conference had been short; there wouldn't be much to tell the media until they had autopsy results or a *bona fide* suspect. MacDonald confirmed that the deceased woman was Lauren Fallon. He acknowledged his office believed a third party was involved, but stated that the exact cause and manner of death were unknown. He said Ms. Fallon likely knew her assailant but wouldn't elaborate on any reasons for that speculation. He said the public should assume that whoever harmed Ms. Fallon could still be in the Lake County area and may pose a continuing danger to the public. Based on an earlier phone conversation between Joe Terranova and Thomassoni, MacDonald announced there would be a $50,000 reward for information leading to the arrest and conviction of any person or persons responsible for Lauren Fallon's demise.

A thunderstorm had rolled through the Arrowhead region a few hours earlier leaving a clear, starry sky above the North Shore with temperatures some thirty degrees cooler than the daytime high. Bell and MacDonald had donned sweatshirts, so they could eat in comfort and enjoy the rain-cleansed night air. Bell told MacDonald about Ricky Holden's visit and his aborted meeting with a wealthy banker from the Twin Cities whose "friend" dressed like a priest and might be an archbishop. Ricky had remembered to send Bell the photos. He even sent one that showed the license plate on the Town Car.

"I'll double-check the ownership of that car," said MacDonald, "but I highly doubt this has anything to do with my case. The fact that this archbishop, if that's who he is, was visiting someone up in Tofte on the same day Lauren Fallon was murdered in Gooseberry is certainly worth pursuing a little."

"What about the rest of it?" asked Bell.

"Rest of it?"

"That the archbishop is a homosexual!" Bell practically shouted.

"I don't see how that's relevant to anything but your ex-husband's voyeurism and obsession with getting back into your pants." MacDonald wasn't sure of the accuracy of that statement but couldn't resist giving Bell some shit. She playfully tossed a small throw pillow at his head.

"You're right about one thing—Rick wouldn't pass up the opportunity to screw any moving object with tits. It took a lot of discipline and restraint, but fortunately I was able to fend him off today, you asshole."

MacDonald took a sip of wine along with a bite of the spicy brown rice and black bean dish Bell had concocted to accompany the tacos.

"Are you familiar at all with the owner of that big place? Rick said McBride is his name." Bell stretched out her long legs, and they landed in MacDonald's lap. She loved touching him.

"I'm not," said MacDonald, kissing the top of her knee, "but I am familiar with that property. It's really a one-of-a kind on the lake, must have cost millions. I'm guessing it's the most expensive single-family home in Cook County."

"I wonder how the guy made his money," pondered Bell. "He must have some connection to the Catholic church."

"We'll have to do a little research on Mr. McBride. By the way, I contacted the BCA today, partly because of Stockman's condition and partly because this investigation could involve a lot of time in the Twin Cities. I think they're going to assign the case to George Redman, the former St. Paul detective who came out of retirement a few years ago to join the BCA. He's got to be in his mid-60s."

"How do you feel about that?" asked Bell.

"Good. Redman's a pro. I've never worked with him, but he's got a reputation for solving tough cases. I met him last year at a workshop. He's a wiry little guy with a dry wit and a foul mouth. He was teaching classes at a community college when the BCA director convinced him to get back in the game. He joined the Bureau under two conditions—he wouldn't have a partner and wouldn't carry a firearm. I know there must be a story behind that, but I don't know what it is."

MacDonald pushed himself up from the wicker loveseat he was sharing with Bell. "Why don't I take care of these dinner dishes?"

Bell grabbed his wrist and pulled him towards her. "Why don't you take care of me first?"

It wasn't really a question.

23

SINCE THE 1920s, the Bureau of Criminal Apprehension, better known as the BCA, has been a specialty division of the Minnesota Department of Public Safety, a division that helps local law enforcement solve crimes. The BCA provides investigative, forensic, technological and training services throughout the state. George Redman worked out of the BCA's main office in St. Paul, though, for the most part, he worked out of his apartment in Crocus Hill and his 15-year-old Jeep.

As soon as Superintendent Rodriquez filled him in on the available details of Lauren Fallon's final hours, Redman left MacDonald a voicemail re-introducing himself and setting up a tentative phone conference for Sunday. Redman knew that the earlier he could get started the better chance he'd have of tracking down the killer.

Never married, Redman shared a second floor, two-bedroom apartment with his long-time girlfriend, Rita Leoni, a forty-something bartender at the oldest steakhouse in the Cities, and his black lab, Barney. With thick, red-tinted black hair and olive skin, Rita was mostly of Italian ancestry, full-figured and very feisty, just the way the cagey veteran liked her. They also shared a love of college basketball and Maker's Mark Manhattans, up with a twist.

As she often did on Saturdays, Rita was working the late shift, so Redman made himself a double and clicked on the 50-inch Samsung suspended from the only full-length wall in their small but, thanks to Rita, tastefully-appointed living room. He reclined on his black leather Lazy-Boy and watched the Twins lose another game before falling asleep with Barney draped over his feet.

24

McBRIDE'S PENTHOUSE CONDOMINIUM occupied most of the 24th floor of The Nicollet, a luxurious residential complex located two blocks west of the Mississippi River and three blocks east of the heart of the Minneapolis business district. McBride was one of the first occupants back in 2010, when he paid $5.5 million for 4,500 square feet of living space and a gold key card to the pool and fitness center that shared the top floor of the building with his condo. To describe his place as opulent was an understatement. With 12-foot ceilings throughout, the apartment had floor-to-ceiling windows that afforded bird's eye views of the Mississippi River and St. Anthony Falls from the great room and downtown Minneapolis from the master bedroom. The floors in the bathrooms and kitchen were marble and heated; the rest were Amish hand-scraped Brazilian walnut adorned with several hand-knotted Persian rugs. McBride worked with a professional decorator to furnish the master and guest bedrooms, a large study/library and the expansive great room that shared a see-through gas fireplace with the master bedroom. The value of the artwork alone, a number of sculptures and original paintings by local artists, exceeded a million dollars.

Governor Bixby had made several discreet visits to McBride's condo over the years. Some to talk business, some for pleasure; though in recent years, he'd lost interest in the more pleasurable aspects of their relationship.

Unbeknownst to everyone but Bixby's accountant and McBride, the last gubernatorial election had drained his bank accounts, even though the electorate still regarded him as a wealthy scion with money to burn. Bixby didn't do anything to dispel that notion. Once worth in excess of $15 million, his messy divorce and several tight elections, including the last Governor's race which he won by fewer than five thousand votes out of nearly 2 million cast, had left him with his condominium, a couple of fancy cars and about a quarter of a million dollars in an IRA. He did have a modest pension based on his years of public service, but Bixby was used to being rich; he liked being rich; he needed to be rich. So, he made a deal with the devil.

Through some clandestine arrangements with a discreet private bank in Geneva, Switzerland, McBride transferred over $5 million to an account to which Bixby had access shortly after the Governor's last election. Coincidentally, Itasca was now managing over $5 billion of the state's money, about half of the firm's total assets under management.

Bixby sat in one of two leather wing chairs that occupied most of a small alcove jutting out from McBride's great room. The intimate half-room overlooked the Stone Arch Bridge that elegantly spanned the Mississippi River hundreds of feet below. It was shortly before sunset, so several bug-size strollers and joggers were still visible in the fading light of a Saturday evening. A mahogany coffee table separated the two chairs. McBride placed a Waterford crystal glass filled with ice and a generous pour of Macallan 18-year single malt on a wooden coaster stamped with Itasca's logo. He admired his own glass of Macallan, no ice, as he sat next to Bixby and took a long draw of the smooth whiskey. Bixby lifted his glass in McBride's direction in appreciation of the exquisite Scotch before taking a drink. He was the first to speak.

"You know I'll be out of office in six months. I've been getting pressure from our analysts to move the money with Itasca to index funds. It's what all the states are doing. Your returns are competitive, but your fees aren't. Even if I can keep the Board from taking action for the rest of the year, you're done as soon as I leave."

"That's not fair, Win. We've beaten our benchmark and the index funds for three years running. Our retail funds have grown ten percent since the first of the year, but there's no way we can replace the $4 million we're earning from the state any time soon. It's not as if you haven't benefited as well."

Bixby thought about changing the subject. He knew McBride would blackmail him in a nanosecond if he felt threatened. He also knew if he disclosed the true nature of their dealings—to the press or the authorities—they'd both go to jail for a long time.

"Look, Jay, I'm just trying to be straight with you. You need to be prepared to lose your business with the state. If Amy wins, she might be inclined to help you, and I know you've made a significant contribution to her campaign, but she's behind by double digits in the polls to that fuckin' fascist Arrington. If he wins, then you're out for sure."

"Then we both need to do everything in our power to prevent that from happening—which I know you'll do." McBride knew Bixby was right but didn't want to think about it. Not today. "By the way, what do you know about the murder of that woman lawyer, Judge Fallon's wife?"

"Only what I heard on the news earlier tonight. What a shame for Charlie. He's a nice guy and a good judge, and now he's lost two wives. Lauren was a beautiful, talented young woman. I knew her a little—she was a contributor to my last campaign. Also volunteered to make phone calls to get the vote out. She was passionate about a lot of things."

"Sounds like that might have been her undoing," mused McBride. "Maybe somebody didn't like the fact that she took on the archdiocese."

"That doesn't make much sense," said Bixby. "That obnoxious little prick Terranova will just pick up the gauntlet. Not that I have any sympathy for the Catholics." Bixby was a non-practicing Lutheran, though he pretended otherwise for political expediency. "I have to admit, though, I was surprised to hear about this latest lawsuit. I thought our local Catholics had put the abuse issue behind them. Have you had any dealings with the archbishop—Lamkin? He reminds me more of a hedge fund manager than a priest, slicker than snot off a doorknob."

"My mother is a fan. She says he saved the Church and has a voice like Dennis Day, whoever that is. I've met him but don't know him well." The fact that he'd kept his relationship with Lamkin a secret all these years made him smirk.

McBride got up to fetch more Macallan while Bixby took his full bladder to the guest bathroom. The Governor had expensive tastes but even he was impressed by the furnishings and artwork in McBride's fancy penthouse. When he returned, McBride had filled their glasses and was consulting his smartphone with a scowl on his face.

"Something wrong, Jay?" asked Bixby.

"Oh, it's nothing," replied McBride. Nothing was a text from Lamkin wondering why he hadn't called him back and asking for the current balance of the fund. The archbishop must be getting nervous.

"So, I'm curious, how much revenue does Itasca produce in a year, $10 million gross?"

"More than that," said McBride, peeved that Bixby would ask. "We submit our audited financials to the state every year, so you have access to that information. Last year we grossed about $15 million."

"You just appear to live so well, Jay. This place with furnishings has to be worth millions. You have your lovely place on the North Shore, a house in Napa and that little villa we stayed in a few years ago in Tuscany. You've shared some cash with me; you drive expensive cars. I'm just trying to do the math."

"Don't concern yourself with my finances, Governor. I've scrimped and saved for years to have what I have today. And neither Itasca nor I have any debt to speak of."

"Sounds like I hit a nerve."

25

THREE PEOPLE KNEW about the fund—Lamkin, McBride and Jenkins. Lamkin had set it up as a secret "rainy day" or contingency fund in the mid-1990s. After observing how the onslaught of pedophile clergy cases had bankrupted other dioceses, Lamkin wasn't about to be victimized by some fortune-seeking lawyers. He instructed Jenkins to underreport the contributions parishes made to the archdiocese for all purposes, from liability insurance to pension funds, by ten percent, and to deposit the funds in a community outreach account. At the end of each quarter, any balance in the account was distributed to various Catholic charities. That's how Jenkins accounted for them on the "official" books. He kept two sets of checks as well and was careful to create a legitimate paper trail to fool the auditors.

In reality, Jenkins transferred the money to McBride each quarter. The arrangement was simple. McBride established an investment account in the name of a shell corporation, Temperance River Partners, at a small discount brokerage firm where McBride maintained his personal accounts. He was supposed to manage the money conservatively and submit quarterly statements to Jenkins. The agreed upon fee for McBride's complicity and services was an annual retainer equal to three percent of the fund's balance, extremely generous by money management standards but commensurate with the risks involved in hiding money and committing fraud.

Over a twenty-year span, Jenkins diverted over $40 million to the fund, and, based on the statements that Jenkins received four times a year, the current balance was over $100 million.

Except it wasn't. Over the years, McBride couldn't resist the temptation to use the fund as his personal piggy bank. Initially, he "borrowed" a few million to set up Itasca and put a down payment on his Minneapolis condo. Though Itasca was successful, he could only take between two and three million a year out of its operation in the form of salary, bonuses and dividends. He needed twice that amount to meet the expenses of his preferred lifestyle.

The brokerage account no longer existed. McBride fabricated all of the statements he sent to Jenkins—a simple task for someone with his knowledge and resources. Temperance River Partners had a bank money market account with about a hundred grand. McBride had opened two accounts in a Geneva Bank, one a joint account with Bixby and one for himself. These accounts had a balance of about $7 million combined. That's it; that's all that was left of the "fund." McBride had squandered, or in his view invested, the rest on creating and maintaining the lifestyle he deserved.

The ostensible success of Lamkin's Project Pedophile (McBride's term) had convinced him the archdiocese would never need the money. That may have been a serious miscalculation, though it definitely was a convenient rationalization. Regardless, he was a highly successful and respected CEO and money manager who didn't appreciate being nagged by a religious twit. He was confident he'd think of some way to deal with Lamkin.

And he was damn sure of one thing: He'd made better use of the money than the archdiocese ever would. No question about that.

26

The 17th Sunday of Ordinary Time

Sunday, July 26th

Wearing his favorite cassock and biretta, Lamkin felt imbued with the spirit and power of God as he surveyed a sanctuary filled with the faithful. They came to see him, to hear him, and to be inspired by him. Bishop McDonough and the lay cantor had prepared them for the homily with hymns and scripture readings. There was only one thing missing—Peter was not in his usual seat in the center section, second row.

Without any notes, Lamkin spread his arms as if to envelop the entire throng and began:

> *My brothers and sisters in Christ, today's spiritual message for the Seventeenth Sunday in Ordinary Time is simple: we must persevere in our living faith. What does it mean to persevere? It means to be persistent, to continue without stopping, without failing. It means to start something and finish it to the end. In what should we be persistent? We should be persistent in our faith. And what does that include?*
>
> *It includes our worship of God, our struggle to inherit the salvation we have received through Jesus Christ who is Lord and God, and our concern for the salvation of our spiritual brothers and sisters in Christ.*
>
> *Reviewing today's first reading from the Book of Genesis, it can be stated unequivocally that Moses had a living faith in Yahweh, God Almighty. The reputation*

of Moses has come down in history as one who continuously feared the Lord Yahweh and who worshipped Him in servitude and obedience in all things. Because Abraham believed in God, it was reckoned to him as righteousness.

As you heard earlier, the Lord God had come down from Heaven to visit the cities of Sodom and Gomorrah because of outcries of blasphemy and sinfulness against their people that were reaching the Heavenly Throne. During this visit, Abraham was concerned that God would destroy Sodom if fifty righteous souls were not found within the city. On behalf of a lesser number of righteous souls, even ten, Abraham secured God's unconditional promise that he would not destroy the city. Unfortunately, as history tells us, not even ten righteous persons could be found, and God destroyed the city.

Today's Second Reading from the Letter to the Colossians reminds us of the need to persevere in our living and believing in Christ. It reminds us to live our lives in Jesus, rooted and built up in Him and established in the faith, just as we were taught, abounding in thanksgiving. In other words, is anything else necessary? No! Starting with the basic truths that most of us learned during childhood, we must build up our faith in the sound Catholic teachings that the Apostles of Jesus handed down to the Holy Church.

There is no benefit, no good whatsoever, that can be derived from listening to false teachers on television or on the internet. There is no benefit in listening to those who sell recordings of their personal interpretations of the gospel or those who publish magazines or books or blogs to entice innocent sheep. We should all reject that. In Jesus, in your Church, we have everything. "For in him the whole fullness of the deity dwelled bodily." The Father, the Son, and the Holy Spirit are all known through Jesus.

Do we need another Advocate? No! Do we need another Mediator? No! Through the Holy Catholic Church, we have the fullness of the Truth that has been given to us through the Spirit of Christ. With the fullness of the grace of God at our disposal, dare we insult the Lord God by looking elsewhere, by entertaining the false teachers whose venom can poison our souls? To do so is to reject the grace of God that is our only hope of salvation. Let this be a warning! It is foolhardy and dangerous to play games with God, with the will of God! If we do, we will find ourselves on the losing side. On the side of perdition.

"You may be hearing and reading more stories in the media in the coming days and weeks about a spurious lawsuit that has been brought against your Church. This is an effort to revive the pain, suffering and scandal that we all believed had been resolved with benevolence, contrition and understanding. This is an action that ignores the strict new protocols we have implemented to ensure the protection of our children, the identification, ouster and prosecution of abusive clergy, and the ongoing education and training of all employees of your diocese.

"The lawsuit is aimed at destroying your Church, all for the financial gain of a few heathens who have no conception of what's best for the victims. I say this to you mindful of the tragic death of a young woman who was one of the lawyers in the case. She is also one of God's children, and we pray for her soul and salvation and for her family. But we also know that her death will draw more attention to this case and may affect our ability to end these distractions without doing irreparable damage to your Church.

"We who humbly serve you at the diocese appreciate your continued prayers and support, as we put our trust in the Lord to guide us through these man-made obstacles."

Lamkin again looked for Peter in his usual spot but was startled to see Billy Hutchinson sitting there, smiling like a Cheshire cat. Holy shit.

"Let us pray. . .."

27

MacDonald met Klewacki and Hakonen in his courthouse office at noon on Sunday to compare notes, review the evidence gathered so far, and consider next steps in the investigation of Lauren Fallon's murder. Redman would be calling in around one o'clock, and MacDonald didn't want to waste his time.

It was a "Chamber of Commerce" day on the North Shore—a little breeze off the lake, not a cloud in the sky, and temperatures in the seventies. Hakonen handed out bottled water and sandwiches while they sat at an oblong conference table and read emails and updates from other law enforcement offices that were assisting on the case. Like Redman, MacDonald believed that thoroughness in the early stages of a difficult investigation led to what others called lucky breaks. He had asked the Minnesota Highway Patrol and Duluth Police Department to inspect dumpsters and trash receptacles at service stations, restaurants and convenience stores along Highway 61 between Duluth to the south and Grand Marais to the north, with additional assistance from the Cook and St. Louis County Sheriffs. A team of Lake County Sheriff's personnel had already "walked" Gooseberry Park. Among other things, they were looking for discarded women's clothing, a cell phone, any kind of weapon and any evidence of a struggle. In other words, the proverbial needle in a haystack.

Klewacki had asked all of the business owners along that route to retain CCTV and other video surveillance that captured customers on their premises between 8:00 p.m. on Friday and 4:00 a.m. on Saturday. She'd also requested copies of all credit card receipts from transactions during the same period. A few of the owners required subpoenas; most did not.

"Anything interesting?" asked MacDonald.

"A couple things," said Klewacki. "Ryan followed up on that license plate you gave me on the Lincoln Town Car. It's registered in the name of the Archdiocese of St. Paul and Minneapolis, and the insurance policy lists James William Lamkin as the primary driver. He is the archbishop, by the way. That's not the biggest find, though. I watched the tapes from the video cameras at the BP station in Beaver Bay this morning. Seems our big-shot cleric pumped his own gas a few minutes after 11:00 on Friday night."

"He's certainly someone Lauren Fallon might have agreed to meet," said MacDonald. "But why would they meet up at Gooseberry on a Friday night. That doesn't make much sense."

"We do have an important new piece of evidence, but it's not as helpful as I'd hoped," said Hakonen. "Judge Fallon was true to his word about the family phone records. We got a call this morning from his service provider who sent me a pdf of Lauren's cell phone billing records for the past six months. During the week before she died, she made 23 calls to a number that was also the last one she called on Friday night at 11:42. Unfortunately, the number is attached to a prepaid burner phone that's probably been discarded and isn't traceable. We know the brand from the number sequence, but they're sold at Walmart and Target among other places."

"What about her computer?" asked MacDonald. "Maybe she sent some emails to this mystery date."

"Her laptop was property of the law firm. Joe Terranova has offered to have his IT guy help us get into her files and email account," said Klewacki. "We've scheduled that for Tuesday of next week. We'll have to retrieve the laptop from the BCA before then."

"Good. I'll ask Redman to follow up with Peter Jenkins and get a hair sample, so we can compare his DNA to anything they find on that condom. George can also set up an interview with the archbishop to check out his story. I have a call into Terranova's office. I want a face-to-face with him myself, so I'll make a trip to St. Paul tomorrow if he's available. Higgins has promised preliminary autopsy results by the end of the day tomorrow. The toxicology reports will take longer, but he didn't think they'd add much. Have we learned anything about this McBride character?"

Klewacki opened an electronic file on her laptop. "I researched him a little at home last night and followed up with some data base searches this morning. He's the CEO and sole owner of a company called Itasca Asset Management. They manage investments for mutual funds and big pension accounts. According to their website, they have over $10 billion in other people's money and twenty-five employees. No criminal record on McBride. He owns real property in Cook and Hennepin Counties with a tax valuation of about $5 million and six vehicles, including two Mercedes and an Alpha Romeo sports car. He's also contributed the maximum amounts over the years to Governor Bixby's campaigns and more recently to Amy Warner's campaign. He's rich and politically connected to the Democrats, but I couldn't find any definitive connection to the Catholic Church or to the archbishop."

"OK," said MacDonald. "I might have the BCA do some white-collar follow-up work on McBride. What about any of the other Scenic Shores guests?"

"All dead ends so far," said Klewacki.

"Shit," said MacDonald. "This was no random attack. It must have been a romantic encounter of some kind that went awry. Lauren Fallon appears to be someone very much in control of her life. She wasn't some vulnerable teenager. But I'm betting she was as surprised by what transpired as we'll be when we figure this out."

28

AFTER PRESIDING AT late morning mass, Lamkin attended a picnic for chancery employees and their families at Hidden Falls Park on the east bank of the Mississippi River. Exhausted and dehydrated in the oppressive heat, he only managed to down a few bites of a hot dog and a dollop of potato salad while mingling and making small talk with his staff.

He gamely tried to watch a spirited (but horribly played) volleyball match between the nuns of Nativity parish and a group of St. Thomas seminarians, but, after fifteen minutes of sheer agony, he politely excused himself to seek refuge in his office and to regroup for the battles ahead.

On Sunday afternoons in July, the chancery offices were usually empty, so the facilities manager set the thermostat at 80 degrees. Lamkin took a shower in the bathroom adjacent to his office and delved into the mountain of reports and budgets strewn across the Peavey executive desk that dominated his work space. He was sparsely dressed in white boxer shorts and a white linen shirt, his pasty thighs sticking to the black leather chair that enveloped his small frame.

Lamkin needed a game plan; otherwise, the depression he'd suffered earlier in life, before discovering his calling as a priest, would return and devour him. He couldn't believe what was happening. He'd worked so hard to rebuild an archdiocese that was the envy of his peers and now the blood-sucking lawyers could destroy everything.

After his apparent success in overcoming the pedophile priest issues, the U.S. Conference of Catholic Bishops had asked him to chair the Committee on the Protection of Children and Young People. At their annual meeting in November, the Conference made him Vice President of the organization that sets strategic priorities for all U.S. bishops. In two years, he would have been in line for the Presidency and, following a three-year term, a likely appointment as a Cardinal by his Most Holy Excellency, the Pope.

But now he faced disgrace and dishonor, especially if this lawsuit forced the Church into bankruptcy. At one time, Zimmerman had actually predicted that Judge Kennedy would dismiss the suit based on the validity of the confidential settlements. But Zimmerman wasn't aware of Peter's betrayal. Now Lamkin had to assume that Terranova knew everything. He might even know about the fund. How could God forsake him in his time of greatest need? He was doing all the right things to save his Church, yet God was fucking him over. He should have stayed in Baltimore, should have worked in the family business, Lamkin & Sons Mortuary, with his father and four brothers. Maybe not. Maybe he just needed a game plan.

Lamkin usually vacationed during the last week of July before beginning the diocesan planning and budgeting process in August. His staff believed he went fishing with a group of bishops in Canada, but he never did. Instead he'd spend a glorious week at McBride's place on the North Shore. He might have to shorten or even abort his vacation this year. He'd scheduled a meeting with Zimmerman for Monday morning. He asked Vicar General Hollander to attend so he had a backup, since Peter could no longer be trusted.

Peter. How could he risk everything they'd so artfully and meticulously built over twenty years for a blonde whore who worked for the devil? Lamkin called him several times after he was a no-show at the Cathedral. He even left a semi-apologetic message.

The diminutive cleric shuffled in bare feet to the wet bar behind his desk. He rinsed out the highball glass he kept in the small metal cabinet below the bar. There were several bottles of Ketel One vodka in the mini fridge next to the sink. He consumed about a bottle a week if he were feeling good, a bottle a day at other times. He filled the glass with ice and was mixing his favorite drink when he heard a light tapping on his closed office door.

"Come in," said Lamkin, as if he knew who was on the other side of the door.

"Hello, Pedro. It's so good to see you."

Pedro Guzman was the handsome, slender 15-year-old son of Lamkin's executive secretary, Rosa. Rosa was a good Catholic, as well as an undocumented alien who was desperate to get an education for her two sons and to keep her small family in the United States. Lamkin met her elder son when he was twelve and suggested that he could benefit from some tutorial sessions on the Catechism.

"Please close the door behind you."

29

Monday, July 27ᵗʰ

REDMAN SAT AT the two-person, formica table in his modest kitchen and sipped a cup of very strong, midnight black coffee. As usual, his breakfast consisted of a banana, two tangerines, and two pieces of whole wheat toast slathered with crunchy peanut butter, which he often shared with Barney.

It was 5:45. Rita wouldn't be up for at least half a day. Redman and Barney had already been on a two-mile walk.

George was frustrated. He'd been trying to schedule a meeting with Peter Jenkins since his briefing with MacDonald and his staff on Sunday afternoon. But Jenkins wasn't returning calls or texts or emails, so Redman decided to make a house call. He and Barney would hop in the Jeep and ride down to Mississippi River Road for a second walk. Then they'd find an empty park bench and share the *Pioneer Press*. Barney would let him know when it was time to visit Mr. Jenkins.

Even an experienced cop like Redman was unprepared for what he saw through the picture window that framed a macabre scene in Jenkins' apartment. Someone should have closed the drapes, thought Redman, as he tried to contact occupants in the other three apartments in the four-plex to gain access to the building.

"Hello?" said a groggy female voice from Unit 3. "Do I know you?" The name on the mailbox was Ashley Panchott.

"Hello, Ms. Panchott. My name is George Redman. I'm an investigator with the Minnesota Bureau of Criminal Apprehension. I believe a serious crime may have occurred in Unit 1 of your building, and I'm asking you to let me into the lobby, so I don't have to break in. I can show you my cop ID if you'd prefer to come down here first."

The only response he got was an electrical buzz signaling the release of the deadbolt lock. Redman entered the hallway and immediately noticed that the white enameled door to Jenkin's unit was a few inches ajar. He punched 911 on his phone and alerted the St. Paul PD of a potential homicide at 528 Summit Avenue, Unit 1, identifying himself as a BCA officer and requesting backup.

Unsure whether anyone was lurking on the other side, Redman opened the door cautiously while crouching in a defensive posture. Seeing and sensing no one, he conducted a quick walk-through of the apartment, checking closets, bathrooms and the backdoor entry-way for signs of life, weapons, blood and any other evidence of foul play. Nothing.

He returned to the living room and took several photos of Jenkins with his cell. He didn't need to check for a pulse. If he were sure of anything, it was that Jenkins was dead. He was literally stuck to the antique loveseat in a sitting but hideously animated position. His neck had been impaled by the steel tip of a long, black umbrella that had severed a main artery before ripping through the couch's suede fabric and ultimately poking out its backing. Jenkins' eyes and mouth were open, expressing a combination of alarm and horror. He was wearing a light-weight tan bathrobe over boxer shorts and a white T-shirt, though all of his clothes were drenched in congealing blood that had stopped oozing from his neck.

Redman surmised that Jenkins may have known his killer, since there was clearly no forced entry into the unit. Moreover, nothing else appeared out of place in the living room. As Redman tried to reenact the crime scene in his mind, he pictured Jenkins sitting on the couch, perhaps having a pleasant dis-cussion with his assailant, when he was the victim of a sudden, surprise attack.

Redman also wondered whether Jenkins had initially been in bed and had been awakened by the perpetrator's call from the entry-way. Why else would he have been in his underwear, wearing a robe?

Within five minutes of Redman's 911 call, four of St. Paul's finest arrived at the scene. Redman saw their flashers and hustled to let them into the building. He knew the two homicide detectives and had probably met the two beat cops but couldn't remember their names.

"We're going to need someone from the medical examiner's office," he said to the group. "This one's kind of grotesque."

Detective Frank Colianni was the team leader. A 55-year-old St. Paul native, Colianni had been on the force for thirty-plus years and had a reputation for thoroughness. It took him about three minutes to assess the situation, dismiss the beat cops and make a call for a forensics unit from the BCA to help process the scene.

"So, who is this guy, and how did you win the prize to find him?" asked Colianni.

"His name is Peter Jenkins. He's a lawyer-type who worked for the archdiocese. I've been assisting the Lake County Sheriff on the Lauren Fallon murder investigation. We know Jenkins spent time with Ms. Fallon on the night she was killed and may have had motive. I'd been trying to contact him by phone and email since yesterday afternoon, so I tried to catch him at home this morning for an interview and to get a hair sample for DNA testing. Given the substantial rigor mortis in his muscles and the volume and crustiness of the dried blood on his torso, I'll bet he died more than 24 hours ago, so sometime early Sunday morning. What I don't get is why none of his neighbors noticed him sitting here in plain sight through the front window."

Colianni shrugged his shoulders. "Not everyone peers into their neighbor's windows on the way to their apartment, Red." He knew Redman's nickname. "By the way, as soon as someone from the medical examiner's office gets here, you can probably get a hair sample if you still want it."

Redman nodded. "Yeah, I still need it."

"What do you think of the murder weapon?" asked Colianni, still shaking his head in amazement.

"Probably just a matter of convenience," responded Redman. "Notice the writing stamped on the handle: 'Property of the Archdiocese of St. Paul and Minneapolis.' It rained on Saturday night, so maybe the umbrella was sitting out."

"Maybe so, but whoever did this was pretty tall, to get enough leverage, and pretty strong."

"And pretty sick," added Redman. "Hopefully, forensics can get some good prints off that thing. Will one of your guys be following up with the neighbors?

Someone may have seen or heard something, or, who knows, maybe one of them is the killer."

"Harrington and I will cover that, Red. I'll share anything we get with you. You think there may be a connection between this freak show and the Fallon murder?"

"It's possible," said Redman, but he was thinking it was probable.

Redman went out to his Jeep to let Barney out for a whiz. He was met by the BCA forensics van and a pathologist from the coroner's office. He returned to Jenkin's condo long enough to get his hair sample and to watch them begin the tedious job of processing a very messy crime scene.

He asked Colianni to keep in touch and then drove to the apartment to drop Barney off before heading to his home away from home, an eight-by-ten cubicle at the BCA. When he called MacDonald's cell to give him the news about Jenkins, he went directly to voicemail. His message was brief.

"Call me, sheriff. Jenkins is dead. Murdered."

30

MacDonald LEFT HIS place at 3:15 in the morning. Terranova had agreed to meet with him on Monday, but it had to be before 8:00 a.m. It was 7:05 when the Tahoe pulled into a visitor's space in the parking lot that served the three-story granite, steel and glass edifice that elegantly housed Joe Terranova & Associates in Shoreview, a tony second-ring suburb of St. Paul and a five-minute drive from Terranova's mega mansion in the gated community of North Oaks.

MacDonald had traveled all over the world and seen many impressive offices, including the oval office in the White House. But when he walked through the opaque glass doors of Terranova's building and beheld a three-story, tinted glass atrium together with massive crystal chandeliers, white Carrara marble floors and plush black and silver leather chairs and couches, he was dumbstruck. Even if Terranova had money to burn, he thought, what did his clients, most of whom were middle class at best, think of this extravagance?

Before he could check in with the receptionist, a well-tanned young woman with the features and demeanor of an aspiring actress, Joe Terranova strode towards him with a wide, toothy smile and an extended right hand.

"Sheriff MacDonald, I'm Joe Terranova. I've got us set up in my conference room with some fruit, pastries and a pot of coffee."

"Thank you," said MacDonald. That's very thoughtful."

MacDonald was surprised by Terranova's physical stature and appearance. He was athletically trim but couldn't have been taller than 5'5". Though he had to be ten years older than the sheriff, his hair was thick and black and perfectly coiffed. Without doing the math, MacDonald figured that between the gold Rolex, Brioni suit, and multi-carat diamond ear studs, the flashy lawyer had invested about

$30k, and that didn't include the Ferragamo shirt with diamond studded cufflinks. Apparently, one man's abuse could be another's gold mine.

MacDonald poured himself a cup of coffee and sat in one of twelve Italian leather chairs that surrounded a cherry wood conference table with a black granite inlay that housed sophisticated electronic and video equipment. He felt a little under-dressed in his standard issue, navy-blue polyester uniform with matching baseball cap, but he'd get over it.

Terranova closed the conference room door and sat at the head of the table, kitty-corner from MacDonald. "I sure hope we can help you, sheriff. I'm in the business of dealing with human tragedies, and this might be the worst of the worst. Lauren was a special person and a wonderful lawyer. We're a small shop, seven lawyers and eight support staff, and everyone loved her, so it's going to be extremely difficult. Her clients adored her, too. And I can't imagine what Charlie's going through."

"I spent some time with Judge Fallon on Saturday afternoon," said MacDonald. "As you might expect, he took the news hard, but he seems like a resilient fellow."

"He's a wonderful man, simply the best jurist we've got in this state." said Terranova, who, MacDonald was thinking, may have a penchant for exaggeration. An occupational hazard or necessity.

"Tell me more about Lauren, Mr. Terranova. Did she have a lot of friends or was she more of a loner?"

"She could have had a lot of friends, but she didn't. She worked long hours. Too long, actually. Lauren was an incredibly dedicated lawyer, always prepared, with a brilliant legal mind and the best presentation skills I've ever seen. Her Achilles' heel, if she had one, was getting too personally involved with her clients and their causes. Obsessed may be a better word. And, unfortunately sheriff, though she loved Charlie deeply and for all the right reasons, and I'm telling you this in strictest, strictest confidence, she would often use her sexuality to compromise men who had something she wanted."

Thomassoni had warned MacDonald that Terranova was on his fourth wife, the most recent a 25-year-old paralegal who no longer worked for the firm. Prepped with this knowledge, MacDonald naturally wondered whether there had been more between Lauren and Terranova than a collegial relationship.

"Did you have something she wanted?"

"Lauren never showed any interest in me in that way, sheriff. When she started working for the firm about ten years ago, I admit I was smitten with her; it was hard not to be she was so special and incredibly attractive. But I quickly figured out she was much more valuable to me as a lawyer than in any other position."

"But she had affairs with others?" MacDonald asked reluctantly, as if he didn't want it to be true.

"I wouldn't call them affairs, and I'm not sure how many there were. To be honest, I've never known anyone quite like her. She cared so much about the vulnerable people in the world. She crossed lines at times that would have ended other lawyers' careers. If she felt it would benefit her relationship with a client, she might be intimate with him, but strictly on her terms. After she ended that part of the relationship, she maintained a friendship with these people in a way that wouldn't work for others. It's difficult to explain because it was so unusual, and I'm guessing Charlie didn't have a clue."

"So, do you think she had one of these relationships with Peter Jenkins?"

"I'm not certain, but it wouldn't surprise me. Let me give you some background information that might be helpful. When Lauren started working for me, she didn't handle sexual abuse cases. She did all of the *pro bono* work for the firm because she loved that stuff, and frankly we needed to do more of it to enhance our reputation. She also represented elderly victims of swindle, fraud and abuse by guardians and relatives. She consistently obtained extraordinary results for her clients.

"During this same time, I led a group of three or four lawyers and several support staff that did nothing but represent victims of sexual abuse all over the country. After Lamkin became archbishop in the Twin Cities, we had virtually no success bringing claims against the fortress he created because no one would talk to us. Take a look at the screen."

Terranova inserted a flash drive into his laptop and after a few clicks of a wireless mouse a video entitled "Ramsey County District Court File No. CIV-98-1232 (John Doe 15)" began playing on the 60-inch Samsung Smart TV on the conference room wall.

The camera was fixed on a well-dressed, pleasant looking man in his forties during the entire ten-minute video. A professional sounding voice in the background asked questions and the man facing the camera answered.

"*Could you state your name and current address for the record?*"

"My name is Noah Madison. I live at 1517 Hawthorn Road in St. Paul."

"*Noah, I understand that you were a victim of physical, emotional and sexual abuse when you served as an altar boy at St. Theresa Catholic Church from 1982 through 1984. Is that correct?*"

"Yes, sir."

"*How old were you at that time, Noah?*"

"I was eleven years old when it began and thirteen when it ended."

"*Can you tell me the name of the priest at St. Theresa who took advantage of his position and did these terrible things to you, Noah?*"

"His name is William Hofmeister, but he was known to me at the time as Father Bill."

"*Do you know what happened to Father Bill?*"

"I know he left Minnesota around 1985 and was convicted of child abuse or sexual assault in Wisconsin in the late 1980s. He served some time in prison and died many years ago."

"*Noah, why are we here today, talking about this difficult time in your life?*"

"Archbishop Lamkin personally contacted me, explained that he knew about Hofmeister's abuse and wanted to talk to me if I were open to it and had forgiveness in my heart. I left the Catholic Church in college. My family and I were attending the Unitarian Church in Minneapolis, where I continue to be a member. Anyway, he apologized to me on behalf of the archdiocese and asked me if I wanted to put this terrible period of my life behind me and move on. He offered me a cash payment of $15,000 and lifetime emotional counseling and therapy that I might need to deal with the abuse."

"*What was your reaction to this offer?*"

"I discussed it with my family and with a lawyer provided by the Church. I've been impressed with what the archbishop is doing to get rid of the abusers and to protect children. Though I'm not returning to the Catholic Church I have accepted the archbishop's offer. I'm not interested in pursuing a lawsuit against the Church or in reliving the nightmare I endured with Hofmeister."

"*And you understand that by signing the Settlement Agreement and Release that will accompany this video and be submitted to the court for approval you will be giving up any right to sue the Archdiocese or St. Theresa in connection with Father William Hofmeister's assaults and other actions against you?"*

"Yes, I do."

Terranova clicked off the video and closed his laptop. "Lamkin and Andy Zimmerman devised an ingenious scheme to have the Court bless over 200 settlements even though not one lawsuit was actually filed. Zimmerman convinced the judge that, because all the victims were minors when they were abused, the Court should approve every settlement, just as the Court would be required to do if the victims had still been minors. It was brilliant, and Judge Kennedy bought the argument hook, line and sinker. They made a video just like the one I showed you for each settlement and presented each one to a judge for approval. Do you follow that sheriff?"

"I hope so," said MacDonald, thinking he'd be an idiot if he couldn't. "So, this Noah Madison. He appeared to have his shit together and clearly had no desire to sue the Church or to obtain a big payoff. Is he one of the plaintiff's in your case?"

"That's one of the reasons I played his video. It was made more than ten years ago. Noah contacted me a few years before he talked to Lamkin but decided not to pursue a claim against the Church, at least not with us. Lauren met with him six months ago and changed his mind. You need to know this story.

"Lauren had a classmate at Washburn High School who was one of the victims. He settled with the archdiocese under similar terms as Madison, but his life was in complete shambles. Lauren met with him several times, did some research and decided, against my advice, to attempt to overturn the settlements. This guy really got to her. She fervently believed, as do I, that these predatory priests robbed their young victims of much more than their innocence and self-esteem. She read everything she could find on the subject and interviewed several child psychologists and experts in the field of post-traumatic stress disorder and other trauma induced conditions. She became convinced that most victims experienced a nearly complete inability to regain to develop meaningful, long-term personal and professional relationships. Then her classmate committed suicide, and she became totally obsessed with this case. She was on a mission to get each of the victims at least a million dollars to assure then they had been robbed of something valuable and to fill what had become an unfillable hole in their lives. She also wanted to punish what she regarded as a cold, heartless, pragmatic institution.

"By the time she sued the archdiocese, she'd convinced about half of the settling victims to join—I think we have 120 plaintiffs. I've gotten calls from ten more since the media reported her death. There are at least 300 more out there who'll never seek redress and may never acknowledge the pain they've endured at the hands of these pious dickheads."

"So, do you think any of your plaintiffs could be persons of interest in Lauren's murder?" asked Macdonald.

"It's possible, of course," allowed Terranova. "Though I doubt it. These men loved and respected Lauren. On the other hand, some of the men who didn't join the suit, especially the devout Catholics who bought into Lamkin's bullshit, might have been motivated to stop her."

"Motivated by what?" asked MacDonald.

"By a misplaced desire to protect the Church. Members of the clergy had manipulated and brutally abused them, but Lamkin made them feel vindicated and worthy and welcomed them back into the flock of the holy. That feeling of belonging to something mystical can be very powerful, sheriff."

Only if you've got an undeveloped ego, thought MacDonald. "Anyone in particular?" he asked. "And, before I forget, can I get a list of your plaintiffs and of anyone you or Lauren met with who declined to become a client?"

"The identity of our plaintiffs remains confidential to anyone not a party to the lawsuit pursuant to a protective order. I'm sure you can get a subpoena to obtain names and contact information, so long as you don't disseminate that data to third parties. Noah Madison consented to my showing you his video. As for the 300 plus victims we don't represent, we have very little information about most of them and no information about many. I'll share what we have so long as you promise not to divulge where you got it.

"After we heard the news about Lauren, my team got together and fly-specked our files, hoping to find something that might shed light on the identity of the killer. Besides Jenkins, who clearly had motive and opportunity, but in my opinion wouldn't hurt a fly, I have two names for you. Two individuals who have a history of violence, although in one case it was justified."

"I agree with your assessment of Jenkins," said MacDonald. "Though I've seen some quiet, seemingly docile men harbor an inner rage that can surface suddenly and explode, often ignited by rejection. Who are the two individuals?"

"They're both victims of tragic circumstances, but the media covered much of their stories, so I'm not betraying any confidences or privileged communications. Billy Hutchinson was drugged and sexually brutalized by maybe the most wicked old fuck ever to be ordained. Billy was a big, strong boy who confronted the old bastard one day after school and then bludgeoned him to death with a silver chalice. He was thirteen at the time. He was never prosecuted, of course, but suffered some severe emotional and psychological damage as well as extended stays in a mental hospital. He's out now, actually works at a local parish as a maintenance man. He's become kind of monk, living in Spartan quarters in the basement of a parish house. He donated his settlement to the Church, refused to meet with Lauren and, I'm told, was furious when he heard about our lawsuit against the archdiocese. He must be fifty by now, but is still a physically imposing man with a volatile temper. Would he have the cunning to set up a meeting with Lauren under some false pretense in order to kill her? I just don't know."

"Fascinating that he's remained loyal to the Church through all this," observed MacDonald.

"You'd be amazed at the number of victims who continue to be practicing Catholics. Anyway, the other potential suspect is Dennis Hedstrom. Denny's life and story are as dysfunctional as they get. His parents were never really together, and his mom was murdered in a drug deal gone bad in the late '70s. Denny lived in foster homes in north Minneapolis and attended St Odelia Catholic School. When he was twelve his foster family consisted of nine kids between the ages of five and fifteen, so let's just say supervision was lax. Denny was a shy, sweet boy who caught the eye of Father Bob Mahoney, one of the priests at Odelia. Over the course of the next few years, Denny was subjected to almost daily abuse at the hands of Father Bob, until a nun who was also the school principal inadvertently walked in on one of Bob's after-school sessions in the parish offices and called the police. Despite counseling and rehab programs, Denny has never really recovered from the horrible abuse he suffered. He attended community college for a few years to become a veterinary tech but didn't earned a degree. He's made a meager living doing light assembly and other factory work but has been in and out of jail for domestic violence incidents. He nearly strangled his first wife to death and has beaten at least two live-in girlfriends to the point of needing orders for protection.

"Apparently Lamkin made several attempts to reach out to him, but he's refused to talk to anyone connected to the archdiocese. Lauren visited him once; he told her the only thing he hated more than the Catholic Church were 'fucking lawyers.'"

"Do you have contact information for these two?" MacDonald asked as he took notes on a yellow legal pad.

"Sure, though I can't guarantee the information is current."

"As far as you know, did Lauren make any other enemies in her legal practice, anyone who had a grudge or ax to grind?"

"I really can't think of anyone," said Terranova. "She could be tough and wouldn't back down in an argument, but she was always professional, never played petty games with opposing counsel. No one treated abuse victims with more kindness, empathy and respect than Lauren."

"Besides yourself, who were Lauren's closest friends or colleagues at the firm?"

"Brianna Steiner was her legal assistant and JoAnn Larson her paralegal. As for the attorneys, I think she worked most closely with Mark Widman. Feel free to interview anyone on our staff, sheriff. Just give them a little notice; they're all busy."

"Thanks. I'll keep that in mind. I also want to confirm that your IT person, I think his name is Max, is scheduled to meet with the County's system administrator and Deputy Klewacki tomorrow to get into Lauren's laptop."

"I think that's right, but we'll check in with Max before you leave today. You won't be able to access our client files on Lauren's laptop; they're all password protected on our cloud server, but you will be able to review her emails, which is what I thought you were after."

"That's fine," acknowledged MacDonald. "I'm curious about the voice on that video. Who's interviewing Noah Madison—is it Andy Zimmerman, the Church's lawyer?"

"No," said Terranova. "Zimmerman's got a much deeper, authoritarian voice. We haven't been able to figure out who that is. Apparently, he's a lawyer hired by Lamkin to provide advice to the victims. Noah and others have said he introduced himself as Sidney Carton, a name that Dickens' readers would know but not the name of any attorney licensed in Minnesota. Apparently, whoever it was wanted to remain anonymous."

"That seems odd to me," said MacDonald, "and not in a good way."

31

ANDY ZIMMERMAN HAD been lead outside counsel for the Twin Cities Archdiocese for nearly thirty years. He was a senior partner at Mason & Fritch, a 200-plus lawyer firm with offices in St. Paul, Chicago and Houston. Zimmerman was an intimidating specimen, standing over 6'4" and weighing close to 300 pounds, with a voice like a fog horn, bushy gray eyebrows and a shiny bald head. Wearing an impeccably tailored three-piece suit and silk tie, as he did every day, he presided at the conference table in Lamkin's chancery office along with two bright but cutthroat female associates. Lamkin was joined at the table by Fred Hollander, the 75-year-old, somewhat addled vicar general. He'd been with the archdiocese for forty years but had served a minor administrative role during Lamkin's tenure. In a private moment with Zimmerman prior to the meeting, Lamkin explained the reason for Jenkins' conspicuous absence.

"I had a rather unpleasant conversation with Terranova last night," said Zimmerman. "He's such cocky little bastard. It's hard to believe he started out as a sniveling public defender, hustling for DWI and domestic assault cases. When he started chasing these abuse cases in the early 80s, no one else would touch them. And now he's the world's foremost authority on how to shake down the Catholic Church. He claims Lauren sent him an email on the night she was killed proposing to set up a grand mediation session to try to settle these claims for the second time."

"Isn't it premature to do that?" asked Lamkin. "I thought you said we'd have a good chance to get rid of the whole thing on summary judgment."

"I did say that," Zimmerman agreed, "but we need to consider a number of factors before rejecting the idea of a quick settlement. First, Lauren Fallon's death does change things somewhat. Terranova claims he's been contacted by a dozen potential new plaintiffs since the news broke, and, if the case survives summary judgment and gets to a jury, there could be a huge sympathy factor regardless of our defenses.

"Second, now that Lauren is gone, Terranova will be the lead lawyer. Lauren was good, but not as obnoxiously aggressive as Joe. He will be relentless in demanding documents and taking depositions, including yours and Peter's. Their case is predicated on showing that you and the archdiocese essentially brainwashed these men into accepting a paltry cash settlement in exchange for a nominal apology and, for lack of a better way to put it, their salvation.

"Third, if this case gets to a jury, the most recent verdicts for abuse victims average about a million dollars a plaintiff. Add in litigation costs and the arch-diocese may be facing a judgment approaching $300 million. We can probably get your liability carriers to cover thirty to forty percent of that, so the net is well over $150 million. I assume you can't come up with anything close to that figure, so we would need to seek bankruptcy protection."

This wasn't really news to Lamkin, but he needed to hear Zimmerman lay it out. The archdiocese had cash and liquid investments of $10 to $15 million and could sell unneeded real estate and other assets worth another $20 million. Add in the secret fund, and he could get close to $150 million. "We might be able to get close to that number, but it would cripple our parishes and schools. And I'm certainly not excited about getting interrogated by Terranova. What's the best settlement we could negotiate?"

"We didn't talk numbers, but he knows that Judge Kennedy could shut him out completely. On the other hand, he has an incredible war chest and might just roll the dice to honor Lauren's memory. If the archdiocese could raise $80 million, I think we can threaten imminent bankruptcy and get Terranova to bite on a total settlement in the neighborhood of $150 million."

"How much of that would he get?" asked Hollander, curious about the law-yer's payday.

"He's been taking twenty percent; if the case goes to trial, at least thirty," said Zimmerman.

"I'd feel a lot better about $50 million," said Lamkin. "Let's agree to medi-ate but make sure we get a reasonable mediator and shoot for a total under a hundred."

"I think that's a good plan," said the lawyer. "Terranova told me Judge Fallon is hoping to have a memorial service for Lauren at the end of this week. They think the medical examiner will release her body today or tomorrow. We can probably schedule the mediation for some time near the end of next week."

"The sooner the better," said Lamkin.

32

"Hello, sheriff, did you get my message?"

"I did. What happened?" MacDonald was sitting in the Tahoe in the parking lot of Terranova's building.

"Best I can tell," said Redman, "is Jenkins was awakened by someone visiting his condo around midnight on Saturday. He let the person in and ended up stabbed to death on his couch. Jenkins' wallet with all of his credit cards and $250 in cash was sitting on a nightstand next to his bed. There's no evidence of a physical struggle. I think the perpetrator delivered one powerful and totally unexpected thrust through Jenkins' neck with the metal tip of a black umbrella. Split Jenkins' carotid artery in half. St. Paul homicide and BCA forensics are processing the scene."

"Did he have any family?"

"I've been researching that this morning. The only known relative was his adoptive mother, and she died twenty years ago. I'd say his boss, Archbishop Lamkin, is the closest thing he had to family. Thought I'd drop in on him this afternoon at the chancery."

MacDonald reminded Redman of Lamkin's visit to the North Shore on the night of Lauren's murder and suggested he inquire into the specifics of that trip as well. He reviewed the highlights of his meeting with Terranova, and said he'd try to track down Billy Hutchinson and Denny Hedstrom before leaving the Cities. They agreed to meet for dinner at Rita's steakhouse to compare notes.

33

GOVERNOR BIXBY SAT at the roll-top desk in his office in the Governor's man-sion and stared in disbelief at the screen on his computer. He'd followed a familiar authentication procedure to access the account he shared with McBride at *Union Bancaire Privee* out of Geneva for the third time and for the third time he received a flashing message in red caps: ACCESS DENIED.

He speed-touched McBride's number on his cell and was surprised to hear a live voice after only one ring.

"What's up, Governor?"

"I can't get into our joint Swiss account, Jay. I need to transfer $50k to my brokerage firm to cover a trade I made this morning."

"I'm afraid you've transferred your last dollar out of that account, Win. I can't afford to give you access to any more of my money."

"Jesus Christ, McBride. Are you kidding me? You can't afford not to give me access to that account. The state will move everything out of Itasca by the end of the quarter."

"I don't think so, Governor. I don't deny I've got a lot to lose if that hap-pens, but you've already taken over $2 million in what can only be described as a bribe. If I lose the state's account while you're in office, you and I can share a cell in Sandstone."

"Fuck you, McBride. I guarantee you'll regret this."

"Fuck you, too, Bixby. The only thing I regret is not cutting you off sooner."

34

THE CLERGY HOUSE next to St. Theresa Catholic Church was a two-story brick Tudor with green shutters, white trim and a red tiled roof, all in need of repair. By far the largest home on English Street, it had five bedrooms, three bathrooms and a custodian's apartment in the lower level. Like the church, it was built in the 1920s on the east side of St. Paul, a couple of blocks from Lake Phalen in what was still a predominantly Catholic, though now ethnically diverse, neighborhood.

The mid-day sun was hot enough to fry an egg on the asphalt pavement, when MacDonald parked the Tahoe in front of the church. He opened the door to exit when Rossini's *Overture* made him sit back and take a call from Redman.

"How's your afternoon so far?"

"I'm at the St. Theresa parsonage, about to pay Mr. Hutchinson a visit. How about you?"

"I have an appointment to meet with the archbishop at three. I said it was urgent but didn't say why. I think it's only right to tell him about Jenkins in person. But I'm calling about Dennis Hedstrom. You can take him off the list of potential suspects; he's been residing at Oak Park Heights Correctional Facility for the past three weeks on a probation violation."

"Thanks for the info," said MacDonald. "I have a call into my office to locate him, but I guess the BCA is the central nervous system of criminal investigations in Minnesota."

"That's almost poetic. See you tonight."

Father Ed Dowling had retired as St. Theresa's pastor several years back but stayed on in an associate or *emeritus* capacity to assist Father Patterson.

He spent six months of the year in Minnesota and the other six with his sister in Fort Lauderdale. Dowling was eighty-two but still sharp and still loved by St. Theresa's parishioners, especially the ones who remembered his days as a history teacher and basketball coach at St. Ignatius High School, where his team set a state record for winning thirty consecutive games.

Dowling had been a three-sport letter winner at St. John's College and had attended seminary in St. Paul. He was of medium height and build, though arthritis had created a noticeable hunch in his posture, with a full head of steel-gray hair, deep-set blue eyes and a wide, gap-toothed smile. The friendly cleric still maintained a rigorous exercise regimen, including jogging twenty miles a week and playing pickle ball at the neighborhood community center. Dowling was never a biblical scholar, but he did represent everything good about the parish priests of his generation. He believed in the Church's mission and in most of its doctrine, but he was also devoted to the well-being of his congregation and infused large doses of kindness and pragmatism into Catholic dogma. He was the only one home when MacDonald rang the clergy house doorbell.

"Good afternoon, young man," greeted Dowling. He opened the outer screen door wide enough to walk out onto a large, open porch, looking out at MacDonald's SUV before looking up at him. "How may I help you on this lovely summer day?"

"It certainly is a beautiful day," replied MacDonald, wondering whether this elderly gentleman in a short-sleeve black shirt with white collar band and black pants was the local parish priest. "My name is Sam MacDonald. I'm the Lake County Sheriff from Two Harbors up on Lake Superior, and I'm investigating the recent death of a woman named Lauren Fallon."

"I read about her in the paper," said Dowling. "She's the young lawyer who was married to a judge, right?"

"That's right."

"What a tragedy, sheriff. I'm Father Dowling, Ed Dowling. I'm a semi-retired priest here at St. Theresa. I'd sure like to help you, but doubt that I can."

"It's nice to meet you, Father. I'm looking for a Billy Hutchinson, and I've been told that he works at St. Theresa and lives with you here at the parsonage."

"Yes, Billy works here and lives with us. As you may know, sheriff, he is a troubled man who's been trying to find peace and meaning in his life. He really struggles at times, but I don't see how he could have had anything to do with your case."

"Is he here at the house now?"

"No, sheriff. Billy borrowed our old pick-up truck and drove up to his Uncle Walter's farm near Hugo. Said he was going to help him get rid of some old tree stumps or something."

"Was Billy home from Friday night through Saturday morning, Father?"

"He worked on Friday night. I convinced him to try some homemade vegetable soup when he came home around ten. He was up before seven on Saturday. He mowed the lawn here and at the church and took a long walk with Father Patterson. He's been cutting himself on the forearm and thigh in the last few weeks, something he hadn't done in a few years, so Father Patterson wanted to spend some time with him. It appears to have had a positive impact because on Sunday morning he was in high spirits. He said God had visited him on Saturday night and helped him plan his future. He packed an overnight bag and told us he was going to Ramsey Hill to attend mass at the Cathedral and then drive up to Hugo. Said he'd be back this afternoon sometime. I'm sorry, sheriff, would you like to come in, sit down, maybe have a glass of iced tea?"

"Thanks, Father, but I need to get going after a few more questions, if that's OK. Do you know whether Billy owns or has possession of any firearms or other weapons?"

"Oh, no, sheriff. We would never allow anyone to bring guns or the like in either the church or this parish house. You're welcome to search his room if you'd like; there's really almost nothing in there. Just some clothes and a bible."

MacDonald was tempted to take him up on the offer but decided against it. "Not right now, Father, but thank you." If Billy were home on both Friday and Saturday night, he couldn't have killed either Lauren or Jenkins, but MacDonald had an uneasy feeling about this broken man. "Does Billy visit his Uncle Walter often?"

"According to Billy, Walter is a bit of a recluse who claims to be an anarchist. He was married once, but his wife left him years ago. Apparently, he's become self-sufficient on his small farm and rarely leaves it. I don't think Billy's seen him since his mother died."

"So why now?" asked MacDonald.

"You'd have to ask Billy that question, sheriff, but I have to say that Father Patterson and I have never seen him as upbeat and animated as he was when we told him he could take the truck for a few days. Whatever the reason, we pray that God is behind it."

"Did Billy ever mention anything about a lawsuit against the archdiocese, specifically his feelings about the lawyer who represents the abuse victims?"

"Oh, now I get why you're interested in Billy," said Dowling, nodding his head. "None of us is too happy about someone dredging up that sad chapter, sheriff. Billy doesn't talk much about any subject, but I do recall him saying something about high-priced shysters out to destroy the church. He may not have used that exact language. Unfortunately, I do think our Billy is still capable of violence. I'm sure you know about his past. But he's made great progress, and I know he prays every day for guidance and strength."

"Does he have a cell phone, Father?"

"Oh, no, sheriff. Billy doesn't use any of those devices. He makes calls from our landline in the house or from one of the phones in the church offices. You don't think Billy had anything to do with that young lady's murder, do you sheriff? I don't know how he could've been involved from here?"

"I don't either," MacDonald agreed, though he wondered if Billy could have slipped out of the house undetected late Saturday night and taken the truck over to Peter Jenkins' place. "I'm more concerned that he might do something in the future. Did he say anything else of significance before he left—anyone else he wanted to visit or anywhere else he was going?"

"Not that I can think of right now."

"And this pickup truck he's driving, can you describe it for me?"

"Sure," said Dowling. "It's a '93 Ford F-150 single cab. It's white but has more rust than paint. I don't think it's worth more than a few hundred bucks, but it still runs pretty good and sure comes in handy to move things every now and then."

"Great. You wouldn't happen to have a current photograph of Billy that I could keep, would you Father?"

"As a matter of fact, I think I do," said Dowling. "I'll be right back."

He retreated into the house and returned a minute later with a three-by-five-inch framed photograph of Billy with his two housemates. He was a head taller than the two priests and had a shaved head and well-defined arm and pectoral muscles that stretched the fabric of his white T-shirt. "Here you go, sheriff. You can keep this if you'd like. I have others and can always take more."

"Thank you. This is helpful." MacDonald studied the photo for several seconds. "Well, here's my card. If you or Father Patterson come up with any other information you think is important, please call me day or night. Thanks again, Father. It was a pleasure meeting you."

MacDonald extended his oversized right hand, and Father Dowling shook it gingerly with his arthritic one.

"Good luck to you, sheriff. May the Lord be with you in all things."

MacDonald acknowledged the benediction with a nod and descended the concrete porch steps. As he opened the door to the Tahoe, he heard Dowling's high, squeaky voice calling his name. He turned back and saw the old pastor jogging down the sidewalk towards him.

"I remembered something, sheriff," he called out with his right arm raised, waving to the heavens. "The last thing Billy said when he left on Sunday morning struck me as odd, especially coming from him. He said, 'I'm off to make the world a better place.' At the time I didn't quite see how removing stumps at his uncle's farm would accomplish that, but, as I said, I was glad to see him happy and with a purpose."

"But what purpose?" MacDonald asked rhetorically, as he pondered what would make the world a better place from Billy's perspective.

35

WALTER ZEMAN WAS Billy Hutchinson's mother's only sibling. They grew up on a dairy farm near Paynesville in central Minnesota. Walter graduated from high school in the early 1960s and immediately enlisted in the army. Though he was a reasonably good student, he had no interest in more schooling and wanted to escape small town, Minnesota and see the world.

After boot camp at Fort Sill in Oklahoma, he spent the next year immersed in field artillery training. Not only did he enjoy blowing things up, he was good at it, so he applied to become an ordnance specialist. After undergoing more specialized training at Fort Lewis-McCoy in Tacoma, Washington, he spent the better part of two years assembling, mounting, loading and firing a ninety-millimeter gun on an M48 Patton tank in Vietnam and Cambodia. He also learned how to defuse unexploded bombs but never utilized that talent in combat.

Walter was honorably discharged in 1969 and parleyed the expertise he developed in the service into a good-paying job as an explosives' engineer with a demolition company in Baltimore. He was lucky to marry the perky young realtor who sold him his first house in Bethesda, and, for a brief time, life was good. Unfortunately, Walter had also developed an affinity for brown liquor in Vietnam, and, ultimately, his love affair with Jack Daniels cost him his marriage and his job.

His wife left him after three rocky years of weekend binges, verbal abuse and broken promises to get help. Amazingly, he was able to keep his job at Commercial Implosions for nearly ten years, mostly because his immediate supervisor was a fellow Vietnam vet who covered for his fellow soldier more than once. Within a month after he moved to California, his replacement fired Walter for being intoxicated on a demolition site.

At his sister's suggestion, Walter returned to Minnesota and checked into Hazelden Rehab Center. It took him six months to dry out, and nothing about it was easy. He sold the house in Bethesda, bought a hobby farm a few miles off Interstate 35 near Hugo, and for the first time in his life began to see everything "clearly." He clearly rejected all forms of religion, all forms of government and all forms of employment, becoming as self-sufficient as a man could be on an 80-acre hobby farm in central Minnesota. He raised a few cows and chickens for sustenance, and, in order to maintain his virtuosity with explosives, invested in a chainsaw, a bobcat and a heavy-duty dump truck and started his own tree and stump removal business.

Walter had only seen Billy a handful of times in fifty years. Then they sat next to each other at Lisa Hutchinson's funeral. Neither man talked much, but Walter learned that Billy's life revolved around his devotion to the Catholic Church and Jesus Christ, whereas Billy learned that Walter didn't like anyone telling him what to do and enjoyed blowing shit up. Neither man thought he'd ever see the other again, until Billy called Walter on Sunday morning. After a brief conversation, the two men discovered they had something in common and might be able to collaborate to make the world a better place.

36

REDMAN AND LAMKIN sat at a small, round conference table in Lamkin's chancery office. The archbishop assumed the "urgent meeting" had something to do with Lauren Fallon's murder, which made him sweat under the collar and tap his right foot nervously under the table. He was surprised to see a police officer wearing a short-sleeve polo shirt and khaki pants, though Redman said he worked for the BCA; maybe they had a different dress code.

"I'll get right to the point, archbishop. I am very sorry to have to tell you that one of your employees, Peter Jenkins, was brutally murdered in his apartment late Saturday night or early Sunday morning. Based on what we know so far, we think Mr. Jenkins knew his killer. The St. Paul police will be interviewing his neighbors and any other persons of interest, but at this time we have no suspects. Since I discovered the murder scene, I volunteered to track down and notify his next of kin. Unless you tell me otherwise, I'm assuming he has none, and that you are the closest thing he has to family."

Lamkin's jaw slackened and his eyes glazed over. He grasped the table with both hands to steady himself and tried to digest what he'd just heard—the violent ending of the earthly life of his closest associate and confidante. Soft spoken, gentle Peter Jenkins *murdered?*

"I don't understand, Agent Redman. Did someone rob Peter?"

"I don't think so, archbishop. Nothing appears to be missing, and his wallet filled with cash was sitting on a nightstand in his bedroom. He was stabbed in the neck with a long, needle-nosed umbrella."

"Was it a black umbrella?" asked Lamkin, a look of recognition displacing the look of disbelief.

"It was black with the words 'Property of the Archdiocese of St. Paul & Minneapolis' carved into the handle," said Redman. He'd already concluded there was no way this scrawny little man had enough physical strength or leverage to be the killer.

Without hesitation, Lamkin exclaimed, "That's my umbrella! I was at Peter's condo on Saturday evening. I brought my umbrella in because it was raining, but I left without it."

"What time did you leave his place on Saturday?"

"Sometime before 8:00. My cook and valet at the parsonage can tell you when I got in that night."

"Thank you. That's helpful. What about any next of kin?"

"Peter had no one. His mother died several years ago; he had no siblings or other known relatives. This is just terrible. Unfathomable."

"What about enemies?" asked Redman, almost rhetorically, but then interrupted himself, "I've been assigned to assist with the Lauren Fallon murder investigation. I went over to Peter's this morning to do a follow-up interview and discovered one of the most grotesque murder scenes I've ever seen."

"How awful," said Lamkin, shaking his head. "Do you think there's a connection between that woman lawyer's murder and Peter's?"

"The thought has crossed my mind. Peter was some kind of an administrator or lawyer for the archdiocese, isn't that right."

"Yes, you could say that. He had responsibility for risk management, human resources and legal matters. But to my knowledge he's never been in any kind of physical altercation with anyone. I can't even remember a heated argument. He had no enemies as far as I know."

"Are you familiar with a Billy Hutchinson?"

Lamkin had a flashback to Sunday mass and the image of Billy sitting in Peter's seat with a contorted smile on his face. "Yes, I'm familiar with Billy, and I assume you are as well, Mr. Redman. He has a history of violence, but my recollection is he was fond of Peter. I can only recall positive interactions between the two at church functions and support groups. Billy was one of several abuse victims who became passionate supporters of this diocese. However,

I do remember Peter mentioning that Billy made some ugly comments about the lawyers who orchestrated the recent legal action against us."

"So, you think he might have been involved in Ms. Fallon's death?"

"I wouldn't want to speculate," said Lamkin, but then he did. "I suppose if Billy knew Peter was trying to negotiate some kind of a deal with Ms. Fallon, that could have upset him and even turned him against Peter, but I don't know how he could have known any of that."

"Anyone else come to mind as a potential threat to Peter or to Lauren Fallon for that matter? Wasn't Jenkins involved in the firing or defrocking of several priests in the midst of all the scandals? I mean couldn't either a disgruntled former priest or dissatisfied abuse victim see Peter as someone who helped to screw him over?"

"I take exception to that characterization and language," Lamkin said smugly, "and you're talking about hundreds of alleged victims and over a hundred priests, though many of them are dead at this point. I wouldn't know where to begin."

"Okay. I'm going to need a list of all your known victims as well as all accused and discharged priests, including any contact information you've got, and I need this stuff ASAP, okay your eminence?"

Lamkin did not like this crass, pushy cop. "Most of that is confidential information, Mr. Redman, so . . ."

"That's just bullshit," said Redman, using his outside voice. "You can produce that information for me by the end of the day today, or I'll be back within 24 hours with a subpoena, and I'll be pissed, and I'll want to know exactly what *you* were doing up in Beaver Bay late Friday night at about the same time Lauren Fallon was murdered in Gooseberry Park."

Lamkin glared at Redman, wanting to lash out. He had battled anger management issues since he was a boy but thought he'd overcome them. Now he felt a surge of rage, a feeling he had to suppress. "How do you know I was up there Friday night?"

"The Lake County Sheriff's office reviewed video and still surveillance photos from convenience stores and service stations in the area, looking for possible suspects. Your Town Car was rather conspicuous as was your priestly attire." Respect for religious authority was clearly not high on Redman's priority list. "Again, what were you doing up there, archbishop?"

"This is ridiculous. I don't have to answer your impertinent questions, especially after what's happened to Peter." Lamkin wasn't used to being cross-examined or having to come up with an alibi to protect his reputation. He didn't like it, though he was quick to concoct a plausible explanation. "I was visiting an important donor to our Catholic charities giving campaign, if you must know. He has a beautiful place on Lake Superior and wanted me to enjoy it while we reviewed our latest fund drive."

Redman didn't believe a word, but at the moment didn't care. "What about the lists? I'm especially interested in the discarded priests who are still living and in the area."

"Come by tomorrow and I'll have our attorneys deliver what you've requested, but you must commit in writing not to share any of the information with the media or with anyone else not connected to law enforcement."

"You get me the information, and I'll protect it and sign anything you want."

"And Peter? When will the authorities let us have him? I could arrange for someone from McKee & Jenson Funeral Home to pick him up for preparation. We need to plan a funeral mass and burial within the week, if that's possible."

"Hang on a minute, Padre. St. Paul homicide is directing the investigation. I'll check in with them later today and share what we discussed, but they may have additional questions for you. Detective Colianni is in charge. Frank Colianni. You can call him directly if you have questions about the body or about the status of the investigation. There'll probably be an autopsy, so don't expect the body to be released before the end of the week.

"You probably think I'm a prick, but I'm just trying to do my job. I am truly sorry for your loss, Archbishop Lamkin. Nobody deserves what happened to your friend Jenkins. Now don't forget that list."

37

B ILLY WAS EXCITED but getting nervous, if not downright scared. His plan was to leave the farm right after lunch and reach his destination no later than 1:30. It was 2:15 when Walter gave him the "thumbs up" to get in the truck. They had reviewed and rehearsed the process twenty times. Billy knew what he needed to do. But Walter had little faith in his nephew. He motioned for him to roll down his window and yelled a final caveat above the sound of the gurgling, spitting V-8:

"REMEMBER, YOU GOTTA BE AT LEAST 30 YARDS CLEAR OF THE TRUCK BEFORE YOU ENGAGE THE FUSES!!"

Billy nodded without really listening and then drove the rusting F-150 down the winding gravel driveway that ended at Northeast 176th Street. Walter had given him directions to Shoreview taking only back roads, so he would be driving through neighborhoods he never knew even existed.

Billy feared the truck would blow up with him in it, even though Walter had assured him the multi-layered explosive device he'd designed and built using pentaerythritol tetranitrate, among other chemicals, was harmless, unless and until Billy pressed the proper sequence of buttons on the black remote detonator. Walter added two ten-gallon containers of diesel fuel to the mix just for good measure. After all, Billy had described a three-story metal, stone and glass structure filled with predatory lawyers. The diesel fuel would ensure they would all burn in Hell.

38

"Jay, for God's sake, why don't you return my calls?" Lamkin hadn't recovered from his upsetting meeting with Redman and was calling McBride from the speaker phone in his office.

"Take it easy, Jim. You're gonna' have a stroke," teased McBride, sucking down the remnants of a dirty vodka martini, including a blue cheese-stuffed olive. "I've been working. We presented to the investment committee at St. Scholastica in Duluth this morning, so I decided to spend a few days at the lake. Why don't you join me? By the way, your name carries a lot of weight with those tight-assed Catholic college administrators."

"Jay, something horrible has happened. Peter was stabbed to death in his apartment on Saturday night, and the killer is still on the loose. I can't believe it. Who would do such a thing? He was a good, gentle servant of the Lord. He always tried to do the right thing, and this is what he gets in return. I'm just heartsick over this. Plus, he handled a lot of difficult assignments for the Church. I don't know how we'll replace him."

"That's awful, Jim, really it is. Peter was a good man, but let's not forget his recent indiscretions that created a huge mess for you."

"I'd rather have him alive with whatever problems he may have caused. That reminds me, you need to be ready to transfer a significant piece of the fund to an account I can access within the next week or so. Zimmerman is scheduling a mediation with Terranova; he thinks we can settle the whole thing for under $100 million. I'm hoping after insurance our contribution won't be more than $50 or $60 million.

"If you want to see any of that money again, you'll have to come up here and spend a few days with me, my friend."

"I don't think that would be very smart," said Lamkin, even though it sounded like a good idea. "The police know I was up there last Friday night. I stopped for gas in Beaver Bay and they captured it on the store video. One of the cops investigating Lauren Fallon's murder asked me what I was doing so close to the crime scene that night."

"What did you tell him?" asked McBride, raising his interest level and his voice.

"Nothing about you, so don't worry. I said I was visiting a major donor who had a place on Lake Superior. He didn't ask any follow-up questions. He's also the detective who found Peter's body. He seemed preoccupied with that."

"Listen. I'm serious. Drive up here tomorrow. There's nothing you can do for Peter in the next few days. Fill up with gas in the Cities and drive straight through to my place. You can go back on Wednesday if you need to."

"I'll think about it."

He had already made up his mind. His world was unravelling. He needed time away from St. Paul to think things through. Why not regroup in the comfort and beauty of McBride's lake home? Plus, he had to ensure McBride would transfer the money to end the clergy abuse saga once and for all.

"I've started to plan Peter's funeral mass," Lamkin said, as if that were a positive development. "You should definitely attend out of respect for the man."

"I wouldn't miss it."

39

AFTER MEETING WITH Father Dowling, MacDonald made a few calls *en route* to Redman's office at the BCA. Redman didn't pick up; neither did Clayton Miller, the Ramsey County Sheriff. He left a message for each and checked in with Klewacki. Always a step ahead, she let him know the hospital would be discharging Stockman later in the day and reminded him of her scheduled meeting with Terranova's tech guy on Tuesday morning and of his meeting with Dr. Higgins to review the autopsy results.

MacDonald asked her to run a quick background check on a Walter Zeman of Hugo in Washington County. He wondered what Billy and Walter were scheming and believed, whatever it was, it had nothing to do with tree stumps.

He turned into the BCA visitors' lot when Klewacki called back and confirmed his worst fears.

"Mac, this Walter Zeman has no criminal record. He's been living at the same address in Hugo for a couple of decades. But did you know he was a munitions expert in the Army and, as recently as three years ago, had a business license to use TNT for commercial demolition purposes?"

"Oh, my God. That's got to be it! I need to go. Thanks."

MacDonald switched on his siren and flashers as he left the BCA lot on his way to Shoreview. He left messages for Terranova and his receptionist to evacuate the building immediately. He was about to make a 911 emergency call requesting that any available officers converge on Walter's farm, when Sheriff Miller returned his call.

"Just listened to your message, sheriff. I'm afraid you're a little late. I'm standing in what's left of Joe Terranova's parking lot up in Shoreview along with

— 123 —

the FBI, several suburban squads and fire units and a shitload of rescue person- nel. Somebody blew up a big chunk of the building and the rest is on fire. I'm guessing you have some information on who might have done this."

"I think I do, sheriff. How many casualties are you dealing with up there?"

"It's too early to tell for sure, but incredibly I think the only fatality may be the dumb fucker who set off the pyrotechnics."

"I'm less than five minutes away. I'll share what I know when I get there."

MacDonald couldn't help feeling sorry for Billy Hutchinson, whose tor- mented, fragile psyche may have been beyond repair. He'd have to make a return visit to kindly Father Dowling later.

40

FOLLOWING WALTER'S DIRECTIONS, Billy drove the old pickup to the north side of the fancy office building to take advantage of a strong northwest wind. The main entrance was on the east side. Unbeknownst to Billy, all but one of the building's occupants, fifteen Terranova employees and four clients, were in the first-floor lunchroom on the far south end having cake, ice cream and soft drinks to celebrate the 50th birthday of Joyce Fahey, Terranova's long-time office manager and former lover.

Driving like someone with a bomb in his bed, Billy carefully negotiated the curb and parked on the grass within two feet of a mostly glass wall. He grabbed the remote detonator from the passenger seat, slid it into his pocket and climbed out of the truck. Walter had instructed him to remove the tarp from the arming device but to leave it over the fuel cans. Record-setting high temperatures over 100 degrees in the Cities on Sunday moderated slightly on Monday due to strong winds out of Canada and mostly cloudy skies. But it was still plenty hot for Billy. He was drenched in sweat from a combination of nervous energy, adrenaline and his outfit, a long-sleeve black tunic with black denim jeans. The truck's lack of air conditioning didn't help.

Billy counted nineteen vehicles when he first entered the parking lot. He assumed the silver Porsche Boxster convertible belonged to the devil's disciple himself. He worried that someone would enter the lot or exit the building while he was making final preparations and interfere with God's plan. For years he had had difficulty focusing on the task at hand. He'd been diagnosed with attention deficit disorder even before the bad times, but with the help of Father Patterson and his therapist, his powers of concentration were improving. Walter told him to envision the structure engulfed in flames while he casually walked the mile and a half to Lexington Avenue and caught a metro transit bus to Lake Phalen. He would be a hero, if only to himself and God and Walter, of course.

But, as is often the case, things didn't go according to plan. A FedEx van pulled into the parking lot and stopped at the outer perimeter, the driver appearing to stare at Billy and the truck. As he pulled the brown tarp off Walter's blinking contraption, a gust of wind blew it out of his hands and onto the glass wall, sticking to it like a giant plastic wrapper.

Billy panicked. He pulled the detonator out of his pocket and started running away from the building. He counted to five in his head, figuring he was at least thirty yards clear of the truck, and then pressed the four buttons in the proper sequence.

Billy saw the initial explosion before he heard it. He never really heard it, since one of the early blasts blew his body into multiple pieces. Billy was only twenty yards from the truck when he detonated Walter's device. Thirty would not have been enough. Walter knew that of course; he never intended for Billy to survive; he didn't trust him to keep his mouth shut.

The FedEx driver was the first to call 9-1-1. He had difficulty interpreting what he was seeing—a muscular man in a black outfit; an old pickup, its bed weighted down with barrels and machinery, parked on the grass next to the building; and, finally, the man running towards him with some kind of device in his hand. He had the perfect seat to watch the ensuing explosions, a series of fiery, mushrooming eruptions, the second or third setting off the diesel fuel and engulfing most of the building in flames. Parts of the structure literally collapsed and nearly half the parking lot on the north and east sides of the building disappeared into a crater filled with burning cars and dislodged auto parts.

Mark Widman was leading the group in singing "Happy Birthday" to Joyce when the lunchroom began to shake as if shifting tectonic plates under the city had set off a massive earthquake. Anything not securely fastened was tossed towards the south end of the room, including Terranova's staff and clients. Those who weren't knocked unconscious heard a series of thunderous blasts that accompanied apocalyptic vibrations. All the lights went out.

After what seemed like several minutes but was under thirty seconds, the fireworks subsided. Sounds of screaming and crying provided a counterpoint to wailing smoke detectors from the hallways and office spaces that hadn't been completely flattened. A few operable ceiling sprinklers showered cold water on terrified victims.

Black smoke billowed into the room. Widman was bleeding from the forehead and right arm but didn't think he was seriously hurt. Whether there'd been a natural gas explosion or terrorists were attacking Shoreview, Widman knew he had to act fast. He yelled for everyone who could stand to form a conga line behind Joyce, who had a few minor cuts and bruises but had already called 9-1-1.

The majority were scared to the point of soiling themselves but, like Joyce and Widman, not critically injured. After some quick self-examinations, they formed a crooked line and managed to follow Joyce down the south hallway and out a service door to the relative safety of the south lot. Two employees were unconscious with more serious head wounds. Widman carried one, a female paralegal who had to weigh 200 pounds, and Mo Hussain, an athletic young summer clerk from Stanford, carried the other. Widman scanned the room one final time for any stragglers before, straining mightily and hunched over, he managed to get himself and the dead weight over his shoulder out of the burning remains of the house that Terranova built.

The group moved like a giant caterpillar to the south lawn to wait for emergency responders, whom they could hear getting closer. Traffic on Highway 96 was nearly at a standstill, drivers and passengers gawking at the smoldering heap that used to be the most upscale office building in Shoreview. The FedEx driver noticed activity on the opposite side of the conflagration and drove around the outer edge of the lot to assist the wounded.

Relieved to be alive and safe, Widman and Joyce embraced. Then, with panic in her eyes, Joyce grabbed Widman's bloodstained dress shirt with both hands and cried out:

"Oh, my God, what about Joe?"

41

"THE WHOLE THING was just fucking unbelievable," howled Clayton Miller in his resonant, baritone voice, as he sat on a high-back vinyl barstool between Redman and MacDonald. He leaned back far enough so he could easily make eye contact with both men.

Miller and MacDonald had spent more than four hours at the scene of the Shoreview firestorm, assisting emergency responders, interviewing survivors, and assessing the cause and extent of the destruction. Physically spent, mentally exhausted and drenched in smoke and sweat, they'd agreed to contact Redman and compare notes after a respite that included a shower and change of clothes. They all would meet for drinks and dinner at Jim Murphy's Steakhouse in downtown St. Paul.

It was a few minutes after 8:00 when Miller walked into the bar area and saw Redman's girlfriend serving drinks to George and the Lake County Sheriff, his new best friend. He greeted the two peace officers, hugged Rita for a second or two longer than he should and ordered a bottle of Grain Belt.

"Which part was the most unbelievable?" asked Redman, who had just received a two-minute briefing from MacDonald after spending most of the afternoon with Colianni.

Miller guzzled two-thirds of his beer before beginning, his brown eyes sparkling and as wide as saucers. "OK, so I had just left a Rotary meeting in Maplewood, where I was giving a speech on gang-related crime in the suburbs. The suits loved it, by the way. I'm driving west on Highway 36 when I hear over the police radio there's been some kind of explosion near 96 and Lexington, a few miles from my location. I'm the second responder on the scene and my mind won't accept what my eyes are plainly seeing. Gas main explosions don't happen in the middle of the summer in Minnesota, and besides, a third of the parking lot was missing. It looked like a war scene, a terrorist attack, but why at a law office in Shoreview?

"A massive crater ten to fifteen feet deep had swallowed about a dozen cars, some on fire, parts strewn everywhere. Two-thirds of the structure had been flattened; the top two floors collapsed onto the first like a mini World Trade Center, and the entire mess was engulfed in flames and black smoke.

"About twenty people were huddling on the south lawn, some clearly hurt and lying down; others comforting them. Miraculously, none of them turned out to be critical. A couple of EMTs from the Shoreview FD were already tending to the injured. Then, out of the smoke and rubble in the middle of the burning mess, Joe Terranova appears like fucking Rambo! He's screaming and running with a pronounced limp, his silk suit ripped apart and his hair on fire. He's also bleeding from a stump where his right hand used to be. The man's in shock. That sight, Red, was the most unbelievable of all.

"Turns out, Terranova had been sitting on the can in the third-floor bathroom when the fireworks started. The stall-surround may have actually saved his life. Instead of getting crushed, blown to bits or burned to death, he fell two floors when everything collapsed and lost consciousness. When he came to, he was still on the stinking toilet. That's when an adrenalin rush definitely saved his rich white ass. Instinctively, he ran towards the light and escaped the burning shitpile. Unfortunately, one of the blasts blew his dick and balls clean off along with his right hand. Makes you wonder what he was doing. Anyway, he was conscious and babbling incoherently when the paramedics prepped him for transfer. They took him to Regions trauma center. I'm sure he'll survive, but I'm not so sure that his twenty-something fourth wife will stick around."

"Why not?" Rita couldn't help but eavesdrop, especially since Miller's voice got louder and his gestures more animated by the minute. "A woman will stick with an older man with money, so long as he treats her well, right Red?"

"Who's an older man?" deadpanned Redman. "And what kind of service is this, sweetheart? Could you bring some menus for three hungry men?"

MacDonald was drawn to both of these smart, dedicated fellows, even though they both could be a little rough around the edges. He had just met Terranova, and though he was a flamboyant poser who flaunted the trappings of his financial success, he certainly acted as if he cared about Lauren Fallon. "You don't seem too heartbroken about Terranova, sheriff. Not a big fan of the counselor?"

Miller shook his head slowly. "I wouldn't wish what happened to him on anyone, fellas, but, in my opinion he's a sanctimonious prick."

"I don't know him well," said Redman. "Thankfully, I haven't had much to do with clergy abuse or other pedophile cases over the years, and that's been his specialty for as long as I can remember."

Miller stood up to stretch his sore knees and back and to give himself more room to pontificate. "When I started out as a neighborhood cop in St. Paul, Terranova was a part-time public defender, always hanging around the court-house trying to pick up a big-time felony case with a paying client. He treated his indigent clients like shit. I know because I arrested plenty of them and knew some of their parents. What a lot of these young idiots needed was a lawyer who cared about them, who would listen to their stories and use the justice system to get them on the right track. Terranova had a reputation for pleading them faster than a goose shits his dinner. He never tried one of those cases—just not enough money in it. You mean to tell me that not one of those kids was innocent, not one deserved a jury trial? Now he portrays himself as a champion of the abused, and that's all well and good, but it's a lot easier to do that when you're making millions off others' misfortunes."

Rita brought a second round of drinks and baskets of shrimp cocktail and onion rings. Redman and Miller ordered steaks with baked potatoes and Caesar salads; MacDonald ordered blackened walleye with wild rice and asparagus. The welcomed interruption also gave Miller a chance to take a breath.

"So, Mac shows up and tells us that the likely bomber is Billy Hutchinson, probably the most tragic sexual abuse victim in history, and I'm thinking, irony of ironies. This guy maims the king of the priest abuse cases and blows up his castle."

MacDonald kept trying to piece together how the mayhem in Shoreview related to the murders of Lauren Fallon and Peter Jenkins. He knew Miller couldn't resist retelling the gory details of Billy's demise for Redman's benefit, even though it made him sick inside and stirred up painful memories.

"Not five minutes after Mac gives us the lowdown on Hutchinson one of the feds finds a severed head on the hood of a minivan. Within fifteen feet of the bloody head, he finds a partial forearm and right hand that is still gripping a remote-control device. We're 99% sure both belong to Billy. Incredibly, everyone believed to be present at Terranova's office this afternoon has been accounted for, and Billy, God rest his tortured soul, appears to be the only fatality."

"That is fucking amazing," said Redman, "especially that no one but the bomber was killed. Mac mentioned that Billy had a munitions expert in the family who didn't have the guts to show up for the party. Has anyone paid him a visit?'

"That was the last call I got before I turned off my phone so I could eat a meal in peace," said Miller. "A couple of U.S. Marshalls picked up Walter Zeman about an hour ago. He didn't put up a fight but has been stone silent. They said he showed no emotion when they told him what happened to Billy, but got a smirk on his face when they described the explosions."

"So, do you think Billy's connected in any way to the other two murders?" MacDonald asked, wanting someone to confirm why he wasn't.

"We've got three dead people and a maimed lawyer in three separate, very different incidents, yet all of them were involved in some capacity in the clergy abuse cases," reasoned Redman. "I'm not buying a romantic rendezvous starring Lauren Fallon and Billy Hutchinson, but what do I know. By the way, Colianni and I interviewed the other residents of Jenkins' building this afternoon. No real suspects in that lineup: A 28-year-old woman who works as a research scientist for Ecolab and shares her condo with at least four cats; a very talkative 70-year-old widow who teaches English literature at Augsburg College; and a young married couple who were on vacation in the Dells over the weekend and just returned today. They all said Jenkins was a pleasant, quiet fellow who kept to himself and had very few visitors."

"Of the four, the professor knew him best and actually provided some useful observations. She had lunch or dinner with him a few times a month. She claims to be spiritual but not religious, so they didn't talk much about the Church, and he never mentioned the clergy abuse cases. Seems Jenkins was an avid reader, so they talked literature. She said he loved to discuss the influence biblical stories and ancient Greek and Roman classics had on modern writers." Redman paused for a moment, sipped his drink, and continued, "Now for the good stuff."

"Yeah, get to the good stuff," urged Miller, who couldn't take his eyes off the vivacious, eavesdropping bartender with the alluring eyes and knowing smile.

"And how about a name for this professor, Red," needled MacDonald, who had wolfed down most of the appetizers while the other two talked.

"Hey, have a little patience, you assholes. Let me get my notes out.

"Her name is Norine, Norine Odden. A few weeks ago, the last time she talked to Jenkins, he confided in her that he was in love with the most talented and beautiful woman he'd ever met. He actually described her as a goddess, but admitted she was married to someone else, so he worried their relationship wouldn't last. He never divulged her name, but I think we can assume he was referring to Lauren. Anyway, on the night he was killed, Norine heard a thud, 'like a door slamming or a heavy object falling on the floor.' Remember, she's an English professor. She also said she's an insomniac, so it doesn't take much to disturb her, even at one in the morning. She got out of bed and peeked through the blinds covering her living room windows. She saw the back of a tall, broad man wearing a windbreaker. He walked through the front yard and turned east on Summit. She couldn't see his face. She assumed he'd been visiting Peter, but thought it was odd that he didn't have a car. That made her think he might be a priest, since he was at Peter's, or someone else affiliated with the archdiocese who lived in the neighborhood. It made me think it was someone hiding his car to avoid detection, maybe someone who'd planned to kill Jenkins."

"What about Lamkin?" asked MacDonald. "Did he have a role in this?"

"You don't think the archbishop is behind any of this, do you?" asked Miller. "That would be a shocker, boys. He's very popular with rank and file Catholics. They believe he cleaned up the mess left by Archbishop Bradley. This latest lawsuit has been the first chink in his armor in twenty years. Being a Baptist, I don't know much about him, though he reminds me more of an accountant than a priest."

"How was your meeting with him, Red?" MacDonald resisted the urge to reveal the hearsay account of Lamkin's extracurricular activity.

"I spent about a half hour with the archbishop this afternoon. First of all, he's even smaller than I am; I'm guessing 5' 7" and no more than 150 pounds. He readily admitted that the murder weapon was his umbrella, but, in my opinion, he's simply not tall enough or physically strong enough to have killed Jenkins with it. Plus, he was genuinely shaken and horrified to hear the details of Jenkins' murder. I can't say that I liked him much; he's haughty and officious, actually kind of a cold fish to be the leader of a huge flock of Catholics.

"After I threatened him with a subpoena, he promised to produce a list with the names and contact information of the abuse victims and, maybe more important, of any priests that Peter had a hand in firing. Though once he talks to his lawyers that may change. Interesting that he couldn't come up with the name of one person who was openly hostile towards Peter or had a grudge against him."

"Billy may be a suspect in the Jenkins murder at this point," MacDonald chimed in. "It's possible that he slipped out of the clergy house after midnight, took the old F-150 and drove over to Ramsey Hill. Peter would have let him in, only to be confronted and startled before he could react. Billy was certainly big and strong enough to do the deed. He could have been back in bed by 2:00 or 3:00 a.m., and those two old priests would never have been the wiser."

"According to Lamkin, Billy was definitely capable of murdering Peter," said Redman, "though he thought it highly unlikely, unless he knew about Peter's relationship with Lauren or felt he'd compromised the Church's position. Lamkin didn't think Billy would turn on someone who had helped him as much as Peter. Lamkin did say Billy had a visceral hatred of Joe Terranova, and we know he was right about that."

"Professor Odden mentioned that the man leaving the scene was wearing a windbreaker, did I get that right?" asked MacDonald.

"That was really the only detail she gave me," Redman replied. "Other than, in her words, 'he was a frightfully large creature,'" which Redman delivered in his highest falsetto to the delight of his companions.

"Billy was a large, imposing man, but also an eccentric one," said MacDonald. "He wore almost exclusively black cotton T-shirts and tunics, both short and long-sleeved. Even though the temperature had cooled into the 60s after the rain, I'd be surprised if he even owned a windbreaker much less wore one on a warm summer night."

"I'm impressed, Columbo," said Miller. "Hopefully, there'll be some decent prints on that umbrella other than Lamkin's." "Sorry to interrupt, gentlemen, but you don't want this good food to get cold," said Rita, as she deftly set three plates in the right order on top of the bar. She'd become too busy with thirsty customers to pay attention to their conversation. Monday night was jazz night at Murphy's, and the bar was filling up in anticipation of the riffs and improvisations of the Connie James Quartet and their sultry female vocalist.

The three men ate in relative silence, engrossed in the simple act of enjoying a tasteful meal, the first one since breakfast for each of them. They were also pleasantly distracted by some familiar jazz and blues standards like "Fever," "Summertime," and "Cry Me a River," seductively styled by a pretty, thirty-something platinum blonde in a body-sculpting black sequined dress, who looked and sang like the reincarnation of Peggy Lee. Miller couldn't take his eyes off her, which made Redman feel better, since it meant he wasn't ogling Rita.

Leaving their server a generous tip, the three mildly inebriated cops left Murphy's a few minutes after 11:00, but not before Miller dropped his business card clipped to a couple of Benjamins in Connie's tip jar. Exhausted but otherwise feeling no pain, they continued a conversation about their intertwined cases while walking to their cars.

"I'm meeting with some of my guys, Homeland Security and a couple special agents at the FBI field office in Minneapolis first thing in the morning," said Miller. "We'll review all of the evidence on the Terranova office bombing and research potential accomplices besides Uncle Walter. Red, I'll bet you fifty bucks that Lamkin doesn't produce a paper clip tomorrow."

"If he doesn't cooperate, he'll worship the fucking devil by the time I'm done with him. He's definitely not used to having a peon like me challenge his authority. We'll see how he responds to a subpoena."

"Let's stay in touch, fellas," MacDonald suggested. "I'll get the Fallon autopsy report tomorrow morning and be in my office by early afternoon.

Red, I assume you'll get an update from Colianni tomorrow, so we can compare notes later in the day."

"Sure," said Redman, as he closed the door of the Jeep, careful not to drop the Styrofoam container of leftover steak he would deliver to Barney.

MacDonald had checked into The St. Paul Hotel a few hours before meeting Redman and Miller for dinner. He'd originally planned to drive home that night but occasionally with age comes wisdom. Finally sliding into bed around midnight, he lamented that his comfortable room overlooking the Mississippi was too nice and too expensive for a five-hour stay. He set his phone alarm for 4:30, texted Leslie good night, and started listening to a voice-mail message from the Mayor of Beaver Bay, Dale Koivisto. Fortunately, he fell into a deep sleep right after the words, "You've got to do something about that crazy old fucker, sheriff. . . ."

42

"I 'VE CALLED HIM at least twenty times. He hasn't responded to voicemails or texts. He's not at his condo or office—I stopped at both places after my speech at the Convention Center yesterday. His secretary claims he won't be back until next Monday, and of course she has no idea where he is. What a lying, worthless sack of shit he is!"

Governor Bixby wasn't happy. He was broke, at least by his standards. His $150k gubernatorial salary barely covered the debt service on his campaign loans. His luxury condo and 401k were mortgaged to the max. He was surviving on his federal pension, but not living nearly well enough. And, his most pressing concern, his broker had given him until Friday to meet a $70k margin call. He desperately needed a lifeline from McBride's Swiss account.

"Just tell me how I can help, Governor," offered Eric Freeman. For the past eight years, Freeman, a lieutenant with the Minnesota state patrol, had been Bixby's driver, personal bodyguard and, in more recent years, confidante. Freeman understood that the Governor wasn't perfect, but the muscular, 6'2" former Marine was mission driven, and his current mission was to serve Winton Bixby. Freeman had been scanning the news wires on his laptop and enjoying a spinach, kale and pomegranate smoothie in his makeshift office, the carriage house adjacent to the Governor's mansion, when Bixby called to invite him into the dining room for breakfast and a new assignment.

"I'd like you to pay a visit to our two-faced, elusive friend up at his cabin on steroids in Tofte," said Bixby. "I think you drove me up there a few years ago."

"Right," said Freeman. "I know where that is, a few miles from the Cascade Resort on 61."

"That's it. What I need is for you to get the password for our shared account. He'll know what that is. Or, even better, I need him to transfer a few million from that account to my brokerage account while you're hovering over him."

"In other words, you want me to intimidate him, and if that doesn't work to coerce him," said Freeman, matter-of-factly.

"He's holding my money hostage, Eric. I just want what's mine."

"Yes, sir. Just give me some details about the account. I'll take care of it. I assume I should handle this at night, so as not to attract attention."

"Perfect."

43

Tuesday, July 28ᵗʰ

REDMAN WAS AWAKENED by a tongue that wasn't Rita's. Unfortunately, it belonged to Barney, who wasn't used to waiting until 8:30 for his morning walk. A combination of a minor alcohol buzz and old-fashioned jealousy had motivated Redman to wait up for Rita as Monday turned into Tuesday. She'd been surprised but not disappointed when old Red started pouring the coals to her at two in the morning.

After their lovemaking, Rita, lying on her back, eyes wide open, had a look of consternation on her broad, beautiful face.

"What's the matter, babe?" asked Redman.

"What's the world coming to, Red?" she asked, turning to face him. "Twenty or thirty innocent people could have been killed in that explosion today."

"But they weren't, and that's pure, dumb luck if you ask me. Lust is the culprit, Rita. Lust for power, lust for wealth, lust for status and lust for revenge. Yet, I still believe there are more decent, well-intentioned shitheads out there than evil ones. That's why I'm still doing what I do."

"I wouldn't mind a little more old-fashioned lust out of you, Mr. Redman," Rita joked while stroking his chin. As usual, though, she couldn't resist sticking him with the verbal needle. "By the way, that Sheriff Miller is sure a big, sexy man. But he's no George Redman."

Rita didn't move a muscle when Redman got up to make coffee and tend to Barney's needs. He clicked on the small TV in the kitchen while Barney attacked his breakfast and slurped up a bowl full of water. All the morning news programs were leading with "an act of domestic terrorism in Minnesota." Both CNN and the local CBS affiliate were speculating that Billy Hutchinson, an unstable 48-year-old abuse victim with a violent past, had gone on a killing spree, murdering Lauren Fallon and Peter Jenkins in bizarre fashion and then conspiring with his uncle to blow up Joe Terranova's suburban office building.

"That's not even half right," Redman said to Barney, who was eying the cinnamon crunch scone on his master's saucer. The only good that could come from such bullshit reporting, thought Redman, is it might make the real killer drop his guard and make a mistake.

Redman shaved, showered and dressed in his best golf shirt and khakis for his visit to the chancery to pick up the promised lists. Anticipating disappointment, he called the number for the archbishop's executive secretary, Rosa Guzman.

"Archbishop Lamkin's office, how may I help you, sir?" she asked politely, recognizing Redman's name from the day before.

"Ms. Guzman, this is Agent George Redman with the Bureau of Criminal Affairs. We met yesterday. It's very important that I talk to the archbishop this morning." Redman sensed rejection in her hesitant response.

"I'm so sorry Agent Redman," said Rosa, with just a hint of a Spanish accent. "The archbishop is not here and will not return to the chancery until Thursday evening. May I take a message, or would you like his voice mailbox?"

"The archbishop was supposed to have a report ready for me this morning. Did he mention anything about that to you, Ms. Guzman? Perhaps he gave you an envelope or package with my name on it."

"There is no envelope or package, but I do see a handwritten note that I think might be a message for you, Agent Redman. It is sometimes difficult to read the archbishop's handwriting, but I think it says: 'For Mr. Redman of the BCA. In light of recent events involving Billy Hutchinson, I assume you no longer need the information. If that's not the case, you can let me know when I return on Friday.'"

"Son of a bitch!" Redman blurted out but not directly into the phone. "Ms. Guzman, I apologize for that, but this is not okay. I need to talk to Lamkin this morning. Where is he?"

"Again, I'm sorry, sir, but I really don't know where he is. I know he's on a brief fishing trip with other members of the clergy. I believe it's up north somewhere, perhaps in Canada, but I'm not certain about that."

"Then at least give me his personal cell number, so I can try to reach him today."

"I'm not allowed to give that to anyone, Agent Redman."

Redman was super pissed, but not at the woman who was doing her best to give him the bad news. "All right, Ms. Guzman, then please would you get a message to the archbishop that I need the information he committed to get me, now more than ever, and I need it today. Tell him to call me on my cell phone as soon as he can. The number is 651-991-2227. Tell him I'm going to obtain a subpoena this morning; that's how important this is. Could you do that for me?"

"Yes, sir," said Rosa, "I will try to reach him this morning and deliver your message. Again, I apologize for your inconvenience."

"Thank you, Ms. Guzman. Thank you very much."

44

MACDONALD SAT IN one of only two booths at the Lakeside Coffee Cafe, sipping a steaming cup of Italian roast. A newly married couple in their twenties snuggled on the same side of the other booth while holding hands and sharing a foamy Frappuccino and a white chocolate croissant.

It was 9:15. Dr. Higgins was late. MacDonald had been awake since 4:30, but the drive up I-35 had been easy and productive. Light traffic and good weather gave the sheriff an opportunity to gather his thoughts and to catch up on some Lake County business.

Among the voicemails and texts from Monday was a message from Joyce Christensen, his executive assistant and the person most responsible for keeping the office running smoothly, informing him that Stockman had been released from the hospital. Apparently, his doctors had disabled him from police work for a minimum of thirty days. If MacDonald had his way, Stockman would be finished as a Lake County detective and Klewacki would fill the vacancy. He knew he could make that happen but wasn't sure whether Stockman would fight it.

A more worrisome message was from Gary Koivisto, the owner of Koivisto Pharmacy and Gifts and the Mayor of Beaver Bay. Koivisto wasn't a bad guy, but he'd become a pain in MacDonald's backside. He kept pushing the sheriff to do something about Theodore Barrett, M.D., the man he claimed was ruining his business.

Dr. Barrett had been a beloved pediatrician in Duluth for some forty years. In 2008, his grandson, Tyler, a 15-year-old sophomore at a private school in the Twin Cities, stole ten Vicodin pills from his parents' medicine cabinet. His father's primary care physician had prescribed the narcotic medicine to help him cope with severe pain after a skiing accident. Of the thirty pills dispensed, Tyler's dad had taken three. The remaining pills sat untouched and available in an unlocked cabinet for over a year. Until that fateful Saturday night.

Tyler and three buddies from the lacrosse team each had an assignment: Find a stash of prescription pain or sleeping pills and bring them to Tyler's house, since his parents would be at a charity fundraiser until after midnight. Tyler contributed the Vicodin, another boy threw in five Percocet, and a third added two OxyContin and five Xanax. The fourth member of the group didn't show up. The three boys tossed fifteen pills into a ceramic bowl and crushed them with a serving spoon, making a crude narcotic salad. Then each boy swallowed a spoonful of the mixture with the help of a few swigs of Budweiser. Tyler's dad would never miss a few bottles of beer.

When his parents returned from the charity gala at 1:00 the next morning, the house was quiet. His mom checked Tyler's room to make sure he was in bed; he wasn't. She figured he was sleeping in the rec room in the lower level with a few of his friends; that was a regular occurrence at their house. Even so, she asked Tyler's dad to check.

Paramedics were able to save two of the boys but not Tyler. His heart had stopped about an hour before his parents got home, and it never beat again.

Even before Tyler's death, Barrett had been an early crusader against the use of opioid drugs for anything except breakthrough pain experienced by terminal cancer patients and acute pain, for up to three months, related to fractures, severe injuries and surgical procedures. He also believed that narcotic scripts should be limited to ten pills and often no more than three to five. In his view, too many people had unused opiates in their homes, and too many physicians were prescribing these drugs to patients who displayed warning signs of addiction.

After Tyler's death, he organized and funded a nonprofit association, Physicians Opposed to Opioid Prescriptions, unwittingly creating the acronym POOP. A typical overzealous advocate for a good cause, Barrett wouldn't tolerate exceptions to a complete ban on opioid prescriptions, believing that ridding the world of these drugs was preferable to permitting limited usage. Few medical professionals agreed with this extreme position, so POOP never generated much interest or funding outside of Barrett and a handful of like-minded doctors and relatives of overdose victims.

After his wife died unexpectedly a few years later, Barrett sold his medical practice and comfortable house in Duluth and bought a refurbished one-bedroom cabin forty miles up the North Shore. With a metal roof, cement siding and wood-burning fireplace, the 800 square foot structure was one of ten virtually identical cabins formerly known as the Castle Danger Motel and dating back to the 1920s. The rustic cabins were scattered in a wooded, three-acre peninsula that jutted out into Lake Superior like a crooked finger about halfway between Two Harbors and Beaver Bay.

Some former colleagues and friends believed the deaths of Barrett's grandson and spouse pushed the 75-year old over the edge of sanity. Others believed he was perfectly sane, but crazy over a worthy cause. Either way, he dedicated his life to ending the *legal* distribution of narcotic drugs. His methods were unconventional and mostly ineffective, though they certainly drew attention to the issue at the local level. He compiled a list of every practicing physician in Minnesota, and one day each week, usually Saturday, he'd write letters, not emails but old-fashioned letters, to ten doctors on the list, outlining the dangers associated with opiates and arguing persuasively that the adverse impacts far outweigh any short-term benefit. A few docs responded to his letter, usually politely.

Barrett was a shade under six feet with a slight build, a long, messy grey beard, and a few scattered white hairs atop a balding head. His silver wire-framed glasses always looked too heavy for his stubby, turned-up nose. Monday through Friday, regardless of the weather, he would ride his three-speed Schwinn to one of the four pharmacies in Lake County to protest against supplying, selling, buying and ingesting opioid drugs.

He would march back and forth in front of the pharmacies holding homemade signs that were half as tall and three times as wide as he. Barrett constructed the signs by gluing or stapling two half-inch sheets of 36 x 48 inch foam core and shoving a sawed-off broom handle up the middle. He used black or blue indelible markers to write the messages:

**OXY, VICODEN AND PERCOCET ARE THE SAME AS HEROIN
DEPENDENCE, ADDICTION, DEATH
OPIOIDS ARE NOT A CURE; THEY'RE A DEATH SENTENCE**

Joey Verchota owned the pharmacies in Two Harbors and Silver Bay. He tolerated and even respected the wizened old doctor and sometimes brought him coffee, hot chocolate and sandwiches. Joe commiserated with the old man's position on narcotics but tried to persuade him that pharmacists couldn't survive if they boycotted drugs that were approved by the FDA and prescribed by licensed physicians. Barrett was undeterred.

Koivisto, on the other hand, was convinced that Barrett was driving away many of his elderly, and most loyal, customers. He'd owned the small gift shop and pharmacy for twenty-five years. The business had been marginally profitable for most of those years but had lost money in three of the last four, mostly because many of his older customers were filling prescriptions via mail order, some from Canada and some through major drug outlets like Walgreen's and CVS. His refusal to do business with national pharmacy benefit management firms like Express Scripts and Optum also had a negative impact on his bottom line. He didn't appreciate their low reimbursement rates, but his formerly loyal customers were willing to drive a few extra miles to Silver Bay to pay twenty percent less for their prescriptions. Besides, it was easier to blame Dr. Barrett's histrionics for his failing business than to accept reality.

MacDonald had a soft spot for Barrett; he admired the feisty old man, kind of agreed with his stance on pain pills, and, most important, didn't think that exercising his First Amendment rights was violating any laws in Lake County. Fortunately, the mayor of Beaver Bay only had so much power and influence.

"Sorry for being late, Mac," said Ed Higgins, as he tossed a leather portfolio on the table, grabbed MacDonald's right shoulder with his left hand, and offered his usual athletic handshake with his right. "I had a breakfast meeting with a couple of county commissioners. They didn't like my proposed budget for next year."

"No problem," said MacDonald. "I needed to catch up on a few things, and the coffee is always good here. Can I get you a cup?"

"No thanks. I've had enough for one morning. By the way, I'll be releasing Lauren Fallon's body to her family tomorrow. I've completed my analysis. The toxicology report will take another week or so, but I doubt it will show anything significant. Mac, I'm going to give you some information that will not make it into the official report from my office."

"I appreciate that," said MacDonald. "Any surprises, official or unofficial?"

"It's clear that the fall killed her; that she was alive and without serious injury before she smashed into the rocky gorge at Gooseberry. No gunshot or stab wounds, no strangulation, and preliminarily, no poison. She probably drank a couple glasses of wine three to five hours before she died but that's it. The principal cause of her death was blunt force trauma to the head, which caused a massive cerebral hemorrhage. She also had multiple skull fractures and a severed vertebra at C-3. As I indicated on Saturday, what is surprising is the severity of her head and neck injuries compared to the damage to her upper extremities—hands, wrists and arms. We know she descended head first. If you're aware that you're falling in that position, the natural response is to extend your arms in front of you to cushion the impact and protect your head. I believe Lauren's head hit the rocks first. From the condition of her upper extremities and the scrapes and contusions on the rest of her body, I'm guessing that most of her other injuries occurred after the initial impact. In other words, she hit the rocks with her head and then flopped down onto the rocks with the rest of her body."

"Wouldn't that indicate she was unconscious and incapable of protecting herself?" asked MacDonald.

"It might, but there are no other signs of prior injury, inebriation or loss of consciousness. I'll give you my theory. You're familiar with airplane pilots who become disoriented in poor visibility and get caught in a death spiral?"

"I think so. Like JFK, Jr. out on Martha's Vineyard several years ago."

"Precisely. The bridge over the river is well lit, but the area below the bridge is not. If Lauren were dragged out of a car and tossed over the bridge, she would have had time to prepare her brain and body for the fall. However, if being thrown over that bridge came as a complete surprise; if she went from feeling safe and secure on a lighted bridge to free-falling in a dark space without any warning, she may have experienced night spatial disorientation, sometimes called somatogravic illusion. For a few moments she lost her sense of gravity, not knowing which direction was up or down. A few seconds is all it takes to fall fifty or sixty feet."

"So, it may be that she was walking with someone she felt comfortable with who flipped her over the bridge suddenly and unexpectedly, at least from her perspective." MacDonald made the statement at the same time he was trying to imagine who that might have been.

"I think that's a likely scenario," Higgins said. "My report will indicate that Lauren had vaginal intercourse within several hours of her death. You probably don't know this yet, but the BCA lab has concluded that the DNA in the condom found in her room at Scenic Shores is a match with Peter Jenkins' hair sample."

"I have to admit I'm disappointed the two of them were having an intimate relationship, but it fits with what Terranova told me and with the rest of the evidence."

"Yes, I guess it does," replied Higgins. "But what doesn't fit and what won't be in my initial public report, but will be in a separate confidential section, is that my examination of Ms. Fallon also revealed some stretching and light bruising of her anal cavity indicative of recent anal intercourse. I examined the area more closely and discovered trace amounts of semen. There was probably no ejaculation, but someone had been inside her without a prophylactic. I sent what I had to the BCA for analysis. We'll see if they can match it with anyone in their database. Do you think that misguided nut-job who blew up the office building could be responsible for this kind of depravity as well?"

"Redman is doing some more digging into that possibility today, but I didn't think he was involved in Lauren's death. If I'm wrong about that, Billy Hutchinson was much more cunning than anyone thought."

45

U NABLE TO SLEEP, McBride was up before sunrise. He fried some jalapeno chicken sausage in a skillet with onions, mushrooms and a couple of fresh eggs, then placed the contents between two pieces of honey wheat toast, the bottom piece smothered in melted Jarlsberg cheese. He sliced a ripe banana and a handful of strawberries on a cutting board and scraped the fruit into a clear glass bowl half-filled with Greek yogurt. A cup of Colombian roast ruined by a few ounces of real cream completed his morning meal.

Arranging his breakfast dishes, laptop and cellphone on a plastic serving tray, McBride navigated his way through the great room to the spacious deck that wrapped around the rear elevation of the manse. Swiping the screened slider open with a bare right foot, he padded onto the deck completely naked, blithely wondering whether the noisy gulls, ravens and robins would notice. Setting the tray on a terra cotta travertine table he'd ordered from an exclusive furniture maker in New Mexico, he was stunned by the cold wind off the lake.

The temperature had dropped forty degrees overnight and was only a few ticks above freezing. "Jesus, fuck," muttered McBride, as he hurried inside to grab sweatpants, a hooded Golden Eagles sweatshirt and a pair of fur-lined slippers.

Returning to the deck, he flipped open his laptop to check the weather forecast for Tofte and Grand Marais. According to weather.com, Tuesday, July 28th, called for mostly cloudy skies and a high of 70 degrees, but cooler near the lake with northeast winds 15 – 20 miles per hour.

McBride was interested in the forecast for later in the day. Lamkin had said he'd arrive by early afternoon, and McBride wanted to make sure his tandem kayak was out of the garage and prepared for a late afternoon or early evening ride. The archbishop wasn't very skilled with a paddle, but he loved gliding on the smooth waters of Superior on a sunny afternoon, especially when McBride was doing all the work. Unfortunately, the forecast also called for cooler temperatures and an 80 percent chance of showers after sundown.

Enjoying the early morning sun, the soothing consistency of the waves lapping against the rocky shore, and his messy egg sandwich, McBride keyed in the password to the Itasca intranet site. Financial markets wouldn't open for a few hours, but he could review the second quarter and year-to-date performance of the firm's managed accounts and mutual funds. He was supremely confident that no one was a better stock picker than he when it came to large and mid-cap value plays in the Midwest. He and the team that managed the state's account had beaten an ambitious benchmark in each of the last five years. Moving the accounts to index funds would be stupid, but Bixby could be a vindictive asshole. McBride hadn't answered any of the Governor's calls or responded to his texts and voicemails. He knew he'd have to throw the desperate fucker a bone, maybe half a million. But he also understood that if Bixby blew the whistle on him, he'd be implicating himself as well. How ironic, he thought, that Bixby was the one who'd urged him to accept Charlie and Lauren Fallon as clients, even though they couldn't meet Itasca's $2 million minimum for an individually-managed account. How ironic indeed.

McBride did some of his best strategizing in the solitude of his North Shore retreat. He'd been working on a plan to retain the state's account, get Bixby off his back and deal with Lamkin and the vanishing archdiocese fund. He worried that he'd have to sell the Italian villa. He'd paid nearly 10 million Euros for the place and dropped another million for landscaping and furnishings, not to mention that it was an incomparable venue for all forms of entertaining. He'd only sell it as a last resort.

According to a poll just released by Minnesota Public Radio, Amy Ryerson, Bixby's lieutenant governor and the DFL's candidate to replace him, had pulled even with State Senator Lee Arrington, the born-again, tax-cutting, pro-life, Mankato insurance agent endorsed by the Republicans. Apparently, she got a major bump based on her landslide victory and dynamic acceptance speech at the party's state convention.

Amy had been a middle school social studies teacher who got involved in the teachers' union and then in Democrat politics. She'd been a three-term state representative from St. Anthony before agreeing to be Bixby's running mate eight years earlier. She was bright, articulate, often even witty, and more pragmatic than Bixby. Her most glaring weakness as a candidate was her husband, Mickey. He was a total jock and a dipshit in most respects, at least according to McBride. Mickey was the head basketball coach at St. Cloud State University, a Division II program that usually finished in the middle of its Midwestern conference. He didn't like politics and was disappointed that Amy did. He participated in her campaigns only when she demanded it, which wasn't often. Their only child was a junior at Arizona State University, so from McBride's perspective Amy was essentially alone and probably in need of the counsel and companionship of an intelligent, politically astute, and fiendishly handsome man.

Amy was in her late forties. She stood a few inches over five feet, with a round, cherubic face, pretty smile and Dorothy Hamill hairdo. In fact, she reminded McBride of the former Olympic skater. She was cute but definitely a few pounds overweight from too much fast food, too many long days and not enough exercise. In McBride's view, that, together with her shaky marriage, meant her self-confidence as a woman might be lacking, which also meant that his brand of unctuous, solicitous charm might succeed. He could be her big brother with benefits. He preferred to seduce men, but he was like a switch-hitting utility infielder, playing whatever position the team needed. Another big campaign check to prime the pump, so to speak, wouldn't hurt either.

McBride checked the bond, stock and currency markets and read the *Wall Street Journal* and *Star Tribune* online editions. There were several stories in the *Tribune* about Billy Hutchinson, a man who unknowingly may have aided McBride's plan by diverting the attention of law enforcement and the media.

McBride wasn't the least bit sympathetic when he read Terranova could be hospitalized for weeks. Gloating would be a better word to describe his reaction, and he wasn't even aware that the lawyer had lost much more than the limb mentioned in the newspaper.

Stiffening up in the cold air, McBride stood up and stretched his limbs. He spied a square-hulled, brown ship in the distance, steaming towards the Duluth harbor from the east. He figured it was an ore boat, moving swiftly through the water because its cargo hold was empty. "Fuck you!" he yelled as loudly as he could but to no one in particular. That made him feel better. He had a plan. Time to get the kayak ready.

46

MACDONALD ARRIVED AT the Lake County courthouse a few minutes before noon. After his meeting with Higgins, he'd stopped in the East Hillside area to visit his mother. Pressed for time, he had picked up a bag of fresh bagels and a cup of her favorite chai tea at a local bakery and promised to take her to brunch at the Pickwick, her favorite restaurant, on the weekend.

He stuck his head into Bell's office to let her know he was back from the Cities and to invite her over to his place for a late dinner, but she wasn't there. Klewacki and Chad Holborn, the County's system administrator and chief information officer, were waiting for him in the large conference room. They'd just spent a couple of hours with Max Schafer, Terranova's technology guru, who'd made the trip to Duluth despite the complete calamity in his employer's world. Max worked out of his apartment on Mondays and Wednesdays, so he wasn't in the Shoreview office when homemade explosives tore the building apart.

In disaster recovery mode, Terranova's staff had rented several rooms at a Roseville motel. Max spent most of the night working to ensure they could get access to the firm's backed-up files in the cloud and had a decent wi-fi connection. He also engineered the purchase and configuration of laptops, portable printers, fax machines and miscellaneous equipment sufficient to meet near-term client needs and court deadlines, though he assumed, given the circumstances, that some parties might cut them some slack, even though they were lawyers.

Max had left Roseville at 5:00 a.m. in his sleek, midnight blue Cadillac crossover. Despite downing a couple of Red Bulls and some rancid coffee, he had to stop at a rest area near Pine City for an e-cigarette and a short nap.

Driving the last eighty miles in under an hour, he arrived in Two Harbors in time to grab a breakfast burrito at McDonald's and stumble into the Sheriff's office half asleep with a few minutes to spare before the nine o'clock meeting.

Only twenty-four years old, Max had long, stringy brown hair and was morbidly obese but carried the extra weight well, or hid it well under bulky sweatshirts and baggy chinos. He looked slow but was fast-talking and brilliant. Within a matter of seconds, he was into the hard drive on Lauren's laptop, impressing Klewacki and even Holborn. The three of them reviewed Lauren's Outlook calendar and email history. They took pictures or printed copies of hundreds of calendar entries and of every email she'd sent or received during the months of June and July. Max had to be back in the Cities by two, so he left at 11:30 but promised to be available by phone or skype and to return if they needed him.

"Find anything interesting?" asked MacDonald, grabbing a bottle of water and a glazed doughnut from a box in the middle of the conference table and easing his weary carcass into the worn, padded chair big Max had warmed up for him.

"Lauren was the consummate professional with her firm laptop," said Klewacki, shuffling through some of the papers on the table and picking out a couple to show MacDonald. "There are very few personal emails and nothing of a personal nature on her Outlook calendar, except for a few lunches and dinners with the judge. There are two emails from a J-Man@gmail.com that might be from the perp. Look at this one first. It was sent on June 8, the day after Judge Kennedy denied the Archdiocese's motion for dismissal in Lauren's case.

To: lauren.fallon@terranovalaw.com
From: J-Man@gmail.com
Date: June 8, 2017
Subj: *Attraction*
Hi. Are you avoiding me? I know you're basking in the glow of a major victory and you've earned that, but I thought we had something special that I hoped would continue beyond a few nights. You are wonderful in ways I can't even describe, and I know I don't deserve you, but I would do anything, **ANYTHING** to keep what we have alive.

J-Man

"Wow," said MacDonald. "This woman was quite the seductress. Did she respond to J-Man?"

"Not via email," said Klewacki. There aren't any emails from or referring to this J-Man until the Friday morning before her death. Read this one.

To: lauren.fallon@terranovalaw.com
From: J-Man@gmail.com
Date: July 24, 2017
Subj: Rendezvous
Looking forward to our midnight date on the North Shore. Call me.
Love you,
J-Man

MacDonald tried to come up with possibilities for yet another man who was infatuated with Lauren and even used the "L" word, but potentially was also her killer. "So, do we have a way to identify this J-Man?"

"Jenkins begins with J," Holborn offered, "but there are several emails from Peter Jenkins regarding the lawsuit that were sent from jenkinspr@archspm. org. Gail doesn't think Jenkins would set up a separate gmail account for personal emails."

"Nor do I think he would ever call himself the J-Man," Klewacki added. "Jenkins is a rule follower. According to Max, whoever set up this gmail account was trying to conceal his identity. He used the name Jasper Frankfurter. There's no one by that name in any directory, census or tax roll in the state of Minnesota. No residential address. Not even a Facebook page. It's a fake name. We sent all of the information Max collected from Google to the BCA to see whether they could begin to construct an identity with it."

"So where do we go from here?" MacDonald asked. "Redman is circling back with the two priests who shared a house with Billy Hutchinson. He's also meeting with Colianni to get a status report on the Jenkins' murder. It sure seems like the three incidents are connected but it's possible they're not."

"It's possible that Lauren hooked up with a boyfriend who's a psychopath," said Klewacki. "I'm guessing Billy had enough rage to kill all three but would never have sent those fawning emails using the name J-Man. He probably never sent an email or text in his life."

"Apparently, Judge Fallon is planning to have a memorial service for Lauren on Friday or Saturday. Maybe I'll pay my respects and see whether anyone who might fit the profile of our Jaspar Frankfurter shows up."

47

LAMKIN DROVE NORTH on I-35 with his cellphone turned off. He knew Redman would be upset and trying to track him down. Not having eaten breakfast, he was famished and felt the emergence of a migraine headache by the time he reached Duluth. Afraid of drawing attention to himself, he slithered through the Wendy's drive-thru on London Road and ordered a cheeseburger, fries and diet coke, not making eye contact with the teenage server and driving off without taking the change from his twenty. When he finally turned his cell back on, he saw that Rosa had called him four times and left two messages. They had to be about Redman.

Dr. Barrett was also getting hungry. He'd spent the morning pacing, protesting and lecturing in front of Koivisto's Pharmacy. At noon, he lugged his sign *du jour* across Highway 61 to the Tettegouche Café, where Maggie Burg made the best grilled cheese, tomato and bacon sandwiches and blueberry crumble pies in North America. Maggie's husband, Wild Bill, had operated the business as the Tettegouche Outpost Bar for forty-five years until he died of hypothermia after falling out of his fishing boat on Lax Lake. He'd been trying to catch the Big One for years. But angling for muskies alone with a bottle of Wild Turkey and no life jacket turned out to be fatal for old Bill.

Maggie stopped selling liquor in his honor and changed the name for obvious reasons. She and the good doctor were about the same age and often dined together to discuss family matters and to commiserate over the pathetic state of the world. There may have been more to their relationship, but no one really cares about the sex life of a couple of septuagenarians. Maggie even contributed a few dollars to POOP when she could.

After a roast turkey sandwich on focaccia with a side of Maggie's German potato salad, all washed down with raspberry lemonade, it was time for Barrett's afternoon shift.

Lamkin was finishing his last few fries when his phone beeped, signaling an incoming text. The archbishop was an infrequent texter; in fact, only two people ever sent him texts and one of them was now dead. Looking down at the message on his I-Phone while driving 75 miles per hour through tiny Beaver Bay, Lamkin never saw Ted Barrett crossing Highway 61. He was startled by the sound of something colliding with his front bumper and grill. At first, he thought it was a cardboard box, but the magnitude of the "thud" convinced him that the box must have contained something substantial. Maybe cargo that had fallen out of a truck and onto the road.

By the time Lamkin looked up from his phone, Barrett's frail, now lifeless body had landed in a muddy ditch on the west side of the highway after literally flying sixty feet through the air like a human missile. He'd lost his grip on the sign at impact, and the wind blew it to the middle of the road well behind Lamkin's Town Car, where a few minutes later a tour bus obliterated it.

Lamkin didn't see any of this. He just kept driving. Under normal circumstances, he might have stopped to see what he'd hit or to inspect the damage to his car, but not on this day. He didn't need to be recognized in the area by some park ranger, deputy sheriff or erstwhile Catholic.

The text was from McBride. It was short:

"Bloody Marys ready. Kayak later. Get here."

After all these years, Lamkin was still a sucker when it came to McBride. As frazzled and stressed as he was feeling, the text both calmed and excited him.

48

THE STRIP MALL that housed Koivisto's Pharmacy had three other storefront tenants: an antique dealer, a consignment shop, and a bakery. The only eyewitness to the hit-and-run crash was Ethel Lindquist, the owner of Lindquist's Bakery & Confectionary. Ethel was taking a short break from decorating a fancy wedding cake. She'd poured herself a glass of iced tea and was casually looking out her storefront window, when she did a double take. Oh my God, she thought, a huge car just barreled into old Dr. Barrett and threw him into the ditch. Her 19-year-old assistant was already glued to her cell phone, so Ethel shouted at her:

"Cindy, call 911! Someone just got hit by a car on 61. I think it's old Doc Barrett!"

Ethel flung off her white apron, threw open the screen door and ran across the parking lot and down to the muddy swale where Barrett had landed. Not yet forty, she had no formal medical training but was smart and resourceful. She knew rudimentary first aid techniques and was certified to perform CPR. She checked for a pulse, couldn't detect one and noticed that Barrett was bleeding from the back of his head. Kneeling in the mud, she started chest compressions, though she didn't think they'd do much good. Forced to stare at the ashen, still face of the sweet old man she'd gotten to know, she began to cry, still pumping on his chest with the heel of her right hand.

By the time the Gold Cross ambulance arrived, a small crowd had gathered around Barrett, including an hysterical Maggie Burg and a somber, somewhat shamefaced Gary Koivisto. Two emergency med techs took over for Ethel, one of them thanking her with a brief hug before beginning his work on the old man.

A Lake County Sheriff's squad arrived on the scene a few minutes later. Hakonen was working the noon to 8:00 p.m. shift along with Mary Pierce, the only Native American deputy on the force as well as the only Ph.D psychologist. Pierce tried to comfort Maggie and a couple of distraught onlookers while Hakonen interviewed witnesses and attempted to recreate the accident scene for his report.

"Did any of you actually see what happened here?" he asked a few minutes after the ambulance had taken Barrett to Lake County Community Hospital, where the coroner would pronounce him dead an hour later.

Ethel tried to compose herself. Her jeans were muddy and soaked at the knees, and sweat from her work on Barrett had bled through her powder blue blouse. She gathered strands of unruly blonde hair with one hand and repositioned the band that secured her ponytail with the other. She gave up trying to tuck her unruly blouse back into her too-tight jeans as soon as Hakonen started asking questions.

"I saw what happened, Ryan," she said hesitantly, hoping someone had a better view of the accident, "but I was looking out the window from the bakery, so I wasn't very close."

"That's OK," Hakonen assured her. "Just tell me what you saw, and I'll take it from there."

"Doc Barrett was crossing 61, I assume after having lunch at Maggie's. He was carrying one of his big signs, so I don't think he had a clear view of traffic in either direction. Anyway, before he made it halfway across, a long, silver car, maybe a Cadillac, came busting through town at about eighty miles an hour. Way too fast, for sure. The car hit him so hard it made me shudder. He flew across the road, bounced hard on the shoulder and ended up in the ditch. His sign shot ten or fifteen feet in the air before landing in the middle of the road."

"Did you happen to notice the license plate number on this silver car?" asked Hakonen.

"I tried to make it out, but the car was moving so fast and I was too far away. I swear the driver sped up after hitting Doc."

"Did you get a look at the driver?" Hakonen asked.

"No, not at all. I think I was in semi-shock when I saw the sheer force of the impact, and then watching the poor old guy fly through the air. I was more worried about him than anything else."

"Sure. Understandable," Hakonen commiserated. "I'm a little surprised nobody else saw the accident. Maybe someone will come forward later. I'll notify the highway patrol and other law enforcement in the area to look for a large silver or gray sedan. I assume there's at least a sizeable dent in the front of that vehicle."

"Given how hard that big boat smashed into Barrett, I would agree, though Doc was just a string of a man, so I don't know how much damage his body could inflict."

"I've investigated a few of these hit-and-run situations," Hakonen said confidently. "You'd be amazed at how much damage the combination of high speed and a collision—even with a small child—can do." The young deputy reflected for moment on what he'd just said to a mother with young children. "Sorry, that was a stupid thing to say."

"That's okay," said Ethel, touching his forearm with her hand. "I get your point."

49

REDMAN WAS HAVING a horseshit day. First, the archbishop stiffed him and then disappeared. Then the two old priests who'd been babysitting Billy Hutchinson turned out not to be doddering old fools. He'd assumed Billy had routinely pulled the wool over their eyes, and, specifically, that he'd left the house late on Saturday night, "borrowed" the pick-up, bludgeoned Jenkins to death and then returned home, all without arousing the suspicion of his sleeping housemates. Tying Billy to Jenkin's murder could have put a tidy end to one murder investigation and possibly implicated Billy in another. The only problem was he didn't do it.

Fathers Patterson and Dowling had insisted on meeting Redman at his office at BCA headquarters when he'd called to schedule an interview. Father Dowling said they were both distraught over Billy's death and felt "morally responsible" for his actions. Redman found this response curious, as if anyone could be morally responsible for a psychopath.

He met them in the lobby at two, and after brief introductions led them to a small conference room on the main floor, where he offered them coffee, soda and bottled water, which they politely declined.

"Thanks for coming over so soon, fellas," Redman said informally, because he couldn't pretend to be deferential to clergy. "I would have been happy to make the trip to your place, but I appreciate the effort."

"It was the least we could do, Agent Redman," said Father Patterson, a burly man in his fifties with thinning brown hair and a salt and pepper goatee.

"First off, as I see it, the only ones responsible for blowing up that office building and maiming the lawyer are Billy Hutchinson and his uncle. The purpose of this meeting is to determine whether Billy may have committed other crimes.

"We understand that, Agent Redman," said Patterson. "But let me tell you what we know about Billy and then you can ask us anything you want."

"Fair enough," said Redman.

It was clear that Patterson would be the spokesman for the two priests. He was nearly thirty years younger than Father Dowling and had made Billy's reclamation as a person and a Christian his personal and professional mission.

"You know that Billy was horribly damaged by tragic events in his life. I won't rehash them now. Over the course of the last two decades, he made incredible progress just to hold a job, co-exist in a home with two priests, and continue the process of healing emotionally, psychologically and spiritually. In fact, he was doing fine until the young lawyer from Mr. Terranova's office tried to recruit him to be part of the lawsuit against the archdiocese. Billy wasn't interested in money. In fact, he strived to be an ascetic, or at least what he considered to be an ascetic, and he refused to meet with her. Though he strongly believed the Church had a moral obligation to cast out pedophile priests and give aid to victims, he bristled at the idea that lawyers could become millionaires by extorting money from the archdiocese, which he likened to extorting money from God.

"After the lawsuit was in the news, I saw the old rage in Billy return. He talked often about wanting to stop Terranova from destroying his Church. Because of his behavior, Agent Redman, Father Dowling and I kept very close tabs on his activities and whereabouts and discouraged him from acting on his negative impulses. I know that Billy stayed in his room on the night Peter Jenkins was killed; Father Dowling and I checked on him at least every two or three hours the entire weekend. I also kept the only set of keys to the truck in my locked nightstand. My mistake was not doing more to investigate the background of Billy's uncle. Ironically, we were pleased that Billy was reaching out to Uncle Walter. I thought it would be a good distraction and possibly the start of a real family connection, something Billy had been missing since his mom died."

Redman followed up with questions about Billy's habits, interest in women, and history of physical violence, but in the end, he was convinced that the very troubled and now very dead man was not a serious suspect in either murder. He escorted the two priests to the BCA parking lot, reassuring them that, in his opinion as a law enforcement professional and secular humanist, they bore no responsibility, legal or moral, for Billy's actions. They promised to pray for him.

Redman's outlook improved when he returned to his cubicle. He'd left his cell phone on his desk and it was vibrating. Colianni. He touched the screen on the last buzz.

"Redman."

"Red, I think we may have a breakthrough in the Jenkins' murder. One of my guys found a soggy but legible receipt from a Holiday store in a lilac bush in front of Jenkins' condo. It's time stamped 11:45 p.m. on Saturday, July 25th, approximating the time of the murder. We figure it probably fell out of the killer's pocket when he entered or exited Jenkins' place. The service station is just off I-94 near Cedar Avenue in Minneapolis. The amount on the chit is about sixty dollars, so it probably included gas or was just for gas. It looks like a credit card purchase with a MasterCard, so we're following up with the store to get the complete number and ultimately the account holder."

"That's great," said Redman, "especially since none of the other residents had any visitors after about nine o'clock that night. I just finished interviewing the two priests who lived with Billy Hutchinson. You'll get my report, but in a nutshell, I've pretty much eliminated him as a serious suspect. That was one fucked-up fellow. Pathetic more than evil, but I guess that's more the rule than the exception these days."

"You're just getting soft, you little bastard," said Colianni. "Anyway, let's hope we've got a serious suspect, as you put it, on the end of this credit card trail. I'll let you know as soon as we trace the account. I trust you'll follow up with Sheriff MacDonald. I think we all still believe these murders are connected in some way."

"You'd think so," Redman agreed. "I'll check in with Mac before the end of the day. I'm still trying to track down Archbishop Lamkin. He was supposed to get me some critical information this morning but probably changed his mind after talking to his lawyers. His assistant read me a bullshit note saying he assumed that Hutchinson was responsible for everything, so I wouldn't need the stuff. When I asked to talk to him, she said he went fishing with some of his fellow clergy. His right-hand man is bludgeoned to death, so he leaves town for a little R and R? What the fuck?"

"Take it easy, Red. I have to confess that I'm still a card-carrying Catholic. Lamkin's viewed as a progressive by many of the faithful. You can't blame him for wanting to protect the Church's assets from Terranova. He probably needed a break after the last few weeks. Why don't you cut him some slack?"

"Maybe you're right," said Redman, "but I still think he's an arrogant little prick."

"Bye, Red."

50

SUFFERING HEART PALPITATIONS and shaking limbs, Lamkin was unnerved by the collision, whatever it was that he hit. Finally checking his speedometer five miles north of Silver Bay, he was alarmed to see the needle quivering between eighty and eighty-five miles an hour. The speed limit was fifty-five. Abruptly decelerating to fifty, he started rehearsing the conversation he'd have with McBride. Even with Lauren Fallon out of the picture and Terranova slowed by injury, Lamkin knew the lawsuit would proceed, and, if it went to trial, the archdiocese would be the big loser. He intended to end it now, once and for all, before an onslaught of negative publicity reversed everything he'd accomplished.

He'd demand that McBride turn over $50 million by the end of the month and the rest by September. He'd let him retain a million or so as a fee, even though he was well aware that his most intimate friend, a man he had to trust but never fully did, would never have achieved the financial success he enjoyed without the early "seed money" provided by the Lamkin and the Church.

After passing through the villages of Schroeder and Tofte, he looked for mile marker 83, the first marker after Cascade Mountain Lodge. McBride's property would be next. Lamkin maneuvered the Town Car down the winding, tree-lined driveway and parked next to McBride's Mercedes SUV, in between the lodge and the separate four-car garage and workshop.

He didn't notice McBride sitting in a red Adirondack chair on the front porch, sipping a tall Bloody Mary while reading something on his I-Pad.

"What in the Hell did you run into?" McBride could see a large indentation in the lower half of the front grill.

Lamkin walked to the front of the car and bent over to inspect the damage. "Holy shit!" he exclaimed. "I must have hit a box filled with lead weights. I had no idea it would do this. I should call my agent at Maguire."

"That's fine, but not right now. I've prepared a batch of Bloodies and a plate of cheese, bread and fruit. Let's enjoy the day on the back deck before the storms roll in and ruin it."

Though the sun was still peeking through layered clouds, the weather had changed dramatically from the hot, humid conditions of the weekend. The thermometer wouldn't climb above seventy for the next few days with intermittent heavy showers and high winds in the forecast.

After his burger and fries, Lamkin wasn't hungry, but a couple of drinks on the deck would provide the perfect setting to discuss the fund. "Let me take a piss and grab a sweatshirt out of your closet. I'll meet you on the deck."

"Sounds like a plan."

Stopping in the kitchen for provisions, McBride filled a tall plastic tumbler with ice for Lamkin's drink then set it on a large serving tray along with a pitcher of Bloody Marys, a basket of sliced French bread and a platter of cheeses, liver pate and hummus. He had a well-earned reputation for generous pours as a host, and his Bloodies were heavy on the vodka and extra spicy. He carried the tray out to the deck and set it on a glass-top table in between two wicker chaise lounges. First replenishing his own glass, he filled Lamkin's to the rim and then settled into his favorite outdoor recliner.

The lake was unusually quiet for a July afternoon, not even a sailboat in sight, and that suited McBride perfectly. Lamkin opened the screen slider leading to the deck and admired the magnificent view before making his entrance wearing a Minnesota Vikings fleece hoodie that was three or four sizes too big. He spread hummus on a crust of bread and sat down next to the man he slept with but never really knew.

"Wow, how much Tabasco did you put in here?" Lamkin exclaimed rhetorically. "It's still good but hotter than I remember."

"There's no Tabasco," McBride said with his usual haughtiness. "It's a mixture of horseradish, clam juice, habanero and cayenne pepper sauces and tomato juice. How do you like the red pepper hummus?"

"It's delicious," said Lamkin, beginning to relax after a few very tense days.

"You look stressed out, Jim. I know things are rough right now, especially with Peter's horrible murder, but you'll get through this. How are the preparations for his service coming along?"

"Fine," said Lamkin. "I'm not sure I can officiate. In some ways, Peter was like a younger brother to me. He was a good-hearted man who loved the Lord and served Him well. I feel terrible for the way I treated him over that fucking lawsuit and his naive transgressions with the lawyer whore. Now it looks like poor, wretched Billy Hutchinson has exacted a twisted revenge on everyone. I prayed for Billy's soul at morning mass today, Jay. I prayed for his depraved, ravaged soul."

McBride rolled his eyes, set his drink on the table and stood up. A swirling wind from the north was accelerating, and heavy cumulus clouds were moving in to hide the sun. He buttoned up his black, nylon windbreaker as he walked behind Lamkin and began kneading and massaging his upper back and shoulders.

"How does that feel?" he asked.

"It feels good," said Lamkin, thinking this probably wasn't a good time to bring up the fund. He'd do it over dinner.

"By the way, Jim, does anyone know you're up here?"

"Of course not," said Lamkin, offended that McBride would even ask. "I left word that I'd be fishing in Canada with a couple of bishops and a guide."

"That's great," said McBride. He lifted a loaded Glock G19 out of his right jacket pocket and fired two quick rounds into the back of Lamkin's head.

"How do you like that Bloody, your Eminence?"

51

FATHER DALY WAS worried about his friend. He'd left several messages for Fallon without a response, so he resorted to a form of communication he eschewed but would use in desperation. His text was short and to the point:

"How about 5 miler on River @ 6? Meet @ O'Shaughnessy. KD"

Sitting at the clunky oak desk in his chambers on the fourth floor of the federal courthouse in St. Paul, Fallon read Daly's message and smiled for the first time all day. Technically, he'd taken the day off as bereavement leave, but he couldn't sit still at home. Too many things in the house on Montcalm reminded him of Lauren, which made him want to cry, or scream.

He'd driven to the courthouse to finalize the details of a public farewell for the woman he adored, and sometimes craved, in spite of her flaws. He'd made up his mind to have the memorial service on Saturday afternoon at the University Women's Club on Summit Avenue. They'd been married in the Great Room. Her choice, of course. She loved the charming Victorian mansion. It was the perfect venue for a tasteful, secular remembrance, an intimate gathering of family and friends.

On his way downtown, Fallon had stopped at Regions Hospital to check on Joe Terranova. Lauren had been very happy with her law practice, and there was no denying Terranova had given her guidance, resources and opportunity, but truth be told, neither she nor Fallon liked him much. Regardless, Fallon felt compelled to see him, especially since irrepressible Joe and Lauren had something terrible in common. They were both victims of inexplicable, inexcusable human violence.

The lead nurse in Regions' intensive care unit made a special trip to the lobby to give Fallon the news. Terranova had just come out of surgery and couldn't have visitors until Wednesday morning. He was stable but just beginning a very long and difficult road to recovery.

Fallon had been spinning his wheels in chambers for about an hour, ostensibly planning Lauren's service, when he heard his phone make the rare three-tone ring that meant he had a text message. He replied without hesitation:

"See you at 6. CF"

52

Father Daly loved to run. He'd competed on the cross country and track teams in high school and college and started running longer distances in Seminary to keep his sexual appetite in check. He'd run 18 marathons, including New York, Las Vegas and Boston, and once even completed a sub 3-hour marathon at Grandma's in Duluth. He was only 5'8" tall and at 145 pounds, weighed less than he did in college.

Fallon, on the other hand, hated running. He'd been a decent athlete at Cretin High School in St. Paul, playing tight end on the football team and catcher on the baseball team, but at 6'3" and 260 pounds, the only sport he'd played regularly during his first marriage was golf. Daly had badgered him to take up running for years, and he finally succumbed after he started dating Lauren Bergmann. He began lifting weights and attending yoga classes at the same time.

Daly still logged thirty to forty miles a week, whereas Fallon might jog fifteen, including a three-miler to the Highland Grill for pancakes with Lauren on Sunday mornings. Daly would reduce his customary seven-minute mile pace, excellent for a 60-year-old, down to nine to accommodate his lumbering companion. Running was therapeutic for Fallon; it cleared his head and relieved the stress that invariably accumulated in the working life of a federal trial judge. It also kept him from crossing the border into morbid obesity.

Fallon could see Daly stretching in one of the auxiliary gyms when he entered the men's locker room, a duffel bag over his shoulder, at the O'Shaughnessy Athletic Complex on the St. Thomas campus. As an alumnus and occasional benefactor, Fallon had locker room privileges, though it didn't hurt to be best friends with the university president.

Fallon never stretched, either before or after running, so when Daly saw his large, hairy friend emerge from the locker room, he jogged out of the gym and gave the judge an unexpected bear hug.

"How you holding up, Charlie?"

"I'm okay, Kevin, but I'll be better after working up a sweat, so let's go."

"We'll take River Road to the Ford Bridge, then up the west side to the Lake Street Bridge and back here. That's close to six," said Daly. "You up for that?"

"Sure," said Fallon. "It's cooler today, so why not push it a little."

Fallon usually struggled for the first mile of a long run, breathing heavily and working hard to loosen up his stiff knee joints, so Daly did most of the talking. There was a tree-lined, asphalt walking/bike path adjacent to River Road, a path where joggers could take in the beauty of the meandering Mississippi River while getting some exercise.

"I'd like you to say a few words at Lauren's service on Saturday, maybe a brief eulogy, if you wouldn't mind," said Fallon, gasping for air between words. "I wish you could have gotten to know her better."

"I knew her well enough, and very well through you, my friend. I'm happy to do whatever you'd like. You know that. Would a few scripture readings and a prayer be out of line at the service you're planning?"

"There'll be some music and poetry, some things I know she liked, but I thought you'd have to throw in something from the Bible. I'm sure somebody will appreciate that."

"Even though you won't. Charlie, maybe it's time to let God back into your life."

"Not today, Kevin. Not today."

They ran in silence for a couple of miles, mostly uphill. Father Daly knew when to keep his mouth shut around Fallon. He wanted to ask about the investigation but not if the subject would be upsetting.

As they approached the Lake Street Bridge and turned east to cross the river, Fallon was hurting. "I'm going to walk for a bit," he said with a sigh. "You keep running, and I'll see you at the gym."

"I'm good with walking, Charlie. You were really picking up the pace on that last mile."

"You're full of shit, but thanks for trying to make me feel better. My body was made for eating, sleeping and fucking, not running."

"I'll try to erase that image from my mind."

"By the way, what do you know about this Billy Hutchinson, the pathetic psychopath who nearly killed Terranova and blew himself to bits?"

"Like you, I know what's been all over the media today, and I'm generally familiar with his sad history. The two priests he was living with are two of the finest men I know. Do you think Billy was involved in Lauren's death?"

"I'm pretty sure he had nothing to do with it. The only thing I feel for him is pity. I don't understand why he felt so protective of the Catholic Church after the nightmare of abuse he suffered. Lauren didn't either. Your archbishop must have gotten into his head."

"I don't know about that. Lamkin is highly respected in the Catholic hierarchy. He's never had much to do with me or St. Thomas, though Peter Jenkins taught some theology and seminary classes as an adjunct professor. I wouldn't be surprised if Billy had something to do with his murder."

"That could be. Jenkins was an odd fellow. He gave Lauren a shitload of data on bad priests and abuse victims. I don't want to think about what she might have given him in return. I guess I didn't know some things about her as well as I thought. God, I loved her Kevin." Fallon could feel tears mix in with the sweat on his face.

"Listen, Charlie. Why don't you take a few months off? Go out to California and visit Shawn. Is she coming to town for Lauren's service?"

"She arrives on Thursday and will be here through the weekend. The truth is, Kevin, I'm thinking of retiring from the bench. I need to take care of some things in the next few months and then I might call it quits."

"You love your job, and you're a great judge, Charlie. I'd take some time off and think about it before giving up a lifetime appointment. You're still a young man."

"Right. There are just some things I need to do."

"On the other hand, you could become a priest," Daly joked, slapping his friend across his broad right shoulder. "It's not too late to dedicate your life to the Lord."

"I could never take a vow of celibacy. Based on your college days, I don't know how you've done it either."

"It's all the running I do," said Daly. "It saps my sexual energy."

"Whatever you say, Father."

It was half-past seven when the two men walked out to the parking lot next to O'Shaughnessy after a quick shower and change of clothes. Fallon's Buick sedan was in the lot; Father Daly always walked to the campus from his small brick colonial on Riverwood Drive.

"Will you let me buy you dinner at the Club?" asked Fallon, wanting to continue the conversation about Lauren with someone he could trust.

"I'll have to take a rain check, Charlie. I have a faculty meeting in about an hour. How about tomorrow, and I'll take you to dinner at the St. Paul Grille?"

"Sure, Kevin, that might work. I'll call you tomorrow. Have a good night."

"You, too, my friend."

53

Father Daly's faculty meeting was in reality an intimate dinner for two at Emily Van Dyke's small but upscale apartment on Grand Avenue, a few miles east of the St. Thomas campus. A petite, subtly attractive woman with close-cropped red hair and copious freckles, Van Dyke was an Assistant Professor of English literature at Macalester College. Her specialty was Chaucer, but she taught courses on Renaissance and 18th Century European literature as well as a popular class on Criticism in the Age of the Internet. She'd been involved with Daly off and on for ten years, beginning when she was an undergrad at St. Thomas. As a senior English major, she'd audited Daly's survey course on comparative religions. Their mutual attraction was both intellectual and physical. It didn't hurt that Van Dyke was an avid runner or that she wasn't interested in marriage.

The most challenging part of their relationship was keeping it secret, which clearly was more important to the "celibate" priest who was also the president of a Catholic university. It provided an aspect of danger and intrigue, which enhanced their natural attraction and the excitement of their intimacy. The fact that they worked for very different institutions of higher learning, conservative versus ultra-liberal, was also a plus, since internal faculty gossip was rampant at both campuses.

Daly brought Thai takeout from Sawatdee for their dinner. Van Dyke opened a bottle of Rombauer Chardonnay. After a light dessert of berries in frozen yogurt, Daly poured them each a glass of Redbreast 12-Year Irish whiskey to share while pleasuring each other in Van Dyke's four-poster queen bed. Aware of Daly's relationship with Judge Fallon, Van Dyke had asked about him during dinner, but Daly had responded guardedly that his friend was grieving but holding up all right under the circumstances. A rapturous encounter with his younger lover made Father Daly loquacious.

"I think Charlie knows who the killer is, but he's keeping it to himself."

"I thought everyone assumed the guy who blew up the law office was the killer," said Van Dyke. "What makes you think Charlie has a different idea?"

"He told me in so many words that Billy Hutchinson didn't kill Lauren. He also said he's considering retiring from the bench. Other than his two wives and daughter, Charlie loves nothing more than being a judge. He would never give that up unless there's something out there that could destroy him professionally."

"Whoa, Kevin. I think you're reading way too much into this. The guy's beautiful young wife has just been brutally murdered. Of course he's re-evaluating everything in his life. Unless you think *he* could have killed her. You don't think that, do you Kevin?"

"I can't think that."

54

Brian Klewacki's family acquired Cascade Mountain Lodge in 2010. The business was one of the oldest commercial ski hill operations in America, its original lodge in the Township of Lutsen dating back to the late 1800s.

Brian's Polish immigrant grandparents purchased a small hotel in Rockford, Illinois in the 1950s. Its success led to the acquisition of several more hotels in mid-sized towns throughout the Midwest all under the Best Western franchise brand. Brian's father and two uncles sold the entire hospitality portfolio, consisting of 29 properties, to an investor group for upwards of $40 million in 2000.

During the ensuing ten years, the Klewackis established a family office in Minneapolis, out of which they made investments in various businesses, including a luxury car dealership, a bank holding company and several commercial office buildings for medical provider tenants. When the retiring owners of Cascade Mountain put it up for sale, Brian was managing a large hotel near the Twin Cities Airport in Bloomington and living in south Minneapolis with Gail and their two toddler sons. His younger brother had recently graduated from Montana State University in Bozeman and was working as a ski instructor in Big Sky.

After crunching some numbers and arranging favorable financing through one of their banks, the Klewacki brain trust added Cascade Mountain Lodge to their column of business assets and recruited Brian, his ski-bum brother and a cousin who was an audit manager at an accounting firm to run it.

Brian and Gail built a new home on the resort acreage, mainly because, commuting from Beaver Bay, Brian was spending about fifteen hours a day at work and the operation was still losing money. For a variety of reasons, the move helped everything and everyone except maybe Gail, whose commute to Two Harbors increased thirty miles each way.

Cascade was a unique property, consisting of five interconnected ski hills overlooking Lake Superior. It boasted over a hundred runs, four high-speed chairlifts, two snow-making machines and a gondola. The sprawling resort also included an 18-hole golf course and a variety of accommodations, from the renovated main lodge and shore condos near the lake to townhomes along the golf course and log cabins and ski villas on Cascade Mountain. Although the busiest season for Cascade was winter, the growing popularity of the North Shore as a year-round vacation destination had dramatically increased the resort's summer revenue.

Nevertheless, on most Tuesday evenings during the summer, the Klewackis were very happy with a 40-50% occupancy rate, and resort attractions and services closed well before midnight.

All canoe and kayak rentals had to be returned by 9:00 p.m. The swimming pool and water slides closed at 10:00, as did the clubhouse at the golf course. The restaurant and bar at the main lodge closed at 11:00 but stopped serving food at 9:30.

Between 10:30 and 11:00, Brian usually toured the property in his Chevy pickup to ensure general compliance with resort rules on fires, noise and trash and to check for any unregistered vehicles at the rental units.

When he walked in the door shortly after 11:00, Gail was upstairs policing their two boys, ages 9 and 11, issuing their final, final warning to be quiet and go to sleep. She had already confiscated smart phones and I-Pads.

Brian grabbed two bottles of Grain Belt from the fridge and sat at the kitchen table. He and Gail had positioned the split log home about halfway up Cascade Mountain. From the front porch, they could see the main lodge and Lake Superior. Two picture windows in the kitchen afforded views of a multi-purpose sport court for their boys, a small vegetable garden, and a row of birch and red maples dwarfed by a forest of blue spruce and pines.

Gail kissed the top of her spouse's shaved head and sat on his knee after gratefully taking her beer. Brian was a bear of a man, six and a half feet tall and nearly three hundred pounds. He had played offensive tackle for Concordia

College in Moorhead, which is where he met and fell in love with Gail Jenson, a criminal justice major.

"How are the rascals?" Brian asked. "You didn't sound very happy with them."

"They're fine, just a little amped up from playing ball out back. How was your day?"

"Mostly uneventful, though I did see something suspicious up at the ski villas that I want to run by you."

"What is it?"

"The parking lot up there is empty, except for a clunky Lincoln Town Car with Minnesota plates that isn't registered at the office. It's got a big crease in the front grill that looks pretty fresh. The weird thing is there's nobody staying in the villas, so the car appears to be abandoned up there."

"Oh, shit, Brian. Did you take down the plate number?"

"Even better, I got a few pictures on my phone," said Brian, handing the evidence to his wife. "What's the big deal?"

Gail stood up and stared at the image on his phone for several seconds, using her right thumb and index finger to expand the photo that included the full license plate.

"This car belongs to the Twin Cities' Archdiocese," she said confidently, returning the phone to her husband. "Archbishop Lamkin was up here last weekend visiting some guy named McBride who owns the big chateaux at milepost 84."

"How do you know all this?" asked Brian, not surprised that she did but curious.

"As part of our investigation of that murder in Gooseberry, we got a security camera shot of the Town Car gassing up at the BP station in Two Harbors last Friday night. We ran the plate and came up with the ownership. Making the connection to this McBride guy was pure luck. You know Hallie, Mac's girlfriend?"

"Sure. We've been out with them."

"Well, her ex, one of the Holden real estate clan, was supposed to meet with McBride about a potential land deal. He made an unscheduled visit to his place last Saturday morning. This Town Car was parked in the driveway, and, apparently, he got a glimpse through a window of McBride and the archbishop in a compromising position, so he left."

"Didn't the man who was stabbed to death in St. Paul over the weekend work for this bishop guy?" asked Brian.

Gail nodded. "Hard to believe he'd come up here to vacation so soon after that, isn't it? Wait just a minute, Brian." She stood up, set her beer on the table and folded her arms in front of her chest.

"I'll bet I know why someone ditched that car. There was a hit and run accident on 61 in Beaver Bay this afternoon. Ryan responded to the 9-1-1 call and made the report. You know who Doc Barrett is?"

"Sure. The crazy old guy who rants outside Koivisto's about drugs. He's harmless."

"He's also dead," said Gail. "According to the only eye witness, a big silver sedan speeding through town smashed into Barrett while he was crossing 61 with one of his signs. Threw him about fifty feet into a ditch and didn't even slow down. At a minimum the driver is guilty of leaving the scene of an accident."

Brian finished his beer and went to the fridge for another. "Not a very smart way to get rid of a car that could be implicated in a crime, especially if this bishop knows the local cops have identified his vehicle."

"You're right about that, Bri," said Gail, reaching in the pocket of her jeans for her cell phone. "Hey, I need to call Mac. I've got a bad feeling about this."

55

McBRIDE WAS CONFIDENT that he had a sound plan, a plan that would forever cut his ties to the Catholic Church, switch his allegiance from a lame duck to the future governor, and maintain his thriving business and lavish lifestyle. Unbeknownst to him, however, his plan depended on a few basic assumptions that weren't true.

He cleaned up the bloody mess around Lamkin with bleach and disinfectant, then wrapped the archbishop in several layers of extra strength cellophane and set him in a seven-foot chest freezer in his garage. He'd purchased the freezer when the lake place was first built to keep mass quantities of seafood and meat for entertaining but found that he rarely used it. He'd intended to sell it last Spring but was glad for now that it had slipped his mind.

Shortly before dark, McBride donned a black, hooded sweatshirt, tossed his mountain bike in the trunk of Lamkin's car, and drove the two miles down Highway 61 to Cascade Mountain Lodge. He searched for an area where no one would pay attention to him or the vehicle and ultimately parked in front of a vacant ski villa half way up Cascade Mountain.

Leaving the doors of the Town Car unlocked, he rode his bike back to his place in the dark, tossing Lamkin's key fob into the Cascade River and smiling inwardly as he envisioned local authorities scouring the Crosby and Cascade Mountain terrain looking for the missing cleric. He didn't know the local yokels had already connected him to the archbishop or that the Town Car had been involved in a crime earlier in the day.

It was beginning to drizzle when McBride placed Lamkin's wrapped, stiffening corpse in a wheelbarrow together with two thirty-pound dumbbells and two strands of nylon rope and trundled down a muddy path next to the lime-stone steps that descended to the lake. There, on a beach of crushed Arizona river rock that McBride had spread to even out the natural shore of larger rocks, he'd already set his 15-foot, tandem polyethylene kayak, a Hobie Mirage, the very best other people's money could buy.

McBride changed into a drysuit and wore a tight-fitting wool ski cap just in case he fell out of the kayak and into the 50-degree water—survivable for short stints, but too cold for him. He could see the lights of an ore carrier several miles out on the lake, but otherwise there was no human activity in sight. A cold wind out of the northwest was gusting up to twenty miles per hour and kicking up two to three-foot waves. The air temperature had settled into the upper forties.

This was not ideal kayaking weather, but McBride had a job to do. He removed a pen-sized LED flashlight from his drysuit and set it on the bow of the kayak with the light facing him. He used a section of nylon rope to tether one of the 30-pound dumbbells to Lamkin's ankles and secured the other one around his neck. Then he slid the lower half of Lamkin's body into the front seat of the Hobie. The dead archbishop weighed about 150 pounds, so with the added dumbbells his carcass perfectly balanced McBride's sturdy frame.

Taking a deep breath, McBride grabbed a paddle and shoved the kayak out into the dark water, holding the flashlight with his teeth. The Hobie featured foot pedals for increased speed and better steering, especially in rough waters. McBride was familiar with the depth of the lake near his property. Although it was over a hundred feet deep a quarter mile from shore, he preferred to drop the body closer to a mile out, where, according to his plan, it would never sur-face and never be found.

Paddling as fast as he could in the cold, rainy night air, McBride didn't like how low the Hobie was sinking in the choppy water. He recalled that the sleek vessel's capacity was about 550 pounds, so with the added weight of the dumb-bells he was approaching the limit.

After disposing of Lamkin, he would secure the cabin and return to the Cities. He needed to placate Bixby in some way and then he should be able to return to his old life, a life without James Lamkin. These thoughts of a more pleasant future kept him going.

Although Lamkin had been bossy and officious, he'd also been McBride's lover, benefactor and friend. Unfortunately, he'd become an irredeemable liability.

After enduring twenty minutes of muted terror, he arrived at a suitable spot for the archbishop's burial at sea, as the drizzle became a steady rain and the wind started blowing it sideways.

McBride slowly turned the kayak 180 degrees, so the bow faced the shoreline. Then he fastened the paddle to the side clips of the Hobie and leaned forward to lift Lamkin out of the front seat. The cellophane was wet and slippery in McBride's cold hands, and Lamkin was much heavier with the added weight of the dumbbells. As he leaned back with both arms around the dead man's chest, he tried to toss the wrapped bundle into the lake by twisting his torso to the left and shot putting the archbishop with his right arm. He executed the maneuver perfectly but lost his balance as the corpse splashed into the dark, heaving water, and McBride followed it, face first into the lake.

Startled and disoriented, McBride sucked water in through his mouth and nose and started choking and flailing his arms in total disequilibrium. He lost the flashlight when his face met the freezing water and was nearly paralyzed with fear when he thought he saw Lamkin's shrouded mug staring up at him a few feet below the surface, even though the weighted corpse had already sunk well beyond his view. He was lucky the Hobie didn't capsize during his ordeal in the water, though rolling waves were carrying it farther out into the lake.

It took several seconds for McBride to regain his bearings and start swimming towards the kayak, which he wouldn't have seen bobbing twenty yards away but for a sliver of light that escaped through a fissure in the thick clouds hiding the moon.

Without the drysuit, McBride would surely have suffered hypothermia, panicked and joined Lamkin at the bottom of the lake. With it, he struggled mightily to keep the tiny vessel in sight, to keep water out of his lungs, and to keep his aching arms crawling forward. It took him the better part of five minutes to overtake the kayak. By the time he clambered back into his seat and unclipped the paddle, he was completely spent but strangely exhilarated.

"Fuck you, Lamkin, you little prick," he yelled triumphantly as he began paddling back to shore while bursts of wind pelted his face with icy raindrops.

The Hobie had taken on a few inches of water but still glided higher and faster without a dead passenger. Because of foresight or good fortune, McBride had left his deck and back yard spotlights on, so losing the flashlight didn't hamper his return to shore.

McBride had more respect for Lake Superior than he had for most humans. As a boy, he'd visited the Maritime Museum in Duluth a few years after a brutal November gale literally snapped the *Edmund Fitzgerald* in half and entombed the big freighter and her crew of twenty-nine. The dark side of Gitchee Gumee intrigued McBride. Over the years, he'd collected books about shipwrecks, deadly riptides and haunted cabins and became obsessed with having a world-class retreat on the largest, coldest, deepest freshwater lake in the world. A lake that, according to legend, didn't give up her dead. Now more than ever, he hoped that was true.

56

MacDonald had hoped to end the long day on a high note—with a leisurely dinner at home with Hallie. A frantic call from her mother nixed that idea.

Long retired, her parents lived in a townhouse in Cape Coral, Florida. Her dad, who recently turned eighty, suffered a stroke shortly after his morning walk and was hospitalized in Fort Myers. According to her mom, if he survived the next 24 hours, his long-term prognosis was good, but he had swelling around the brain and doctors had placed him in an induced coma to get it under control.

Hallie hurriedly packed an overnight bag and drove to Duluth. MacDonald's mom then drove her to Sky Harbor Airport where she caught the 5:00 p.m. Delta flight to Minneapolis and secured a seat on a 7:30 connector to Fort Myers. MacDonald learned all of this via a series of texts and voicemail messages while they were both on the run.

After meeting with Klewacki and Holborn, he'd spent over an hour at Stockman's bungalow in Silver Bay trying to convince him to transition from disability leave to retirement. The meeting became uncomfortable when Marlys asked why his heart attack wasn't covered by workers' comp, since in her words: "it happened in the line of duty when he was investigating a murder." Obviously, Stockman had avoided giving her an accurate description of the activity that precipitated his myocardial infarction.

Arriving home about 7:00, MacDonald was too exhausted to make dinner and too happy to be home to go out. He'd been up since four in the morning, so the smart thing to do would have been to catch up on his sleep. Instead, he "revived" himself by going for a five-mile run. After a long, hot shower, he feasted on a tuna salad sandwich accompanied by leftover fried rice and an icy cold bottle of Castle Danger Cream Ale.

He downed a second beer while re-reading the Fallon evidence file stretched out on his favorite overstuffed recliner in the cozy, cedar-paneled family room overlooking the lake. Within ten minutes of his last swallow, he was snoring softly.

Startled by the tinny ring of his cell phone, MacDonald, swiped the irksome device off a side table and answered the call, just as his grandmother's antique cuckoo clock was cooing ten bells.

Redman was in the Jeep accompanied by Barney. He was on his way to the North Shore and had made reservations at the cheapest motel in Two Harbors.

Colianni had confirmed late in the afternoon that the credit card number on the receipt from the Holiday station belonged to a MasterCard corporate account owned by Itasca Asset Management, LLC, and assigned to its chief executive officer, Jay Robert McBride. Of course, Redman was already familiar with McBride after his weekend debriefing with Klewacki and MacDonald. He knew McBride was a business guy who handled a slice of the state's money and contributed big bucks to political campaigns. He knew McBride was tight with Governor Bixby, and he knew McBride might have been *in corpus flagrante* with the archbishop's *veretrum*; that is, unless his two semesters of Latin in college had betrayed him.

At Redman's request, Colianni had added him to the Jenkins' murder investigation team. He had to agree with the old fart that the murders of Jenkins and Lauren Fallon were somehow related even if the killers weren't the same person.

Redman had snooped around McBride's downtown penthouse and office earlier in the evening; both were locked and dark. However, the voicemail message on his direct line for investors indicated he would be out of the office until Friday, "at his cottage on the lake."

Redman intended to review all of the data Klewacki and the BCA had collected on McBride at the motel. He would make the drive to the "cottage" in Tofte shortly after sunrise to question McBride about his whereabouts on Saturday night and his relationship with Archbishop Lamkin and Peter Jenkins.

MacDonald really enjoyed Redman's wry, irreverent wit. He invited him and Barney to stay at his place instead of a motel. They could discuss the Jenkins' case and he could update Redman on the information they'd retrieved from Lauren's computer, scant though it was. Besides, given the brutal nature of Jenkins' murder and the fact that McBride was now a suspect, Redman might appreciate a "temporary" partner at his morning interview.

Redman accepted both invitations and then spent a few minutes ranting about "that evasive little fucker, Lamkin. Not only did he fail to produce my shit, he also left town for a few days to go fishing and drinking with a bunch of redneck bishops."

They both got a belly laugh out of that one, and they both agreed on one thing for sure—Lamkin was lying. He wasn't fishing; he wasn't a fisherman; he'd probably never fished in his life.

57

MACDONALD WAS TIDYING up the kitchen and guest bedroom in anticipation of Redman's arrival when he heard his cell and saw his deputy's number on the caller ID.

"What's up, Gail? It's almost midnight and I know you're not on duty. You should be getting some rest."

"Sorry, Mac," said Klewacki, "but this couldn't wait until morning, and I didn't want to get Cook County involved in our business."

"What business is that?"

"Remember the silver Town Car that the bishop, that Lamkin guy, drove up here last weekend?"

"You don't see many of those anymore," said MacDonald.

"Well, someone abandoned that car at the resort, in front of a vacant ski villa. The plates match Lamkin's and there's a fresh crease in the front bumper and grill. I would bet my paycheck against yours that this Town Car is the big sedan that Ethel Lindquist saw smash into Doc Barrett. So, we've got potential negligent homicide and vehicular manslaughter charges against this bishop. At a minimum, he's guilty of leaving the scene of an accident."

"Not to mention potential murder charges against his friend, McBride," MacDonald added.

"For Lauren Fallon?"

"No, but I suppose that's possible, too. Detectives found McBride's credit card receipt for gas purchased at 11:30 on the night of Jenkin's murder in the bushes near the entrance to his condo. That's why George Redman is on his way up here as we speak. Cascade Mountain Lodge is an odd place to scuttle a hot vehicle, unless whoever abandoned it didn't know it had been involved in a hit and run. Redman and I were planning to visit McBride's place tomorrow morning, but I think we'd better check out what's going on up there tonight."

"I can be there in five minutes," said Klewacki.

"I don't think that's a good idea, at least not by yourself. I can meet you there in thirty minutes, and we should probably give Sheriff Rovainen a heads-up call. He might have a squad that's a lot closer than I am."

"Are you concerned about our jurisdiction?" asked Klewacki, not sure why he was reluctant to let her go alone or why he wanted to call the old coot who'd been Cook County's sheriff for thirty years.

"We've got a possible fleeing felon from Lake County, so we've got jurisdiction. I'm just worried that this McBride may have gone rogue for some reason, probably having to do with money. He's a suspect in a vicious crime and, for all we know, he's dispatched the archbishop as well. He may not even know we've connected him to Lamkin. Why would he—that tip from Holden was serendipitous. In fact, if he's the one who abandoned Lamkin's car, I'd say he doesn't. Bottom line, Gail, I'm concerned for your safety."

"So am I, Mac, but I think time may be critical. You're right about the Town Car; it's crazy that some big shot would just leave it up here with its bumper bashed in, so how about I drive over there and park on 61. I'll monitor the place from a safe distance until you get there."

"O.K., said MacDonald, still with reservations, "but be careful. Stay out of sight and keep me posted. I'll leave here within the next five minutes."

"Me, too."

58

Eric Freeman wore a dark navy windbreaker with the USMC emblem prominently displayed over his heart. The jacket covered a black sweatshirt and jeans. Freeman was an intelligent, efficient, no-nonsense, no-humor, no-conscience machine. More marine than cop, he didn't want anyone but McBride to know that a decorated member of the Minnesota State Patrol had paid him a visit on a rainy Tuesday evening. The only state-issued parts of his ensemble were a pair of Tactical Research black boots and the Glock 22 zipped into an inside pocket of the windbreaker. He even drove his personal vehicle, a black Chevy Silverado 1500 LT.

Never married and with no family he cared about, Freeman left his apartment in Burnsville after an early dinner and arrived in Tofte about an hour after sunset. He parked about two hundred feet down the service road on Holden's land just east of McBride's. Before exiting the truck, Freeman put a black USMC baseball cap over his blond crew cut to complete his disguise and to provide some protection from the rain.

A Mercedes SUV was the only vehicle in the driveway, and it appeared that several lights were on in the sprawling log home. Freeman pressed the doorbell as he tried to open the oversized double doors. Locked. No one was answering, and Freeman couldn't detect any movement in the house with his highly-trained ears or through the kitchen window with his penetrating eyes.

He walked around to the back yard. A couple of floodlights on the deck were aimed at the shoreline, though he didn't see anyone or anything down there. Conditions weren't suitable for small watercraft on the lake, so what was going on and where was McBride?

Freeman jogged up the stairs to the wraparound deck. He was getting wet and impatient. Fortunately, for him, the sliding glass door to McBride's great room was unlocked. With deadly efficiency, he searched every room for signs of life and noted there was a desktop computer and Bloomberg terminal in the small office next to the master bedroom and a laptop on the kitchen table next to a nifty little Glock 9mm pistol. He examined the Glock, concluding that two rounds had recently been fired. Slipping the gun in his back pocket, he wondered whether McBride had been shooting squirrels or larger prey.

Returning to the great room, he spied a pair of pricey Swarovski binoculars sitting on top of the grand piano. Just another reminder of what a smarmy, pampered prick McBride was, thought Freeman, more convinced than ever that he was on a righteous mission.

He grabbed the expensive binoculars and walked out to the deck to scan the area one more time before trying to contact the Governor for further instructions. Looking out over the lake, he focused in on what appeared to be someone paddling a tandem kayak towards the shore, but battling rough waters and pelting rain. Could it be McBride? Did the fool have a death wish?

Freeman took out his own Glock, descended the deck stairs and scampered for cover behind a clump of birch trees near the water. By the time he was in position with weapon at the ready, the kayak was a hundred feet from shore. Now he was sure it was McBride. He waited until the husky man in the drysuit hopped out of the kayak and flipped it over on the rocky beach to drain excess water.

"You can just leave your toy boat right there," ordered Freeman, walking out from behind the trees with his gun barrel trained on the man's head.

McBride looked up and squinted, momentarily blinded by the floodlights. Still disoriented from his harrowing kayak adventure, he tried to focus on the large man wearing a baseball cap and pointing a gun in his direction. He'd met Freeman once or twice and seen him around Bixby often. There could only be one reason for his visit, and it wasn't a good one.

"Eric, is that you? Is the Governor with you?" McBride was trying to sound nonchalant and wondering if Bixby were watching the festivities from the deck or the great room.

Freeman ignored the questions. "What were you doing out there, McBride? Disposing of a dead body? That was no pleasure ride."

McBride froze. There's no way Freeman could have seen anything that far out on the dark lake, he thought. "I was just testing my new Hobie. It was much calmer earlier in the evening when I took her out."

"That's just bullshit," sneered Freeman, "but I really don't care what you were doing. The only thing I care about is what you're going to do now—get on your computer and transfer a couple million to my bosses account at your Swiss bank."

"I can't do that, Eric. The money's gone."

"More bullshit, McBride. I have current information on your accounts. I just need your password. Let's go up to the house and get this done." He nudged McBride in the shoulder blade with the Glock and then shoved him in the back with his free hand.

"That's not necessary," McBride recoiled indignantly. Totally exhausted, he struggled to make his way up the stone steps, up the stairway to the deck and through the sliding glass door.

"Let me grab a bottle of water out of the fridge before we do this," whined McBride.

"I'll get us both some water while you go fire up the computer in your office," said Freeman. "And, by the way, I've confiscated that cute little pistol in case you were getting any grandiose ideas. Looks like it's been fired a few times today. What was the target?"

"No target." McBride had to think fast. "I cleaned it and test-fired a few rounds into the woods. Hey, at least let me shower and change out of this suit."

"Listen, asshole, I'm about to lose my shit. It's almost midnight, and I have to drive back to the Cities tonight. I'll meet you in your office in five minutes; you'd better be logged into your Swiss bank."

Freeman used a burner phone to call the Governor's private cellphone number and let it ring three times—that was the signal for Bixby to log into the Swiss account that he'd established to make it easier to move money from McBride's accounts to his. At Freeman's suggestion, there were to be no text messages and no phone conversations between the two of them, except in a dire emergency. Once the funds showed up as a pending transaction in Bixby's account, he would "return" Freeman's call with a three-ring confirmation.

Freeman found bottled water and a case of Diet Coke in McBride's fancy refrigerator. He'd already been through the office and master bedroom looking for additional weapons and found none, though some of the sexual paraphernalia he came across made him want to vomit.

Not trusting McBride to follow his instructions, he hurried through the dining area and great room to McBride's office, a room that resembled an old English library. Freeman wondered how many of the hundreds of books lining the white, enameled floor-to-ceiling shelves McBride had actually read. That was a fleeting thought, however, one replaced by utter revulsion.

59

"Hi," Bell barely whispered into her phone.

"Hi. Where are you?" asked MacDonald, surprised to hear a live voice but happy she took his call.

"Sitting in my dad's hospital room. He's doing much better. Was actually awake and talking about an hour ago. I told mom I'd stay with him for a few hours while she went home to rest. The doctors say if he continues to improve, they'll transfer him to a rehab facility in a few days. I might be able to fly home Thursday or Friday."

"That's good news," said MacDonald.

"What's going on up there? Anything new on the Doc Barrett hit and run?"

"Believe it or not, it's likely that Archbishop Lamkin's Lincoln was the car that hit Barrett. We don't know whether he was driving, but we do know that his Town Car, with a damaged front grill, was abandoned up at Cascade resort. And his friend McBride has been implicated in Peter Jenkins' murder in St. Paul. I'm on my way to meet Gail up at McBride's right now. I shouldn't keep you any longer. I'll call tomorrow."

"OK, but please be careful. If something big happens, you can still call me tonight."

"Sure."

MacDonald checked in with Redman. He and Barney were about twenty miles south of Duluth. MacDonald told him about the abandoned Town Car and about his plan to meet Klewacki at McBride's. He suggested that Redman just drive to his place and wait there but knew he'd want in on the action.

"I'll just head straight to McBride's," Redman said. "Call me when you know more."

MacDonald knew better than to argue with the old fart.

The Cook County Sheriff was a much different old fart. Re-elected for a ninth consecutive term in 2016, 72-year-old Wilho Rovainen was the direct descendant of a Finnish immigrant who, back in the 1880s, began working in an iron ore mine in Tower, Minnesota at the tender age of twelve. Against his parents' wishes, Matti Rovainen married a beautiful Chippewa girl from the reservation near Bemidji a few years later. Her father was an avid fisherman who shared ancient tribal secrets for catching various species with his son-in-law during their frequent outings on Lake Bemidji and Leach Lake.

Preferring fishing to mining, Matti decided to try to make a living as a commercial angler. He and Abequa settled in Grand Marais, the Cook County seat on the shores of Lake Superior, where Matti eventually prospered as a commercial fisherman. Thereafter, more than three generations of Rovainen men made a respectable living catching whitefish, trout and walleye in the big lake. By 1960, Rovainen's Fish House had become the No. 1 seller and exporter of smoked whitefish in the Western Hemisphere.

Wilho, better known as Will, loved Grand Marais but couldn't stand the smell or taste of fish, especially smoked fish. Forsaking the family business, he went to community college in Hibbing and joined the Cook County Sheriff's Department in 1965 as one of two deputies. Even though he didn't fish, he was an accomplished marksman, becoming president of the Cook County Gun Club in the 1990s. Like most Club members, Will spent much of his free time hunting birds, deer and even bear from time to time.

With fewer than two thousand residents, Grand Marais was a close-knit community, and the Rovainen family occupied a highly respected place in it. Will's younger brother, Jessie, managed the Fish House, and Kathy, his wife of forty years, kept the books and ran the shipping department. Four of Will and Kathy's five children were employed by the Cook County Sheriff's Department, three as deputies and one as a probation officer. Cook County residents were very comfortable with this degree of nepotism. Violent crime was rare in the county, and the name Rovainen was synonymous with safety, stability and family. Outsiders like Gail Klewacki believed that unchecked nepotism led to favoritism, discrimination and mediocrity. MacDonald didn't disagree, but so long as the citizens of Cook County kept electing Will by a wide margin, he didn't have a problem with it. Besides, he appreciated the difficulties associated with recruiting and retaining talented law enforcement professionals in the tundra of Northeastern Minnesota.

MacDonald didn't expect Rovainen to answer his cell phone.

"Sheriff Will here," he said almost cheerfully.

"Will, it's Sam MacDonald in Lake County. I expected to get your voice-mail this late on a Tuesday night."

"Oh, no. I'm a night owl, Sam. Just finished watching the Twins lose to the Angels. I thought I might hear from you about the murder of that lawyer over the weekend. I hope my folks got you everything you needed."

"I'm sure they did, Will. We're making slow progress on the murder investigation, but I've got something else. I don't know if you heard about the hit-and-run fatality in Two Harbors this afternoon. A local doctor was the victim."

"You know, I think my son, Terry, mentioned something about it. Didn't know the victim was a doctor. Who was it?"

"A retired family doc from Duluth. His name's Ted Barrett. Anyway, we suspect someone abandoned the car that hit Barrett on the Cascade resort property, and we have evidence that Catholic Archbishop James Lamkin from the Twin Cities may have been the driver."

"You're shittin' me!" Rovainen exclaimed.

"There's more," said MacDonald. "We think Lamkin may be visiting a wealthy banker type from the Cities who has a fancy log home on the lake north of Tofte, at about mile marker 84. His name is McBride."

"Jay McBride?" Rovainen asked, with skepticism in his voice.

"Yeah, you know him?"

"Not well, but I sure as hell know Jay McBride. A couple of years ago he hired Todd, my youngest, the one who has his own security company, to check on his place once or twice a week when he's not up here. He insists on paying him twice his normal rate. Then last fall he noticed all the campaign signs on 61 for Mick Sertich, the dickhead undersheriff from Carlton County who bought a house on Devil's Track Lake and thought he could just move up here and take my job. McBride asked Todd if he could host a fundraiser for my campaign at his cottage, as he calls it. Not only did he feed over a hundred people, but he also gave me a very generous contribution. Just a helluva' nice fellow. Maybe a little pretentious, but we're happy to take his big city money up here in Cook County."

MacDonald recalled that Sertich had only lost by a few hundred votes. He was having second thoughts about enlisting the help of the Cook County Sheriff.

"I'm on my way to McBride's right now, sheriff. One of my deputies is going to meet me. We need to see if Lamkin is laying low up there or worse."

"Why don't you just call McBride? I've got his cell number; I could call him for you."

"That wouldn't be a good idea, Will. McBride is now a suspect in the murder of the archbishop's assistant in St. Paul; you may have heard about it over the weekend. We're concerned that Lamkin may be in danger."

"I didn't hear about that one, but there are so many murders down there in the Cities it's hard to keep track. Anyway, it's hard to believe that the Jay McBride I know would murder anyone, much less someone who does the Lord's work."

"You know as well as I, sheriff, that under the right circumstances anyone is capable of violence. Anyway, I wanted to give you a heads up because we'll be operating on your turf. Plus, I wanted to know if you've got any squads in the area as potential backups if we need assistance."

"We should have a regular patrol in the vicinity--within fifteen miles of McBride's place for sure—until 2:00 a.m. I'll let my dispatcher know that you might be needing backup as soon as we're done."

"Thanks, Will. I appreciate it."

"And I appreciate the courtesy call sheriff, but I'll bet you dollars to doughnuts that McBride's not involved in any violence. To tell you the truth, I think he might be a little light in the loafers, if you know what I mean."

MacDonald didn't respond.

60

KLEWACKI CHANGED INTO her uniform, augmented by a Kevlar vest, light-weight rain slicker and Lake County baseball cap, and drove her newer Ford Explorer the three miles to McBride's fortress at milepost 84. Thinking like the smart cop she was, she drove down the service road adjacent to the Holden parcel, where she spotted the black Silverado. Wanting to check the license but not having access to one of the county's on-board laptops, she parked thirty yards ahead of the pickup and called in the plate number. She didn't have time to wait for results.

Staying low, which wasn't too difficult for someone 5'5", a pair of mini-binoculars hanging from her neck and a compact LED flashlight in her right hand, Klewacki stalked the perimeter of McBride's property, trying to avoid well-lit areas and on the lookout for surveillance cameras. She observed lights on in the kitchen and main living area but couldn't see any human forms or movements. Unfortunately, heavy blinds covered most of the windows on the front of the log home. There was a black Mercedes SUV in the driveway and an expensive mountain bike leaning against the steps of the front porch.

As she approached the rear elevation, she was surprised to encounter a backyard bathed in artificial light. The walkout lower level was dark inside but multiple spotlights and floods on the second story illuminated the deck and sloping terrain all the way down to the lake. She was curious about the over-turned kayak near the shoreline but knew she'd be visible to anyone in the house if she tried to check it out.

Seeking the cover of a grouping of blue spruce in the side yard to the east of the house, Klewacki lifted her cell from a jacket pocket and called MacDonald. She was miffed when the call went directly to voicemail.

"Mac, I'm on McBride's property. It's difficult to see any activity in the house, but lights are on everywhere and McBride's SUV is in the driveway. I parked on the service road. There's a newer, black pickup parked there as well. I called in the plate number and assume whoever was in the truck is in with McBride. At this point I'll just wait. . ."

Her message was interrupted by the distinctive pop of a gunshot reverberating from inside the house.

"Gunfire from McBride's, Mac. I'm going in. Get here!"

She shoved the phone in her pocket, unbuttoned the holster hanging from her belt and pulled out her service revolver while running up the stairs to the deck. Crouching down to create a small target, she opened the sliding glass door, scanned the massive great room and shouted:

"Sheriff!"

61

"WHAT THE HELL is wrong with you? I leave you alone for thirty seconds and this is what you do?"

McBride was sitting in his office chair facing a 30-inch computer screen. He had logged into his Swiss account, just as Freeman had directed, but was completely naked.

"I was boiling in that fucking drysuit," McBride explained, hoping that the straight-laced cop would be repulsed by his appearance and just leave.

"Let's get on with it, McBride. Bixby gave me this account name and number. He opened an account at your Swiss bank to facilitate the transfer. He said if you move two million to this account tonight, he'll do everything in his power to keep the state's money with Itasca, and he'll consider your personal business with him to be finished."

"You can see the balance in this account right here," said McBride pointing to an "available balance" figure on the screen of $2,752,300.00. How about we each take half?"

"I said I don't have time for your bullshit, McBride. Move the money now!"

"I don't get it, Eric. Why are you even involved in this? How much is Bixby paying you to risk your career to do his bidding? You tell him I only had a million in the account and I'll give you a hundred thousand."

Freeman pushed the barrel of his Glock against McBride's left ear. "You're beginning to stink, asshole. I'm going to pretend I didn't hear your weak attempt at a bribe. Move the money or I'll start shooting your fingers off and move up or down from there."

McBride was pretty sure Freeman wouldn't actually shoot him but wanted this over as much as he did. Now that Lamkin and Jenkins were gone, McBride was the only one who even knew of the existence of the fund. He could afford to give Bixby $2 million, especially if the Governor followed through on his promise.

"All right," sighed McBride as he focused on the banking transaction and started typing. "It's 8:15 in the morning in Geneva and the two million will hit Bixby's account in just a minute or two."

After a few minutes, Freeman felt his phone vibrate. It was the signal from Bixby that the money had been transferred.

"Good," said Freeman. "One last item and I'll be gone."

"What do you mean one last item? What else to you want?"

"I need a little insurance." Freeman lifted a sheet of Itasca Management stationery from a bin on the desk and placed it in front of McBride. "You're going to write a short confession that won't be used unless you turn on me or the Governor."

"That's bullshit, Freeman. I've done nothing wrong. What do you want me to say?" McBride picked out a ballpoint pen from his top desk drawer, sensing he wasn't going to get rid of Bixby's strong-armed bagman unless he capitulated. He worried that Freeman would figure out that a tiny camera at the top of his monitor was recording the proceedings.

"Just a couple of simple lines."

"Saying what?"

"Put today's date on the top right-hand corner. Then write this down:

I deeply regret what I've done, but I can't undo it now. I hope someday that those I have hurt will forgive me. I can't forgive myself.

"Now sign your name."

McBride followed Freeman's instructions, but was perplexed by the wording of the so-called confession. After signing the short note, he reread it. "This sounds more like a suicide. . ."

Freeman fired a bullet from McBride's Glock 9mm into his left temple from close range, the round exploding in his brain before he could complete the thought, before he could finish the sentence, before he could face his executioner.

Freeman wiped the gun down with a handkerchief and was about to place it in McBride's dominant hand, his left hand, when he heard footsteps on the deck.

"Oh, fuck!" he muttered under his breath, wondering who in heaven's name would visit Jay McBride on a weekday after midnight. Then he heard a female voice call out:

"Sheriff! Come out in the open with your hands in the air!"

Freeman knew he might be fucked if there were more than one cop on the scene, but he had to make a plan and commit to it. He kept McBride's gun and moved quickly but stealthily into the dark master bedroom, getting down on all fours on the plush carpet and pinning himself against the wall just inside the double doors. He deftly peered out into the light-filled great room, keeping his head within inches of the floor.

A cold, calculating narcissist, Freeman wasn't used to unpleasant surprises. Even as he contemplated his next move, he was analyzing logical reasons for this intrusion. The closest neighbor was a half-mile south, and there was no way anyone driving on 61 could have heard a gunshot from inside McBride's place, so the only explanation was a security check. That was it. McBride paid one of the locals to check on his expensive property. She heard the shot and responded. If that were true, she would have called for backup. He needed to act fast.

He detected movement behind the grand piano and could make out a pair of black boots and dark pants below the wide body of the instrument. He could also see two hands clasping a pistol, but the head and torso were hidden. A lithe, female figure slowly raised first the bill of a baseball cap and then her forehead above the polished ebony piano, high enough for Freeman to aim and fire a 9mm round right between her eyes.

Klewacki heard the shot at the same time she felt a burning sensation in her head and then a black nothingness as she collapsed in a heap on the hardwood floor. It took less than a minute for Freeman to wipe off the pistol, place it in

McBride's limp hand and scurry through the great room, down the deck steps and out to his truck. He didn't have time to check the condition of the intruder, but he was both relieved and worried to see a white, unmarked Explorer parked on the service road near his truck. Relieved, because it appeared to be a personal vehicle, not a squad, corroborating his theory that it belonged to a local cop for hire. Worried, because the lady cop might have called in his plate number.

Opening the driver's door to the Explorer, Freeman checked the interior looking for anything that would identify her or her employer. There was nothing of interest, no phone, no wallet, no police scanner. There was a basketball in the back seat, a tin of mints and some wet wipes in the center storage compartment, and a flashlight and owner's manual in the glove box. That was it. Fuck.

Freeman hopped into his truck and drove out to Highway 61. Instead of turning left towards Duluth and the Twin Cities, he turned right, heading north towards the Canadian border.

62

MACDONALD WAS ONLY ten miles from McBride's when he heard his deputy's frantic message. He activated the siren and flashers on the Tahoe and jammed the accelerator to the floor, popping the needle past ninety and careening down the dark, vacant highway.

He was anxious, agitated and perplexed. Klewacki had called in a license plate for a truck parked on the service road near McBride's. Unable to reach her, the dispatcher radioed MacDonald with the information. The truck was registered to a Rodney Eric Freeman from Burnsville, Minnesota, a senior officer with the Minnesota State Highway Patrol on special assignment to Governor Winton Bixby.

What was the Governor's driver doing at McBride's place on a Tuesday night? Was Governor Bixby with him? Why wasn't Freeman driving an official state vehicle? Who fired the shot and at whom? Why couldn't Klewacki wait for him to get there?!!

These questions swirled in MacDonald's brain as he tried one last time to reach Klewacki on her cell. No answer. He sped down McBride's driveway, stopping inches from the front steps. Exiting the Tahoe, he took a Colt M1911 out of his side holster, climbed the stairs two at a time and pulled on the front door handle. Locked. He blasted the dead bolt mechanism with a couple of well-placed shots and kicked in the double doors.

The chandelier in the two-story entryway lit up the foyer and kitchen revealing no one. The only sound he heard was the whirring of a ceiling fan in the great room. Moving fast with senses alert and gun drawn, he spotted Klewacki sprawled on the floor between a grand piano and open sliding glass doors leading to the deck. He called 9-1-1 demanding the closest emergency responders in either Cook or Lake County and knelt down to check on his unconscious deputy, sensing no one else was in the house but not caring at all for his personal safety.

Klewacki had fallen on her stomach, her arms outstretched, her gun just beyond the reach of her left hand. Her head was cocked to the right, and a small pool of blood had formed on the floor under and around her face. MacDonald felt a weak but steady pulse in her neck and observed that she was breathing regularly. Having extensive training in first aid in the air force and secret service, he examined the wound on her forehead and was relieved to see that a small caliber bullet had entered there and then exited about two inches above her hairline, where droplets of blood were coagulating near the exit wound.

MacDonald surmised that whoever shot his deputy did it from a kneeling or supine position, which was a very fortunate circumstance, since the upward trajectory of the shot caused the bullet to enter her skull at about a 45-degree angle, implicating only a small section of the brain before departing out the top of her head. MacDonald knew that her chances of survival, and survival without residual neurological or cognitive deficits, were all much better without a bullet lodged in her brain. That the blood was oozing rather than gushing from her wounds was also a good sign.

Figuring he couldn't do any more for her until paramedics arrived, he stood up and began searching the rest of the house. Klewacki had responded to a gunshot. MacDonald suspected he'd find Archbishop Lamkin's body somewhere in McBride's unholy manse.

He checked the lower level first, flipping on lights in the wine cellar, billiard room and movie theater. Nothing. A search of two bedrooms, a laundry and the mechanical room also yielded nothing. His attention was diverted by bright lights in the back yard and the overturned kayak, but he decided to complete an inventory of the inside before going out.

Back on the main level, he spied muted light seeping from a half-opened door on the south end of the spacious great room, adjacent to what appeared to be the master suite. Leading with the Colt, he cautiously entered the book-lined study and encountered a bizarre sight—a well-built, completely naked man sitting on a leather executive chair, his upper body literally dead weight slumped over an antique wooden desk. The man's blond head was face down in a puddle of blood on the desk top, both arms extended as if signaling a final touchdown. But for the pistol in his left hand, he resembled a swimmer doing the butterfly in mid-stroke. One thing for sure, he wasn't Lamkin.

Feeling no pulse in the man's neck, MacDonald examined the bullet hole in his temple and the blood-stained note that was partially concealed by his head. He was reluctant to move the body or anything else until a crew from Cook County, or more likely the BCA, could process the scene. Nevertheless, he could see enough of the short note to discern what it was intended to be. And he could make out the signature—Jay McBride.

Though he'd never met McBride, he'd read more than one description— tall, medium build, blue eyes, blond hair, possible sociopath. The dead man matched that description. But if McBride had shot Klewacki and then killed himself, there was still the matter of the shot Klewacki heard.

The "suicide" appeared staged to MacDonald. He had a hunch that Bixby's man Friday had something to do with it. He'd never met him either.

The computer monitor on McBride's desk was dark, and the tower next to it was off, but MacDonald noted that both machines were hot, meaning McBride had probably been conducting some kind of business earlier in the evening. There could be some pretty valuable evidence in there, he thought.

Still wondering what happened to Lamkin, MacDonald moved to the master bedroom and switched on the overhead chandelier, a bronze and glass monstrosity that probably cost as much as he made in a year. There were no signs of life, or a dead archbishop, in the bedroom, walk-in closet or palatial bathroom. There was, however, a black leather duffle bag on the king bed with gold embossed lettering: Archbishop James Lamkin.

The blaring of sirens interrupted MacDonald's search. He hustled out to the great room to greet the paramedics.

63

FALLON SAT AT the kitchen table in his boxer shorts and sipped Irish whiskey straight from the bottle. He'd hoped the run with Daly would help him sleep, but his tortured mind wouldn't give his tired body a break. Now he was thinking about how comfortable his life had been with Mary. They'd met at the University of Minnesota when he was a second-year law student and she was a senior majoring in architecture.

In many ways, Mary and Lauren couldn't have been more different. One was petite, barely five feet tall, with dark brown hair, often worn in a ponytail, a delicate, button nose and warm, empathetic smile. Mary was modest and coy, yet possessed a wonderfully wicked sense of humor that reeled Fallon in like a big, dumb northern pike. She excelled at her chosen profession—commercial interior design—but was also a gourmet cook and devoted mother.

Lauren looked like a model, only much more athletic. Close to six feet tall, she was naturally blond and, in every respect, captivating. Her extra-long but undressed eyelashes shaded enchanting blue-green eyes, and her high cheek bones and wide smile gave her a sensual, feline aspect that she used to her advantage. She was confident, outgoing when it suited her objectives and always a patient, and sometimes even artful, listener, unusually inquisitive about the lives of others. Fallon came to believe that this characteristic was mostly an act, an act that enabled her to discover other people's secrets while camouflaging a level of passion and intensity that was often close to boiling over.

Fallon had loved both women, but only one of them betrayed him. He screwed the cap on the whiskey bottle and fingered the shattered iPhone he'd retrieved from his brief case. The phone didn't work, but that didn't diminish how nervous he'd been when Sheriff MacDonald interviewed him while this battered phone screamed silently in his pocket.

Lauren was the opposite of pretentious and wasn't fond of jewelry; Fallon had been more excited than she over the stunning two-carat diamond engagement ring he'd given her. However, she thoroughly enjoyed a well-played gag gift, so when Fallon gave her a graphite crystal "bling" iPhone case for Christmas, she not only got a good laugh over it, she used it. He would smile broadly every time he saw her caress it with her long, handsome fingers. But no more. The case was cracked in several places, and most of the crystal chips were missing, casualties of a violent act. At this point, Fallon wasn't sure what he should do with the phone or with himself.

64

REDMAN AND FREEMAN had a shared history, and it didn't end well. A decade earlier both had been employed by the St. Paul police department, Redman as a detective in the homicide and robbery division, and Freeman as an undercover cop in the narcotics and vice division. Freeman had earned a reputation as a sniper in the Marines, so the commander of St. Paul's elite special weapons and tactics team had recruited him to be a member of that unit as well.

After the retirement of Redman's longtime partner in the late 1990s, he was paired with an earnest and idealistic young officer who'd impressed the power suits in the department so much that he rose to the rank of detective in just three years. His intelligence, thoroughness and work ethic impressed even Redman, who was highly skeptical of the value of any cop with fewer than ten years of seasoning.

Gary Bostic was a St. Paul native. Both he and his yoga instructor spouse were graduates of Hill Murray High School. The Bostics and their two young children attended the same Catholic parish where Gary had been baptized, confirmed and married. Though Redman wasn't Catholic, he was impressed with and somewhat envious of the close-knit young family, especially when he observed their genuinely loving interactions. Not having any close relatives of his own, Redman was more than happy to be called "Uncle George" by the Bostic children.

It was New Year's Eve 2008. The stock market was in the tank and the banking system had nearly collapsed. George W. Bush was presiding over the worst recession since the 1930s and was about to hand the baton to the first African-American President in the history of the Republic. Wall Street was not celebrating, though Main Street was still hopeful and resilient.

At the time, Vince Marcus was president and chief executive officer of Marcus Capital Partners, a Minneapolis-based hedge fund that had invested heavily in securities backed by subprime mortgages. Vince was supposed to be in New York City from December 29th through January 4th meeting with several bankers he'd hoped would lend him $40 to $50 million to keep his sinking business afloat until the mortgage and real estate markets recovered.

Vince, overweight and hypertensive at fifty, and his second wife, Lindsay, well-endowed at thirty, lived on Mississippi River Boulevard in St. Paul. Three years earlier, when the housing market was booming, they'd torn down a 1950s era rambler and replaced it with a five-bedroom, six thousand square foot "craftsman cottage," with a pool, hot tub and outdoor kitchen, not to mention an indoor basketball court for Vince's two teenage boys, who spent every other weekend with their dad.

By the end of the day on December 30th, Vince had accepted the harsh reality that no one was willing to extend the kind of credit and terms he needed to avoid a reorganization under Chapter 11 at best or, more likely, a complete liquidation of his highly leveraged company. He'd be better off spending his time with bankruptcy lawyers than subjecting himself to further ridicule and rejection by tight-assed bankers who were too shell-shocked and risk averse to envision his brighter future.

Strapped for cash and overextended, he would have to sell the house and fancy cars and get his outrageous alimony and child support payments reduced. And the worst part, he would have to explain all this to Lindsay, who, at least for the short run, might have to return to her former occupation as a hostess at an upscale restaurant.

He decided not to tell Lindsay he'd be home a few days earlier than planned. She would have asked a bunch of questions he wasn't prepared to answer just yet. When he'd asked her about her plans for New Years' Eve, she'd said a few women in the neighborhood were meeting at the Club for a glass of wine to toast the New Year. She'd be home by ten.

Vince's flight landed at MSP at 9:30. He'd been depressed for months, especially because he felt he couldn't share his heavy burdens with Lindsay, who still believed he was a financial wizard, which he was. The prospect of one last night of fun with his young wife before the truth came out made him feel amorous enough to pick up an expensive bottle of champagne at Highland Park Wine & Spirits before driving home.

Wearing a light wool suit with no overcoat or gloves, Vince was woefully underdressed for the weather—five below zero with a nasty northwest wind making it feel like twenty below. As he approached his driveway, he could hear rock music reverberating from his house. Surprised, he lowered both front windows and recognized a famous Eagles tune on Lindsay's favorite playlist. He also noticed a new Acura sedan parked on the river side of the boulevard. No one ever parks there, he thought. He killed the lights and engine of his 750i sedan and left it at the end of the driveway. Ignoring the frigid air, he walked up the driveway and peered through the front picture window. He couldn't hear himself think, the music was so loud. There was no activity in the formal living room, though it seemed like every damn light in the house was on. A party with no guests?

There was a three-inch layer of new snow on the ground that had hardened into an icy, slippery crust. It made a crunching noise as Vince awkwardly trudged to the back of the house.

He'd been wrong about the lights. There were no lights on in the family room, just a blazing fire in the authentic $50k river stone fireplace. Lindsay was on the leather sectional facing the fire. She was naked, her long, shapely legs spread apart, and a heavily-muscled, half-naked African American man was busy pleasuring her.

A flood of emotions, none of them positive, filled Vince, still unaware that he was freezing his ass off. Wearing polished black oxfords, he fell to his knees a couple of times as he raced back to the BMW and retrieved a loaded Smith & Wesson .22 caliber pistol he kept in a hidden compartment in the back of the glove box. Given the decibel level of the music and the distraction provided by her kneeling houseguest, his wife would never hear him coming through the front door. She didn't; she'd even left it unlocked.

By the time Lindsay looked up and recognized her husband's beet-red face, Vince had shot her young lover twice in the back. When the startled fellow turned to see his attacker, he took a third hit, this one in the mouth.

He collapsed face down on the Marcus' imported Persian rug. He wouldn't be getting back up.

Lindsay screamed and screamed and screamed and then screamed again, believing she'd be Vince's next victim. Neighbors on each side of the Marcus house heard the gunshots and Lindsay's response. Both called 9-1-1.

Vince was momentarily stunned by what he'd just done. He'd never shot anyone, or even any living thing, before, and he felt sick to his stomach. Then he looked over at his naked wife, and the rage returned. She was responsible for this. He snatched a fistful of her thick, artificially blond hair and pulled her off the couch.

"You fucking bitch, you fucking whore!" he shouted into her anguished face, his stinking breath from a combination of airplane food and Irish coffee making her want to retch. Part of her just wanted him to get it over with, to kill her quickly. She knew nothing she could say or do would mitigate the hatred in his eyes or the pain in his heart, but she had to try something.

"Please, Vince," she begged, struggling with both hands to pry his fat fingers from her hair, "can't we just talk about this? I can explain!"

While all of this was going on, Redman and Rita were on their first extended vacation together in the Oro Valley, just north of Tucson. Not having as much tenure, Redman's partner was on duty on New Year's Eve, a night when squads spent most of their time dealing with drunken drivers and rowdy partygoers, not responding to reports of multiple gunshots.

Nursing a cup of cocoa in the break room of the Highland Park duty office, Detective Bostic volunteered to respond to the 9-1-1 calls from Mississippi River Boulevard. Officers Adams and Freeman would bring one of the S.W.A.T. vans from downtown to assist.

Meanwhile, Vince knew it was doubtful he'd make it to 2009 alive, but he wanted to make sure that Lindsay wouldn't either. On the positive side, he'd avoid the humiliation associated with the failure of his business and the infidelity of his treacherous wife. His only feelings of regret came during passing thoughts of his two boys, but his ex and her new boyfriend would care for them. He needed to tend to the matter at hand.

"You want to explain this?" he seethed. Grabbing Lindsay's left wrist, he led her to the two-story foyer, where he swung her roughly in a semi-circle, causing her to lose balance and fall ass first onto the cold, marble floor. He pinned her arms down with his knees and sat across her ribcage with his full weight, over 250 pounds, making it difficult for her to breathe.

Shoving the barrel of his pistol in her mouth, he shouted, "Let's hear it, then!"

Sensing her demise was certain, Lindsay resorted to the truth.

"You haven't been around for months. I have needs. What did you expect me to do?"

Vince wasn't listening to Lindsay. The sound of sirens distracted him. He didn't want to spend any time in jail but wasn't sure he could pull the trigger in Lindsay's mouth or in his own. Maybe the cops could help. In one motion, Vince wrapped his left arm around Lindsay's waist and lifted her off the floor, resting the barrel of his pistol against her right ear. He then opened the front door and pushed his naked wife out unto an icy concrete stoop.

"Oh my God it's cold, Vince! Please, please let me go back inside. Jesus fucking Christ it's cold!"

"Shut the fuck up, you whore!" Vince growled, as he compressed her rib cage with his forearm and moved the tip of the gun back to her mouth. He was oblivious to the cold, but oddly excited to see an unmarked squad car, its blue and red lights flashing, stop at the end of his driveway. A tall, thin man wearing a navy leather jacket and black gloves slowly emerged from the driver's side and gently flipped the door closed.

"Mr. Marcus, I'd like to come up to the porch and talk to you," Detective Bostic called out, using a loud but friendly voice.

"It doesn't matter," Vince responded, disappointed that the cop wasn't brandishing a weapon.

Bostic walked in a steady rhythm toward the small, rectangular porch, a concrete block framed by two white wooden pillars. He stopped about twenty feet short, where he could attempt to have a calm, rational conversation with the target. He observed that the naked woman was convulsing and that her bare skin was turning red. She had a look of despair on her face, accompanied by resignation in her eyes.

"Does anyone inside the house need help, Mr. Marcus?"

"No," said Vince. "The black bastard who was doing my wife is dead."

"Mr. Marcus, you don't know that for sure. I understand that everything seems bleak now, like there's no way out of this situation, but I assure you things aren't as bad as you think. I'd like you to give me your weapon, so we can go inside and talk. Find a way to work things out. I don't believe you want to hurt anyone else tonight."

His voice was soothing to Vince, who was beginning to feel the icy wind penetrate his thin layer of clothing. Lindsay was starting to feel heavy against his chest. She wasn't shivering any more, just crying softly.

A sudden gust of wind nearly knocked Vince off his feet at precisely the same time a shot exploded out of the darkness and a metal projectile whistled within an inch of his head. The bullet ricocheted off an antique iron knocker on the front door, then cut through Detective Bostic's neck like a knife through warm butter and obliterated his left carotid artery. He barely felt a thing, only the rush of his life's blood, hot and steamy, against his cold skin for an instant. And then he was gone.

Startled by the blast, Vince instinctively pulled the trigger of his pistol. Before he could appreciate the fact that he'd completely missed Lindsay's head from a distance of about three inches, he, too, was gone. The bloody mess that had been his head resembled a ghoulish Halloween mask, his lifeless carcass collapsing into Lindsay, his dead weight knocking her to the ground. For several minutes, she was in a state of surreal consciousness, somewhere between shock, relief and utter horror.

A black, S.W.A.T. team van had been idling on the walking path on the west side of River Boulevard. Freeman's partner had used the van's fancy computer to disable all the street lamps in the neighborhood. The two sharpshooters had been in "sniper" position atop the van, roughly fifty yards from Marcus' front door but shrouded in darkness. In all, six rounds were fired, all from Freeman's Remington 700.

In his statement to St. Paul homicide, Freeman contended that Vince had raised his voice, turned towards Detective Bostic and raised his weapon to fire, prompting Freeman to shoot. Officer Adams corroborated this version of events in his written report and in subsequent interviews.

Redman cut his vacation short and returned to St. Paul. He was nearly overcome with grief and highly skeptical of Freeman's account of how things went down at the Marcus residence. He spent six months investigating his partner's last night on the job. An investigation conducted on his own time.

In the end, he couldn't prove shit. Freeman and his partner were tight. Lindsay probably knew the truth, but she couldn't remember anything after her husband executed her boyfriend. In Redman's opinion, she suffered from one of the few truly legitimate cases of PTSD he'd ever seen, exacerbated by a sudden change in her socio-economic status. By the time creditors, lawyers and the IRS were done picking over Vince's insolvent company and mortgaged assets, she was forced to return to the restaurant business and could barely afford a one-bedroom apartment. Freeman actually tried to comfort her with his little dick, but she preferred poverty and a vibrator to his company.

Redman was deeply affected by the loss of his protégé and friend. He refused to take on another partner and told his boss he would no longer carry a firearm. That didn't sit well with the police chief, who transferred his best detective to a permanent desk job. Within two years, Redman took early retirement. At about the same time, Freeman met Governor Bixby and applied for a senior position with the state patrol.

Redman was a few miles south of McBride's when he connected with MacDonald.

"I'll be there in five minutes," Redman said. "What did you find?"

"A total shit-show. Klewacki's been shot in the forehead, but I think she's going to survive. The paramedics are stabilizing her for transport to St. Mark's. I found McBride sitting at his computer in his birthday suit, a bullet hole in his temple and a suicide note on his desk. No sign of Lamkin, but it looks like someone from McBride's may have taken a kayak out on the lake in this lousy weather, so the archbishop might be fish food."

"So, McBride shot Klewacki and then killed himself?" Redman asked skeptically.

"That's how someone wants it to look, but at least one other person was here when everything went down. Do you know the Governor's driver from the state patrol, a guy named Rodney Freeman?"

"Yeah, he goes by Eric and he's a fucking asshole, why?"

"Gail reported that a pickup truck was parked on the service road near McBride's when she got here. My folks checked the plate number, and the truck is registered in Freeman's name. About fifteen minutes later, she reported hearing a gunshot in McBride's. That's what prompted her to go inside to check things out. Some of your friends from the BCA will be here soon to process a very unusual scene. We need to track down this Freeman character and see what he knows. I'm putting a statewide APB out on his truck. It's possible the Governor is somehow involved in this as well."

"I bet I know where that trigger-happy bastard is hanging out. You don't need me at McBride's; I'm heading up to Trestle Pine Lake."

"Trestle Pine Lake? My dad used to take me fishing for rainbow trout near there."

"Freeman has a small cabin up there; it's more of a hunting shack, right off Trestle Pine Road on the south end of the lake. No one knows more about Eric Freeman than I do, Mac."

MacDonald didn't have time to delve into why that was so. "That's great, Red, but you have no business going up there alone and unarmed. Drive over here and we'll discuss the best way to approach this guy."

Redman clicked off his cell and stroked the top of Barney's head.

65

Bixby would be furious when he learned about the execution of Jay McBride, but Freeman didn't like loose ends, and he certainly didn't trust McBride to keep quiet about the evening's transactions. The intrusion of the lady cop complicated matters and made him vulnerable. However, even if local authorities connected him to McBride's place, they had no way to prove he fired McBride's gun.

He needed to spend a few days off the grid in a place with no wi-fi, no phones, no traffic. He'd picked up some provisions on his way up the shore. He loaded the cabin's mini-fridge with beer, bottled water, eggs, bacon, cheddar cheese and salami, then placed a loaf of wheat bread and some steel cut oatmeal in one of two cupboards above the single metal sink in the kitchen.

He began building the primitive, three-room cabin a month after 9/11, thinking at the time he might need a refuge in the event of a foreign invasion. He spent a few weeks each summer making incremental improvements to the remote hideaway. One of those improvements was supposed to be indoor plumbing. Though he had running water and even a decent shower, he still used the ancient wooden one-holer he'd inherited from the previous landowner.

Freeman liked the sound of rain drumming on his steel roof, but he didn't like the damp chill that infiltrated the poorly insulated walls of his glorified shack. With the aid of an old edition of the Cook County Herald and a squirt of lighter fluid, he ignited a fire in the wood stove that was his only source of heat and picked out one of two Montecristo Double Edmundo cigars that were aging in a makeshift humidor on the Formica kitchen countertop. The $20 Cuban was still surprisingly moist, which made Freeman smile as he opened the back door and made his way to the decrepit outhouse to take care of some pressing business and have a smoke.

He finished the cigar while gazing at the widely scattered lights around Trestle Pine Lake from his truncated aluminum dock. In stark contrast to Lake Superior, Trestle Pine was a small, shallow body of water, not quite a hundred acres and about thirty-five feet at its deepest point. Most of the lake was in the Superior National Forest, where there was a well-maintained campground and seldom-used public boat launch. Once or twice each summer, Freeman came up to fish for splake and bluegills from his old but still reliable boat, a 16-foot Lund Rebel with a Yamaha 50. His was one of only four private cabins on the lake, and, by choice, he had never met the other property owners.

Bothered by the increasing intensity of the cold rain, he flicked a smoldering butt into the lake and took the worn, dirt path back to his cabin. A brown tarp covered a neatly stacked woodpile about ten yards from the back door. Recalling that the firewood rack next to the wood stove was nearly empty, he lifted the tarp and cradled a bundle of birch and pine in his long arms to ensure that he could sleep in relative warmth.

Before reaching the cabin, he heard an engine accelerate and saw the flicker of car lights on Trestle Pine Road and then, in an instant, complete silence and darkness. He let the logs fall to the ground and pulled his Glock from his jacket pocket. A vehicle had turned onto Trestle Pine from County Road 27 and then stopped. Since his was the only property within a mile of the intersection, he was naturally curious, especially at one o'clock on a Wednesday morning.

Freeman was very familiar with the terrain near his property, even in the dark. He scampered through the woods, using the flashlight app on his phone to avoid colliding with a tree. He made it to County Road 27 in under a minute but decided to stay off the road, running along the brush parallel to the tree line to the intersection of Trestle Pine. There he discovered an old Jeep parked on the shoulder, its occupant or occupants not in sight but most likely headed towards his place about a quarter mile up the road.

He stayed low and hustled up the grassy shoulder. Several yards from the gravel driveway, he heard a hard knock on his screen door—he'd left the inner storm door open.

"Freeman," shouted a vaguely familiar voice. "BCA officer. We need to talk, now!"

Hiding behind an oak tree at the edge of the driveway, Freeman focused in on a short man wearing a baseball cap and standing on the cement stoop in front of his cabin, a black lab at his side. After waiting several seconds for a response, the man said, "I'm coming in, Eric," then opened the door and walked in with the dog.

Oh my God, thought Freeman, as he ran up the driveway, I know who that is. Quietly pulling back the screen door, he pointed the Glock at the chest of the man coming out of his bedroom.

"Redman, what the fuck are you doing here?"

Before Redman could even open his mouth, Barney charged the man endangering the life of his master and leapt up just as Freeman fired two quick rounds into his chest.

Barney let out a short yelp and collapsed at Freeman's feet. By the time he looked up from the dead dog, Redman had dived at his knees, grabbing his calves and literally flipping him backwards off his feet and onto the thinly carpeted floor. When Freeman lost his balance, he also lost control of his gun. It bounced on the floor behind his head.

Redman was still a capable fighter at sixty, but even with adrenalin coursing through his system and righteous vengeance on his side, he was still no match for this younger, stronger adversary. That didn't stop him from winding up, leaning in, and punching Freeman squarely in the nuts.

"You're a disgrace, you fucking prick!"

Freeman cried out in agony but reflexively sat up and hit Redman in the jaw with a right cross that knocked him half way across the room, giving Freeman time to recover his gun and take aim at Redman's head.

Shuddering from a new blast of gunfire, Redman braced for the inevitable pain, or worse, that would follow. Instead, he saw Freeman examining a bloody right wrist while screaming a string of unintelligible expletives and frantically searching the floor for his gun. Within seconds, MacDonald was on top of him, giving him the *Miranda* while cuffing his wrists behind his back and wrapping the bloody one with some kind of tape. Redman was amazed at how easily the big sheriff handled the former Marine. He had the irresistible urge to kill Freeman then and there, but he knew that wasn't going to happen. Dizzy and in pain, his jaw probably broken and his gut aching, he sat up and looked over at his brave, four-legged friend. The he started to sob.

MacDonald leaned over and squeezed Redman's shoulder with his right hand while holding Freeman by the handcuffs with his left. "Red, are you O.K?"

Redman nodded. "Yeah, I'll be alright."

"Listen. I'm going to secure this asshole in the Tahoe and drive your Jeep up next to this dump. Then I'll come back and help you with Barney. Give me your keys."

Five minutes later MacDonald returned with a folded wool blanket. Redman was sitting on the floor holding Barney, tears streaming down his cheeks.

"You open the back of the Jeep," MacDonald directed. "I'll bring Barney."

Redman did as instructed. MacDonald wrapped the lifeless dog in the blanket and carried him out the door. He carefully placed the bundle in the back of the old Wagoneer while Redman stood in silent disbelief.

"Red, here are your keys and the key to my garage. I need to take Freeman up to the Cook County jail for processing. They won't charge him with anything until tomorrow. You can leave Barney in the blanket in my garage. There's plenty to eat in the fridge and the guest bedroom is ready for you. Try to get some rest and, if you like, we'll find a good spot to bury Barney in the morning. I'd suggest you get your jaw examined by the emergency room doc at Lake County Hospital, but I doubt you're interested in doing that tonight."

"It can wait," said Redman. "And Mac, thanks. I mean that. I'm just a fucking old fool."

66

THE FIRST-FLOOR ASSEMBLY room at the St. Paul College Club was filled beyond capacity. Over three hundred people had shown up on a hot, sticky afternoon to commemorate the life of Lauren Bergmann Fallon. A Georgian Revival home originally built in the early 1900s for a wealthy industrialist, the College Club was also home to the American Association of University Women, an organization of which Lauren had been an active member. The official Governor's residence was immediately to the east of the Club, and, although Governor Bixby didn't attend the service, he watched the procession of mourners with more than idle curiosity from his second-floor study.

The old stucco mansion's air conditioning system was losing its battle to offset the heat. Fallon was sweaty and uncomfortable in a small, white folding chair in the front row, seated next to his daughter and her spouse. His brother, Patrick, and his family were also in the front row along with Father Daly and Fallon's long-time assistant, Molly Perkins.

Lauren had been a big fan of both Bach and the Beatles, so Fallon had arranged for a pianist friend who taught at MacPhail Center to play excerpts from the *Goldberg Variations* for thirty minutes prior to the start of the service. Patrick's oldest boy was an accomplished guitar player with a pleasant singing voice, and, like each of Patrick's four kids, he adored Lauren. When Fallon had asked whether he could perform *Imagine* or *Blackbird,* he quickly replied, "Uncle Charlie, I could play both."

One of Patrick's daughters read poems by Robert Frost, Emily Dickinson, and W.H. Auden, and two young partners from Terranova's firm told brief, touching stories highlighting Lauren's unique combination of lawyerly skills and compassion. Miraculously, Joe Terranova arrived in a motorized wheelchair, accompanied by his wife and two nurses. Heavily bandaged and sedated, he slept through most of the program.

Even though Fallon had created a program devoid of biblical or other religious references, he'd asked a Catholic priest to officiate, which meant that Father Daly would have the last word. Near the end of the service, he asked whether anyone from the audience would like to share a story or sentiment about Lauren. Nine of her clients, all plaintiffs in the clergy abuse cases, came forward to talk about the woman who gave them the strength and conviction to tell their stories and, possibly, to restore some of what they'd lost.

It was at this point that Fallon had intended to address the assemblage, but he couldn't do it. He signaled to Father Daly to move on to the end of the service. Daly led the crowd in a spirited rendition of Leonard Cohen's *Hallelujah* and then delivered the *23rd Psalm* from memory, which wasn't in Fallon's program but was perfect.

There was a catered reception in the Parlor Room after the service. Fallon forced himself to participate in the receiving line, where he was somewhat surprised to see the Lake County Sheriff.

"Hello, sheriff. Thank you for coming."

"It was a beautiful service, Judge. This is my friend, Hallie Bell. She's a lawyer with the Lake County Attorney."

"A pleasure to meet you," said Fallon, extending a slightly shaking right hand to Bell.

"You as well, Judge Fallon. I am so sorry for your loss."

Fallon wanted to ask MacDonald about the progress of his investigation, but this wasn't the time. He'd read about the violence at McBride's, the disappearance of the archbishop and the alleged involvement of Governor Bixby's bodyguard, but the media hadn't connected any of that to Lauren's murder, at least not yet.

"Thank you," Fallon said. "By the way, how's your deputy doing, sheriff? Sounds like you've been pretty busy up north."

"She's recovering remarkably well, Judge. Thanks for asking. If you're up to it, I'd like to have a follow-up conversation with you sometime soon."

"Sure, sheriff. I'll have Molly call you to set something up."

Fallon shot a quick glance down the long line that remained and noticed Beth Liscomb wearing a short black dress and holding David's hand. What a fucking hypocrite, he thought. The sight of her made him physically sick. He'd already decided to resign from the bench. Deep in his gut he knew what else he needed to do to make things right.

67

"MCBRIDE'S COMPUTERS HAVE yielded a treasure trove of information," said MacDonald, as he added a few logs to the crackling blaze in the fire pit overlooking the lake.

He'd invited Redman and Rita to spend Labor Day weekend with Hallie and him at his rustic home on Lake Superior. They arrived in time to witness a magnificent sunset over the water from his screened-in porch while enjoying rib-eye steaks and root vegetables cooked to perfection on MacDonald's mesquite pellet grill.

Redman had picked up two mouth-watering pies, a French silk and mixed berry, from Betty's Hometown Bakery north of Two Harbors. Braving forty-degree temperatures on a clear, calm night, the two couples carried pie and Irish coffees out to the backyard, where MacDonald had built a roaring fire shortly after dinner. They sat in a tight semi-circle in white Adirondack chairs that bordered the circular, stone pit.

The swelling in Redman's severely broken jaw took a few weeks to subside, but it never stopped him from talking. "I'll bet Freeman shit his pants when his lawyer told him about the camera. McBride recorded his own murder, committed with his own gun."

"This berry pie is fantastic," said Rita, not wanting to change the subject but unable to restrain herself. "I thought McBride was the bad guy here. Didn't he kill the bishop?"

"There are multiple bad guys, actually," MacDonald said. "The BCA found the archbishop's hair and traces of his blood and skin on McBride's deck and in his kitchen and garage. The Lamkin and McBride cases are under Cook County's jurisdiction, but the County Attorney has asked the BCA and Attorney General's office for assistance in the investigation and prosecution. Everyone assumes Lamkin's body is in Lake Superior, but professional divers with sonar equipment haven't been able to find him.

"And that's not all. As you know, Red's been investigating the murder of Lamkin's assistant, Peter Jenkins. We had decent evidence linking McBride to Jenkins' condo on the night of the crime, but no clear motive. The BCA's computer forensic staff uncovered hundreds of transactions where Jenkins was funneling archdiocese funds to McBride. The total amount is in the tens of millions. Apparently, McBride was supposed to invest the funds to create a war chest to protect the Church against future claims of clergy abuse. Instead, he blew through most of the money on an incredibly lavish lifestyle, including an Italian villa, a beach house in Monterrey, a penthouse condo in Minneapolis, a yacht in Cabo San Lucas, fancy cars, expensive art and the beautiful retreat up the shore.

"He was taking $3 to $5 million a year in salary, bonuses and dividends from his investment business, but apparently that wasn't enough. He squandered another $30 to $40 million of the archdiocese's money. And until Lauren Fallon came along and started picking at some old scabs, I have no doubt McBride thought he got away with it—that he was in the clear."

Hallie hadn't heard about the BCA's recent discoveries in McBride's hard drive. She'd been spending three or four days a week at her parents' place in Florida. Her mother still needed help while her dad slowly recovered from the stroke. Trying to keep up with work at the county, she hadn't been spending much time with her boyfriend. The tangled web of deceit spun by McBride fascinated her nonetheless.

"Did anyone at the archdiocese other than Lamkin and Jenkins know about this defense fund?" she asked.

"We don't think so," said Redman. "Lamkin must have pressured McBride to return the money after Judge Kennedy ruled against the archdiocese. He and Jenkins knew the Church would have to come up with serious cash to settle with the plaintiffs.

Lamkin probably told McBride that the *femme fatale* was screwing his pudgy little assistant to get information, which naturally made McBride worry that Jenkins would disclose the existence of the war chest."

"The *femme fatale*? You're such a romantic, Red," Rita said sarcastically, punching him in meaty part of his narrow shoulder.

"I get why McBride thought he needed to get rid of Jenkins and Lamkin," said Bell. "But do you think he murdered Lauren, too? What did that do for him? There are plenty of lawyers at Terranova's firm to keep pursuing the abuse claims."

"Red and I have spent hours going over this," MacDonald explained with a pained look on his face. "We've come to the conclusion that McBride was a high-functioning sociopath with an insatiable lust for the finer, or should I say finest, things. Somehow, he lured Lauren up to Gooseberry with a promise of inside information about the archdiocese. He'd already decided to eliminate Jenkins and Lamkin but wasn't sure whether Lauren knew about the fund. We'll never know what he learned that night, or whether he decided to kill her for some other reason. There's no question that her death, and the revelation she and Jenkins were having an affair, drove a wedge between Jenkins and Lamkin that ultimately helped McBride isolate and murder them as well."

"That theory makes everything neat and tidy, but I'm still not sure I buy it," Redman said. "Plus, there's the whole butt sex thing doesn't fit as well as I'd like.

"The butt sex thing?" Rita and Hallie asked in unison.

"Wait a minute!" Rita exclaimed, waving an arm in the air as she spoke. "The headline in this morning's *Pioneer Press* was *Governor Resigns in the Wake of Indictment*, and the article said the state was accusing Bixby of accepting a bribe from this McBride guy.

"On the way up here, Red told me that the reason Bixby's "asshole bodyguard"—that's Red's description—was at McBride's on the night all this stuff happened was to force McBride to transfer money to the Governor. I voted for that guy twice. So, before you get to the butt sex thing, and believe me I want to hear about that, can you explain to me exactly how our Governor was involved with a sociopath?"

"I'll say it again. We probably wouldn't know any of this without McBride's computer," said MacDonald. "Not only did it show transactions between the archdiocese and dummy accounts McBride set up to hide the fraud, it also included statements from a couple of Swiss bank accounts he opened to move some of the money out of the country. Bixby had access to one of these accounts for a while and withdrew over a million dollars. At some point, McBride cut off Bixby's access to the account; that's when Freeman paid him a visit."

"This is the best part," said Redman, standing up to continue the story. "Initially, Freeman wouldn't talk to us. His lawyer said he visited McBride to negotiate the repayment of a personal loan the Governor had made to him a few years ago. He claimed they had a drink and agreed to meet again in the Cities in a few days. Then we showed Freeman and his lawyer the video of Freeman blowing McBride's brains out. After that, the fucker was more than ready to sell out his boss to save his own bacon.

"Because of all the potential charges and jurisdictions, there was a huge confab involving multiple county attorneys, the FBI and the U.S. Attorney. We all finally agreed to recommend no more than a 25-year prison sentence and to drop attempted murder and assault charges involving yours truly and Deputy Klewacki, if, and only if, Freeman pleads guilty to second-degree murder with respect to McBride and provides evidence that leads to a felony conviction against Winton Bixby. I think he's going to take the deal, even though I personally believe his sentence should involve burning in Hell.

"Governor Bixby claims McBride owed him money from an earlier loan, but there's no documentation or evidence whatsoever of money flowing from Bixby to McBride. What the evidence does show is that Bixby influenced the State Investment Board to place billions of dollars with Itasca Fund Managers. In more recent years when other Board members wanted to move the money to a couple of index funds, Bixby resisted and strong-armed the Board into keeping the funds with McBride's firm. In return for his efforts, Bixby ultimately received close to $4 million. Where I come from, that's called bribery."

"Though all that seems pretty damning," MacDonald chimed in, "the chief prosecuting lawyer told me they have less than a 50/50 chance of convicting Bixby of state bribery or federal money laundering charges. And even with Freeman's cooperation, I doubt they'll charge him with conspiracy to kill McBride. With most of the players dead and a popular public figure who might testify about things the state can't disprove, I think a deal is in the works with Bixby, and I'd be surprised if it includes jail time."

"That's really a shame," said Bell

"It's a terrible shame," echoed MacDonald. "The good news is they're going to appoint a special administrator to liquidate McBride's estate. Most of the proceeds will go back to the archdiocese. I assume Bixby will have to disgorge whatever is left of the $4 million either as restitution or as part of a civil lawsuit.

"I wouldn't be surprised if it's already been paid to his lawyers," said Bell

"Let's get back to the sex thing," Rita suggested. "I'm starting to get bored."

MacDonald and Redman stared at each other for a few seconds, then Redman said, "You know more about that than I do."

"No surprise there," teased Rita.

"Ed Higgins' autopsy report, the detailed version that I reviewed," said MacDonald, "included a finding that Lauren likely had anal intercourse on the night she died. Only trace amounts of semen were found, but there was some bruising and chafing in the area. Based on other evidence, we believe she and Jenkins may have had intercourse in her room earlier in the evening, but the other act occurred shortly before she died."

"So, you think McBride raped her before he killed her?" asked Bell. "I thought he was gay?"

"We're not sure of his sexual orientation," said MacDonald. "He might have been bisexual or more of a sexual chameleon, where he became whatever he needed to be to achieve his objectives. By the way, his staff at Itasca are shocked by all of this. To a person, they said he was the consummate professional, highly ethical and client focused. They all thought he was straight because he dated several women.

"What's even more of a curveball is the anonymous call Thomassoni received from a woman who would only identify herself as a friend and former classmate of Lauren's. She claimed Lauren told her she was having an affair with someone a few weeks before the murder. She insisted she didn't know his identity but thought we should know."

"Why wouldn't she identify herself?" Bell asked.

"She said she didn't want Judge Fallon to find out about it, that he'd been hurt enough already."

"How do you know the Judge didn't already know about this affair?" asked Rita.

"That brings me to the Klewacki theory of the case," said MacDonald. "Gail has been recuperating at home for the past few weeks. She's itching to get back to work but still has residual headaches and double vision from the gunshot wound, which damaged her optic nerve and killed a few of her surplus brain cells but otherwise did no permanent damage. She's either bored or obsessed with Lauren Fallon's murder or a little of both, because she's pored over every shred of evidence a hundred times. She believes Fallon knew about Lauren's extra-marital activities but didn't confront her because he was afraid of losing her and because he didn't think they meant anything to her. Until one did."

"I don't get it," said Bell. "I thought he had a tight alibi on the night of the murder."

"That's the part I haven't told you yet," said MacDonald. "Last week, at Gail's urging, Red followed up with the Judge's neighbor regarding Fallon's alibi. The Judge said he had dinner at his club and then went home. Dinner at the club checked out; he was definitely there until about eight o'clock. But Fallon said he ran into his neighbor and a car full of kids getting home from a concert after midnight. Turns out that concert and the encounter in the driveway occurred on Thursday night, not Friday. The neighbor had no recollection of seeing Fallon or his car on Friday."

"So, have you confronted Fallon with this information?" asked Bell.

"I did," said Redman. "I met him in his chambers the next day. When I asked him about the inconsistency, he shrugged his shoulders and said he was in shock when he told Mac about seeing his neighbor; that he must have mistaken the two nights. But he insisted that he was home all night and left early on Saturday morning to have breakfast at his club."

"Obviously, you two believe him," said Rita, pouring whiskey into her empty coffee mug.

"It doesn't matter whether I believe him," said Redman philosophically. "We have absolutely nothing to link him to the crime scene, and Sheriff Miller told me Fallon's reaction to the news of Lauren's death was as authentic as he's ever seen. Klewacki's home reading murder mysteries and doesn't have enough to do."

"I'm not convinced McBride's the culprit," MacDonald admitted, "but I'm afraid it might be the best explanation we're ever going to have."

"Wow," said Redman, pointing out at the lake. "Look at all the lights on that ore boat! Someone must be having a big party out there."

"That's not an ore boat," chuckled MacDonald. "It's what we call a saltie, an ocean-going ship that's probably carrying grain to some foreign destination.

"Let's hope you're better at identifying murderers," said Rita.

68

Tuesday, July 14th

"THANKS FOR MEETING me for lunch. It's been a long time."

"More than three years I think, but we've both been busy. Me, sleeping my way to the top of the Criminal Division at the U.S. Attorney's Office, and you, as Joe Terranova's star litigator and relentless advocate for the abused and oppressed."

"I see you've retained your sick sense of humor and gift for exaggeration."

"Just survival tools, girlfriend. I'm glad you called. We used to be so close. Roommates in law school and housemates during our first few years as lawyers. Now I'm saddled with a horny, workaholic husband and two messy kids and you've got the chief federal judge and challenging but I assume gratifying work. Did you just want to catch up or is there something serious we need to discuss?"

"I could use some advice, Cheryl. Now that Gramps is gone, you're the only person I can trust to maintain confidences and give me honest feedback. I'm so embarrassed to say this, but I've fallen hard for another man. I can't tell you much about him, but he makes me feel alive in a way no one ever has. I know that sounds corny and trite, but I don't know how else to describe it.

"Wow. I'm shocked, Lauren. I thought you and Charlie were the perfect couple."

"I love Charlie. That's part of the problem. He's the finest, most generous man I know. But, honestly, sometimes I feel like I'm married to a benevolent uncle. I married Charlie because I admired him so much and knew he loved and respected me as much as anyone could, but, honestly, I've never had that deep in the gut, sensory attraction to him or anyone, and I never thought I would.

I'm afraid I'm not totally in control of my feelings, but I'm also not ready to give up the great life I have with Charlie."

"You *are* screwed up. Sounds like you want to have your cake and eat it too. Can't you just have a discreet affair with this guy and see how it plays out?"

"It looks like that's where this is headed, but I'm really afraid of hurting Charlie if I can't extricate myself soon. If he finds out, he'll be devastated and justifiably angry. You'll think this is terrible, Cheryl, but I've often regarded sex as nothing but a tool to be used to gain an advantage with men—information, compliance, even love. That's because it's meant nothing to me; I could take it or leave it. But not with this guy."

"I don't know what to tell you, my friend. You may be incredibly bright, but you will get burned if you're not careful. My advice—give this guy up sooner rather than later and stick with Uncle Charlie."

"That's good advice, Cheryl. Really good advice."

69

I T WAS WHAT they used to call an Indian summer day in St. Paul. Fallon had invited his brother Patrick, Father Daly and David Liscomb to join him at Town & Country for his first round of golf since Lauren's death. Patrick couldn't make it; he had plans to take his sons to the Vikings game against the Bears. The other two men hadn't seen Fallon since Lauren's funeral. They'd each heard, from different sources, that Fallon had resigned from the federal bench effective October 1st. The news had made local media outlets, and speculation about the reason abounded. Fallon's resignation letter simply stated he was leaving the best job he had ever had for "personal reasons."

Daly was excited to see this friend. He'd made efforts to connect with him shortly after the funeral, but when Fallon had responded to a voicemail message with a polite but distant email saying he "needed some alone time," Daly decided to back off for at least a few weeks.

A cloudless afternoon with temperatures in the sixties helped motivate Fallon to walk the mile and a half to Town & Country. The Club stored his golf equipment during the summer months, and he always kept a change of clothes in his locker.

Liscomb and Daly were shocked when they saw Fallon standing on the first tee, joking with two teenage caddies. He'd lost over thirty pounds in two months and looked ten years younger.

"Look at you!" Father Daly literally shouted, slapping Fallon on the shoulder and giving him a bear hug. "You've been running without me!"

"Haven't run once since the last time we were out," Fallon confessed. "I've taken up biking and healthier eating. I have to admit I feel great."

"Good enough for a little $50 skins game this afternoon?" Daly asked.

"Betting on Sunday? Sure, if David's up for it."

"Of course," said Liscomb. "I haven't played in a month, so I'll probably kick your ass."

Daly loved to bet on golf, partly because when money was on the line he always played better than his seven handicap, partly because he got a rush from gambling, but mostly because he got a bigger rush from trying to cheat once or twice a round without getting caught. After all, who's going to accuse an old priest of cheating at golf?

By the time the threesome reached the 18th tee, Daly had won nine $50 skins, Liscomb three, Fallon three, and three were riding on the final hole. Eighteen was a 175-yard par three from the blue tees. The shot needed to carry a steep ravine with a creek running through the middle, and the green was long and narrow with deep bunkers on the right and left. Liscomb was first to tee off, having won the 15th hole with a bogey/net par. His caddie handed him a five iron, which he quickly rejected in favor of a six.

Fallon didn't think that would be enough club for Liscomb to get to the green but was always reluctant to give unsolicited advice on a friend's golf game.

"It's getting dark," needled Daly, growing impatient while Liscomb adjusted his stance and fidgeted over the ball.

"Wait a minute," Fallon interrupted, just as Liscomb was about to swing. "If I win the final skin, you two gentlemen can buy me dinner in the card room. If either of you wins, dinner's on me."

"I'm in on that," said Daly.

"Fine," grunted Liscomb, not happy with the interruption.

When Liscomb finally swung, he dug the face of his six iron into the turf about an inch behind the ball, producing a low, sputtering shot that bounced twice before diving into the ravine and ending up in the creek.

"Motherfucker!" Liscomb cursed while embedding the heel of his club in the ground to the side of the tee box. "I knew I should have hit the five."

"With that swing, you wouldn't have made it to the green with your driver," Daly said in his matter-of-fact-you-suck voice. He placed his ball in the middle of the box without a tee and smoothed a five iron over the hazard and onto the green about twenty feet beyond the pin.

"Nice shot," said Fallon, whose game was rusty but getting better with each hole. He used a broken tee to wedge his ball about an eighth inch off the ground and stroked a towering shot with his seven iron that landed softly in the long shadow cast by the pin and came to rest about three feet from the hole.

"Is that my ball or a fallen leaf within gimmie range of the hole?" Fallon asked one of the caddies.

"That's no leaf, sir," replied the lanky, freckle-faced teenager, trying to keep a straight face. "Heckuva shot, sir."

"But it's certainly no gimmie, Charlie," said Daly. "You'll have to earn your dinner."

70

A FTER SINKING HIS birdie putt to win the hole, Fallon gave each of the caddies
a generous tip and then quizzed them about their schools and families,
as he always did. The sun had set by the time he followed Liscomb and Daly
into the locker room, where Daly had already set one of the Club's famous
Boilermakers (a double shot of bourbon poured into a frosted glass of wheat
beer) on the bench next to his locker.

By the time the men showered and changed it was 8:00. Three couples
were still in the dining room having dinner, a handful of regulars sat at the bar
watching a football game, and Fallon's threesome was the only group in the
more intimate card room. The Club was not a hopping place on Sunday nights
in October.

They sat comfortably in leather upholstered chairs at an antique oak card
table. Fallon took the lead and ordered drinks and a couple of flatbreads for
starters followed by three chicken Caesar salads, a Club specialty. Father Daly
couldn't help himself; he started pumping Fallon for information.

"You didn't think I was going to talk politics and the weather all day, did you
Charlie? I mean, how many times and in how many ways can I say that Trump's
an asshole? You said you've been riding a bike, and I can see the obvious benefits,
but now that you've left the bench, what else are you going to do with yourself?"

"For starters, I'm leaving tonight on a week-long biking and camping trip
around our beautiful state. Then I'm going out to California to spend a week
with Shawn. When I return, I'm planning to open a small law office on Grand
Avenue, doing mostly *pro bono* work and some mediations. Fortunately, I have
the financial means to do whatever I want. I have a generous federal pension;

I've lived pretty modestly, and, ironically, our investment account at that monster McBride's firm has performed quite well. But that's enough about me. How are Beth and your boys doing these days, David?"

"We're empty nesters, and we're not even fifty. I'd like to sell the big house in North Oaks, but Beth wants to remodel the lower level and build a third house in Palm Desert as an alternative winter getaway. I guess I'll have to work till I'm eighty."

"Don't you have a place in Naples, too?" asked Fallon.

"Sure," said Liscomb, "but you just can't count on the weather in Florida in January and February."

"I didn't think this could be true," said Fallon, hesitating before completing the thought, "but an Assistant in the U.S. Attorney's office told me you've been retained by Winton Bixby. I told her I didn't think your firm ever took on criminal cases."

"Wait a minute," said Daly. "I thought I read that Mack Gehan was representing Bixby." Gehan was a solo practitioner and hotshot criminal defense attorney with a reputation for histrionics in the courtroom and hung juries in cases nobody should win.

"I went to law school with Larry Haugen, the lead Ramsey County prosecutor assigned to the state's case," said Liscomb. "Bixby retained Gehan just in case I can't negotiate a plea bargain with Haugen that doesn't involve jail time."

"The old good cop, bad cop routine," said Fallon. "And the firm is okay with your handling this kind of case? I mean I could understand if the charges were just bribery and money laundering, but conspiracy to commit murder is pretty unseemly."

"Freeman is a lying, and everybody knows it," Liscomb protested. "There's no way the Governor even imagined that he would kill McBride. That piece of shit told the feds that Win ordered him to transfer the money, whack McBride and make it look like a suicide. If the charges were restricted to the money transfers, which Bixby claims were legitimate loan and repayment transactions, we'd have already made a deal. Frankly, I'll stake my reputation on the Governor's innocence of any wrongdoing."

"No offense, David, but I think your client is a piece of shit," said Fallon. "And I used to consider him a friend."

"On that positive note, I need to take off, fellas," said Father Daly, folding his napkin and getting up from the table. "David, good luck representing our wayward governor. I admit I voted for him twice. Charlie, I can't believe you're going on a bike trip. I really failed you as a running coach. Be safe and call me when you get home. Good night, gentlemen."

"I wish I lived a block away from this place," said Liscomb.

"You still wouldn't play more than once a week," said Fallon. "By the way, I walked over here this afternoon, but I'd really like to take my clubs home tonight. The golf season is over for me. Do you think you could give me a lift?"

"Sure, Charlie. Be happy to."

71

LISCOMB PULLED INTO Fallon's driveway and popped open the trunk of the S7. Fallon hoisted his golf bag out of the trunk, and Liscomb lowered the front passenger window to say goodbye to the judge.

"Say, David, do you have a minute? I'd like to show you something in my garage."

Without saying a word, Liscomb got out of the car and followed Fallon through the service door and into a dimly lit two-car garage. The nearest parking space was vacant; Fallon's Buick occupied the other one. Liscomb thought it odd that an eight by twelve foot polyethylene tarp covered the concrete floor.

"You working on some kind of project in here?" he asked.

"Not really," Fallon replied, fidgeting with something in his right pants' pocket. He expanded the built-in tripod on his golf bag and set the clubs down next to his workbench, then reached up and pulled on a long cord that hung over the bench, activating two overhead fluorescent lights. Opening the top drawer of the workbench, he grabbed Lauren's battered smart phone and handed it to Liscomb.

"Recognize that?" he asked.

"Jesus Christ! Where did you find this?" Liscomb's right hand shook like a palsy victim's as he stared at the phone and then at Fallon in disbelief.

"Lauren often wore a unique and wonderful Joy perfume. That scent on her made me crazy. When you gave me a ride to Duluth, I smelled it in your car. At first I thought it was just my imagination, but it got stronger and stronger. When you stopped to take a piss, I searched the car for some other sign that

Lauren had been there. I found her phone in the glove box wedged inside your owner's manual."

Liscomb thought about making something up, but, after a moment or two of calculated introspection, he went with the truth, as he recalled it.

"After I destroyed the sim card and smashed the phone a couple of times on concrete, I thought I put it in the canvass bag she left in my car. She had a bottle of red wine and a couple of plastic cups in there. Maybe some dark chocolate. I stuffed her clothes and glasses in there after the accident. On my way back to the Cities, I stopped at a rest stop near Rush City and poured gasoline over the bag in an old fire pit. By the time I left, there was nothing but ash in that pit."

Liscomb's detailed recounting made Fallon cringe, but he needed to know the rest. "Several months ago, in April or May, Lauren confided in me that she was going to meet with you. Apparently, Peter Jenkins told her that Lamkin had paid you over two million dollars to act as "special counsel" for all the abuse victims who didn't have a lawyer. He said your job was to convince these men that their claims had very little value or merit and that the Church was offering them a fair settlement. Is that true?"

"What difference does that make now, Charlie? Why didn't you ask me about the phone when you found it? And why haven't you turned it over to the police?"

"Because I wanted to know the truth first. I wasn't ready to confront you at that point. I was too upset and still in a state of disbelief. I needed to know how and, more important, why you killed her, and I didn't trust some country sheriff to figure it out. And then there was the avalanche of crap that followed—Jenkins' murder, the explosion at Terranova's office, Lamkin and McBride, and even the fucking Governor is mixed up in this.

"You want the truth? The truth is I didn't kill her. The truth is I was infatuated with her. Maybe obsessed is a better word. And you of all people should be able to appreciate that. You also must know that she liked rough, kinky sex. We met at the park, had a few glasses of wine and started making out. It's two o'clock in the morning and she wants me to bend her over the bridge railing, so she can hear the roar of the falls while I'm holding her by her hips. We were hot and sweaty; she slipped out of my hands and went head first into the darkness and onto the rocks."

"Then why did you run and destroy evidence?"

"Really, Charlie? I knew there was no way she could survive that fall head-first, and even if she had somehow survived, there was no way to get down into that gorge. Besides, who would have believed what I just told you?"

"I know I don't," said Fallon, still trying to parse Liscomb's version of the truth. The image of Lauren in any kind of intimate embrace with Liscomb made him seethe. "I think Lauren wanted you to help her overturn those settlements, but you had no intention of doing that. Part of your story might be true, David, but I'm not buying that it was an accident."

"Well, you can go fuck yourself, Charlie. Today, the media and everyone who counts think a dead man, Jay McBride, murdered Lauren, and there's no good reason to change that. You can try to implicate me, but you have no proof whatsoever except this phone, which I will properly destroy tonight, thank you very much.

"Just let it go, Charlie. For everyone's sake, especially your own. Just let it go." Liscomb stuffed the phone in his jacket pocket and turned his back on Fallon, but before he could take two steps towards the service door, Fallon lifted the persimmon driver out of his golf bag and swung it with incredible, adrenalin-fueled strength in the direction of Liscomb's skull.

The face of the driver struck Liscomb's head just above his right ear, crushing the bones that protected his brain. Reeling yet not comprehending what had just happened, he took a step back towards Fallon. His legs stopped working and folded beneath him, causing him to bounce face first on the tarp. Both repulsed and energized by this violent act of revenge, Fallon knew without checking that Liscomb was dead.

He bent over and rearranged the lifeless body of his former law partner to facilitate transporting him in the canvass tarp. He wondered how anyone could stomach handling dead bodies for a living. Once Liscomb was snuggly wrapped up and secured with a bungy cord, Fallon walked out the service door and scanned the neighborhood for activity. It was 9:30. Though the sun had been down for a few hours, a full moon, a clear, star-filled sky and several streetlamps shed more light on Fallon's property than he wanted.

None of his neighbors or anyone else was in sight, as a solitary vehicle, a minivan, drove by his house, heading south on Montcalm without braking. He opened the trunk of Liscomb's fancy car. Returning to the garage, he gazed down and shivered as the reality of what he'd done sunk into his now very alert psyche and tense physiognomy. With no time to lose, he picked up the two-hundred-pound bundle and, unable to lift it above his waste, carried it awkwardly but as fast as he could out to the driveway and deposited it into the trunk. Liscomb didn't fit perfectly within the space, but Fallon couldn't think of a reason to be careful as he stuffed everything in and slammed the lid shut.

Lights were on in his living room and kitchen. He'd set timers on several lamps earlier in the day and taken his dog to a local kennel. Unlocking the front door, he ambled through the living room to the kitchen, where he'd outfitted a 64-liter backpack that included a sleeping bag and portable tent. He took a tiny digital voice recorder out of his pocket and hit the stop button. He had rarely used it to dictate letters or orders to his assistant, preferring instead to type his own documents, but it sure came in handy to record admissions of guilt. He pressed the rewind button and listened to his conversation with Liscomb. Perhaps no one else would ever hear it, but just in case he needed it in the future, he slipped it in the top drawer of the roll-top desk in his den.

Fallon closed up the house, picked up the backpack and, just before returning to the garage, caught a glimpse of himself in the full-length mirror that Lauren had hung in the mudroom. He was in the best shape of his adult life, but the combination of weight loss, grief and anxiety had aged him in other ways. The wisps of hair on the top of his head and two-day stubble on his face were pure white, and there were new and deeper creases and wrinkles on his face and neck. This is now the face of a murderer, he thought.

He exchanged the golf sweater he was wearing for a heavy Gophers sweatshirt he'd intentionally left on a hook in the mudroom along with his favorite cap, a souvenir from the 2011 Masters. A pair of high-top sneakers and light leather gloves completed his outfit. He removed his cell phone from the front right pocket of his jeans and set it on the laundry table. Better off without it, he decided.

Back in the garage, he eyed the compact, collapsible Montague road bike he'd purchased from a specialty cycle shop a month earlier. He hoped it would perform half as well as the salesperson claimed.

Preferring not to examine the head of his driver too closely, he picked it up, broke it over his knee, and then severed the head with wire cutters. He put the metal rods in his recycling bin and the head in his backpack.

The bike and backpack easily fit in the backseat of the S7. Opening the driver's side front door, Fallon remembered that he hadn't retrieved a car key from Liscomb's pockets. He was relieved to see a black key fob sitting in a cup holder between the front seats along with Liscomb's smart phone. Two text messages were displayed on the phone, both from Beth.

Thought you'd be home by 9:00?

Where R U??

He truly hated Beth, but seeing the messages diverted his thoughts to Liscomb's two kids. He didn't know them well, but he couldn't help feeling some regret for causing innocents to experience pain.

The neighborhood was eerily quiet when Fallon backed the Audi out of the driveway. The gas gauge displayed a full tank, so thankfully there'd be no stops along the way. He drove a few miles per hour over the speed limit and took Interstate 94 to US 280 and then I-35 to Duluth, where the interstate ended and merged into US 61.

He arrived at Gooseberry shortly before 2:00 a.m., driving the last twenty miles without seeing another vehicle. Parking Liscomb's car on the shoulder about twenty yards north of the bridge, he set up his bike in the grass and hid it and his backpack in heavy brush. As soon as he opened the trunk, he spotted headlights in the distance from the north. He closed the trunk and crouched down on the shoulder, using the car to shield his body from view. If it's a cop or if anyone stops, he thought, I could be screwed.

Whoever it was drove by without even braking. But more lights appeared, this time from the south.

Fallon started to sweat, though he was surprisingly calm thanks in part to the constant roar of the falls. An old pick-up truck with a belching muffler shot by at about eighty miles an hour.

Fallon needed a three to four-minute window. Deciding to go for it, he opened the trunk and lifted the tightly-wrapped body. He lugged it about thirty yards and set it down on the bridge walkway, close to the spot where he thought Liscomb had somehow jettisoned Lauren. Unfurling the tarp and removing Lauren's phone from Liscomb's jacket, he glanced up and down the highway. No vehicles within earshot or in sight. He leaned Liscomb's corpse against the railing, lifted it by the ankles and tossed his former partner headfirst into the wet, rocky abyss.

He carefully placed Lauren's phone in the cup holder next to Liscomb's and then folded the tarp and secured it between his back and his backpack. He would burn it at the first campsite.

Thankful for the absence of traffic on 61, he mouthed a short prayer to no one in particular as he hopped on his bike and started pedaling.

72

"GOOD MORNING, *DETECTIVE*," said Redman. "I sure didn't expect to hear from you today. Congratulations on the big promotion. How are you feeling?"

"Thanks, Red,' said Klewacki. "I feel pretty good. Good enough to do some follow-up on the Lauren Fallon case that I thought might interest you."

"Why am I not surprised by that? I don't suppose the Sheriff suggested that you give me a call."

"He might have. Anyway, remember the name J-Man?"

"Sure, the crypto guy who sent the love-struck emails to Lauren. I remember."

"I think I know who he is. An associate from Terranova's office has subpoenaed a bunch of Archbishop Lamkin's personal files related to old abuse cases. She's discovered the identity of the lawyer Lamkin hired to brainwash—I mean represent, the victims. His name is not Sidney Carton; it's David Liscomb, David *J.* Liscomb, a big-time litigator with Judge Fallon's old law firm."

"Okay," said Redman. "I think I've heard of him in some context, but how is that information related to this J-Man?"

"David Liscomb's middle name is Jasper. How many Jaspers do you know? And, he was the recipient of the Justice Felix Frankfurter prize for legal writing at the University of Michigan Law School. If you recall, Chad Holborn said J-Man's gmail account was registered in the name of Jasper Frankfurter, but no one in Minnesota, lawyer or not, is cursed with that moniker. Chad says that people reaching for aliases to open Facebook pages or sign up for dating sites or secret email accounts often combine parts of their real name with something fictitious. Plus, this guy probably had some reputational and ethical reasons to keep Lauren from exposing his involvement in the abuse cases."

"I get the connection, Gail. Nice piece of detective work, though it might just be a very odd coincidence. I'll bet you and your boss think I should have a talk with Mr. Liscomb, potentially our J-Man, before the Lauren Fallon murder becomes a cold case."

"You are a mind reader," said Klewacki.

"Maybe I'll visit the now retired Judge Fallon on Monday and see what he has to say about his former partner."

"Sounds like a good place to start."

"Thanks for giving me something to do," joked Redman. "All kidding aside Gail, it'd be easy to pin Lauren's murder on that bastard McBride, but I've never been comfortable with it. Maybe your extra research will lead us to the real killer.

"You, Mac and I are all on the same page on this, Red. Have a great weekend."

73

Monday, October 19ᵗʰ

FALLON WAS EXHAUSTED. Stopping only for a few short bathroom breaks, he had ridden through the darkness and well into Monday. Exiting Highway 61 in Silver Bay, he had taken a circuitous route on old county highways and backroads to get to the Willard Munger State Trail in rural Carlton County. All told, he'd biked about seventy-five miles in nine hours when he stopped at Gordy's High-Hat Drive-Inn in Cloquet for a chocolate shake and a couple of bacon cheeseburgers. Though he looked rough and smelled ripe, he figured he'd fit right in with Gordy's regular patrons. For the most part, they completely ignored him, which was a victory of sorts for a man who'd never been camping or on an extended bicycle trip in his life.

Two super-sized Carlton County Sheriff's deputies shared a bag of donuts and a pot of coffee in the booth next to Fallon's. He thought he heard them mention something about Gooseberry Park before one of their beepers went off and they left so fast that one of them spilled his coffee and took the Lord's name in vain. Fallon was relieved to see them go.

His plan was to take the Munger trail into Jay Cooke State Park, where he would set up camp, get some sleep and then explore the St. Louis River basin for a a day or two before riding west. He was in no hurry to get back to St. Paul.

After inhaling the burgers and taking advantage of indoor restroom facilities at Gordy's, Fallon stretched his aching quads and glutes, bought a bottle of water for the road and hopped on his bike. He smiled just a little as a southerly breeze blew warm, fall air into his face. For the first time all day, he allowed himself to appreciate the incredible beauty surrounding the tree-lined trail.

He felt a strange combination of remorse and liberation, accomplishment and fear. He was opposed to the death penalty because he didn't think the state had a right to take a man's life. But he wasn't the state, and he wanted to believe that Liscomb got exactly what he deserved.

Did Fallon commit an act of justice or just revenge? He thought he knew the difference. He was a judge, after all. But for the first time in his life, he'd been the executioner as well. This wasn't perfect justice by any means, but it was a justice he could accept. And besides, all this exercise in the open air was sure to do him some good.

ABOUT THE AUTHOR

R. T. Lund is a lawyer and writer. He lives in Minnesota with his spouse and loyal dog, Charley.

CPSIA information can be obtained
at www.ICGtesting.com
Printed in the USA
LVHW101925190922
728751LV00003B/359

9 781793 185693